PERFORMANCE

D1639478

PERFORMANCE

by

DOUGLAS CLARK

LONDON
VICTOR GOLLANCZ LTD
1985

First published in Great Britain 1985
by Victor Gollancz Ltd,
14 Henrietta Street, London WC2E 8QJ

British Library Cataloguing in Publication Data
Clark, Douglas, *1919–*
    Performance.
    I. Title
    823'.914[F]   PR6053.L294

    ISBN 0–575–03600–1

Typeset at The Spartan Press Limited, Lymington, Hants
Printed in Great Britain by
St Edmundsbury Press, Bury St Edmunds, Suffolk

Chapter One

DETECTIVE CHIEF SUPERINTENDENT George Masters and his immediate assistant, formerly DCI Green, but now wearing the hat of Senior Scene of Crime Officer, were shown by his secretary into the office of the Assistant Commissioner (Crime).

"Well, George," said Anderson, gesturing them to take seats opposite him as he sat at his desk, "have you come up with anything? You've had a week to think about the problem, and though I've studiously refrained from chasing you, I had expected a report of some sort by now."

Masters put the file he was carrying on to the corner of the desk. "We've taken a little longer than we had originally expected, sir, but we have, actually, devoted all our time to the job. The written report should be done tomorrow. It will be very detailed. . . . "

"Meaning you've found something? I mean, if it were just a nil report, it wouldn't be very long, would it? You haven't gone into detail over failure, I hope."

It was an off-beat job Masters and his team had been given. What Masters himself called desk investigation. The Northern Counties police had a serious problem. It was now late November, and every month since January, up to and including the present month, there had been a murder, so far unsolved, of a woman. It was not a Ripper case, despite the sex of the victims. They were women of widely differing ages; of different ways of life; no one of them related to another; none having mutual friends; none a low-lifer; and the murders themselves had taken place in widely differing areas of the northern counties. Even more puzzling for the divisions that were combining in the investigations was the fact that each victim had been murdered in a different way. This had led a number of the more senior officers in Northern Counties to maintain that the deaths were not the work of one killer, but eleven. They based this belief on the common practice of all villains — including multi-murderers — of repeating their methods, if not exactly, at least with recognizably similar features. Their viewpoint had been upheld by computer checks. No common factors had appeared on the print-outs. In desperation, and in the face of rising public disquiet at their lack of success, Northern Counties had asked if Scotland Yard would be willing to go over the files and reports on the eleven cases. They had intimated in advance that they considered it a forlorn hope that even fresh eyes would discover anything new or any facet that had not been thoroughly investigated and rechecked several times. The files had, naturally, been put on the desk of the AC (Crime). Anderson had handed the job to Masters and Green, with their two detective sergeants, Reed and Berger.

"Northern Counties have been on to me," said Anderson. "They're getting twitchy, and virtually accused me of lying down on the job." He pushed the cigarette box across the desk towards Green. "And because I haven't been breathing down your necks, I had no good reply for them. I need hardly say I'd like to be in a position to call them back with something they can get their teeth into."

"You'll be able to, sir," said Green confidently, helping himself to a cigarette and leaning across for the table lighter.

"I'm glad to hear it."

Masters spoke.

"To begin with, sir, let us deal with the number of murderers involved. The Northern Counties people are thorough and efficient. Their files prove that, and so does their past record — except perhaps for the mistakes we all make from time to time. Our belief is that had there been eleven murderers, they would have caught at least some of them by now."

"Good point. They'll like hearing that as your considered opinion. But if not eleven, how many? Can we narrow the number down?"

"Working on that premise, sir, nobody could say for sure what the number is. There may be copy-cat criminals involved, but we believe that what goes for eleven would go for four or five."

"So you think there could still be several murderers?"

"I didn't say that, sir. Based on the argument just put forward, we feel we can be sure in saying there are not eleven at large. Nor any number approaching eleven. There's a weakness in numbers in a business like this. The fewer the number, the less likelihood of detection. Logically, therefore, one could assume that where there has been no actual apprehension or, indeed, any scrap of positive evidence to point to there being a number of villains, there should only be one of them."

"So, despite the fact that no evidence has been unearthed to link any of these crimes together, you would go nap on all of them being the work of one man?"

"Two points, sir. First off, making this report is not an easy business, because our conclusions were built up as we went along. We made assumptions, we tested them; we discarded or accepted them. The ifs and buts were endless. So, let me say at this point that, based on the single fact that none has been caught so far, we cannot stipulate that there is only one murderer. That was an assumption, because we had to start somewhere. Later on we will show how we tested the assumption."

Anderson grunted a grudging acceptance of this point.

"My second point, sir, is that Bill and I do not agree that there are no links between the cases, despite Northern Counties' failure to find them and the best efforts of their computer."

Anderson stared at him for a moment or two. Then: "You've got something, George. What?"

"Let us call them strongly held opinions, sir. The result of a hell of a lot of thought, a great amount of reading and hours of phone investigation. We've been pretty thorough, that's why your report will be detailed."

"But something has come to light? Something to re-energize the Northern Counties people?"

"It would sting us into action if we were handling the business," grunted Green. "But NC may not think so much of it as George and I do."

"Let's have it," urged Anderson.

"There are the names of eleven women to juggle with, sir. We

7

found that an impossible task, so we've called all by their professions or whatever we have discovered their activities to be. Doctor, lawyer, deaconness, councillor and so on. It's become much easier using that system."

"Understood. What did you turn up, dammit?"

"One report mentioned that a girl had won a tennis tournament just before she died."

"So what?"

"There was very little in the way of information like that about any of the victims. NC had looked into their past histories pretty closely and all seemed absolutely blameless, but you know what reports are like, sir, they often leave out the apparently trivial, intimate little scraps such as the bit about the girl winning her local singles title. I thought nothing of it, really, but nevertheless it stuck in my mind. And then I saw a report on the young woman town councillor. Because she had been involved in initiating and pushing through her council a controversial bit of local legislation — against all the odds — the reporting officer had mentioned it, just in case she had made some enemy among those adversely affected by the new law."

"Go on."

"We decided to look very closely into the last few days of the lives of all these women, sir."

"You said you had found a link, George."

"We did, sir. A common factor." He looked straight at Anderson and uttered the one word. "Triumph."

"Triumph? What are you on about now, George? Triumph!"

"I'll explain, sir. I warned you this would be long and detailed."

"All right, you've made your point. And as you don't usually talk tripe . . . get on with it."

"None of these women was a really well-known personality, sir, except perhaps in their own areas, even though some of them were members of learned professions. But in the last hours or days of their lives, each and every one had achieved something. They had all become big fish in their own particular little ponds. As I said, the idea came to me from reading a note about the tennis player and the mention of the councillor's success.

"One girl was an athlete and had just won a one-hundred-metre sprint at a country meeting. Triumph. She died the next day. Knifed.

"The town councillor dead within two days of her triumph. Bludgeoned.

"A small-part actress in local rep suddenly got a chance to appear in a TV ad. It appeared for the first time on a Thursday evening. Triumph. She disappeared on the Saturday, to be found about a week later gagged and bound to a tree, having died from exposure."

"They're all like that?" asked Anderson. "All . . . er . . . triumphs, as you call them?"

"Yes, sir. We spent long hours on the phone establishing the facts. One swam Morecambe Bay successfully, another won a beauty contest."

"That's six so far," corrected Anderson.

"They're all alike."

"Another young lass did her first singing gig, or whatever they're called," said Green. "Anyhow she got her first chance to appear on stage with a group."

"Then there was the deaconness, sir, who preached her first sermon on a Sunday morning and died that same night on the way home from evening service. The solicitor won a difficult case in court. We haven't yet discovered whether it was her first appearance, but it was a controversial business and she won it despite the fact that older and more experienced colleagues believed she had no chance of pulling it off. She was beaten up in her own flat a night or two later and died, sprawled on her bed."

"That's nine," said Anderson. "What about the other two?"

Masters paused a moment before replying. "We are not on quite such firm ground with the last two, sir. However, we learned that the young woman journalist had just been appointed football correspondent of the local paper on which she had worked for a number of years. We felt we could stretch a point and credit her with a triumph in that, although she had merely changed her job on the staff, she had broken into what I must assume must always have been a male preserve. Whether you'll accept that or not, I don't know.

"That only leaves the woman doctor, sir. She had sat for and gained her MRCGP. As I understand it, that is not an earth-shattering event, but obviously it was a qualification she wanted otherwise she would not have bothered to prepare for and sit the exam. She passed it, and her local paper put a couple of column inches in its mid-week edition, mentioning her success. So I suppose, in a way, it was an achievement and, hence, a triumph. During the night following the appearance of the report in the paper, she was called out to a case and was missing for several days. She was at last found in a derelict building, having been killed by the simple expedient of having been injected countless times with every drop of every fluid medicine and drug she had been carrying in her bag. In other words, she was given massive overdoses, by means of one of her own syringes, of a number of toxic substances."

"Eleven," said Anderson grimly. "All killed after personal triumphs, petty or otherwise." He sat back. "Devilish," he muttered.

After a pause, Masters continued. "The triumph theory alone has given Bill and myself good cause to believe that one killer alone is responsible for all the deaths. We have already told you we don't think there are as many as eleven murderers, now we are stating we believe there is only one. We are convinced of this. However, the Northern Counties people are not us. They could well prefer harder facts."

"Which you can't give them presumably?"

"Have a heart, sir," growled Green. "In desperation the NC turned to you, just for another viewpoint because this started best part of a year ago and has gone on, getting worse all the time, without them getting any nearer an answer. You handed us their files with an instruction that we should go over them on the offchance that we might see something new. Nothing was likely to be glaringly obvious, was it, sir?"

Anderson frowned. "I wasn't being censorious, Bill. Not intending to be, anyhow. You've done very well. It seems likely that this triumph business should open up new avenues for investigation even if the Northern Counties people do find it a bit . . . well, theoretical, shall we say?" He turned to Masters. "Was that your intention, George?"

"Just that, sir. Our one murderer has had to get around, not only to kill his victims, but to learn about their successes. Some he could certainly have read about in northern local papers. Possibly all of them. We haven't had time to decide that. But we think there is a possibility, if not a probability, that he didn't always wait to read their names and success stories."

"I don't get you, George."

"For instance, sir, let us say that he actually attended the tennis tournament, knowing that he was going to kill whichever girl won the singles title. He could have planned that trip weeks or months before, because such events are arranged and advertised long in advance. The same goes for the athlete, the beauty queen, and the swimmer, perhaps. The others may have been played off the cuff, but with new ideas such as these to chew over, I would have thought NC could start afresh with added impetus."

"I'll put it to them in that light. If they're as bogged down as they appear to be, anything that gets them moving again ought to be welcome. So, is that the lot, gentlemen?"

"There are a few more points, sir. As I said, all four of us have been working hard for a week on this and other things cropped up."

"Like what?"

Masters turned to Green. "Computer study, Bill?"

"Ah, yes," said Green, helping himself to another of Anderson's cigarettes. "I've been asking our computer a few questions, sir."

"Covering the same ground the Northern Counties officers did?"

"We didn't waste time doing that. I got our operator to feed in all the murders in the Smoke in the last five years and then asked the computer to divide them at random into groups of eleven."

"Why?"

"So that I could see if any eleven came out with a different method of killing in every case. None did. No group showed more than five different methods. Our group has eleven different methods."

"What conclusion did that lead you to?"

"A statistical answer which the Northern Counties can't cast aside as fanciful. There's just one nutter going to great lengths to devise different methods of killing to make investigating officers think they have eleven villains to contend with. You can safely tell NC, sir, that you have statistical proof that if there were eleven killers at large, some of the more common methods of murder would have been repeated."

"A relevant point, Bill. If it won't actually convince them on its own — which I hasten to add I believe it should — then added to the point that if there were eleven different killers some of them would have been caught by now, the Northern Counties people should be thoroughly assured that they are looking for only one man."

Green grunted his appreciation of this approval and carefully lit the cigarette he had taken earlier. Masters looked at Anderson speculatively. "There is a final thought we've worked on, sir. You may find it too whimsical to pass on."

"One of your bright ideas is it, George?"

"It is certainly my idea, sir. I take full responsibility for pursuing it." Masters took from his file a sheet of paper on which were typed several columns of words and figures. Before handing it to Anderson, he said: "As you would expect, we looked for a pattern in the dates of the killings."

"Pattern? One each month from January to November inclusive is a pattern, isn't it?"

"I meant a more precise pattern involving the actual days of the month, sir. For instance, they could have all been on the thirteenth day of each month, or the third Tuesday or some such. Days or dates which might indicate that our man could have been in a position to carry out his schemes at certain times."

Anderson frowned. "Explain that a bit more fully, please, George."

"If all the murders had taken place on the third Tuesday of each month, sir, we could have concentrated on finding somebody who had that day off. Just as an instance, think of a postman who gets a day off each week. He might get Saturday off in the first week, Monday in the second and Tuesday in the third, and so on. Employers — like us — juggle leave days about in this way so that people sometimes get long weekends and sometimes not. Likewise, there are commercial reps who do specified runs on specified days. What we looked for was a pattern which might just give a hint of something like this."

"You failed, I take it. I mean that would have been an obvious one for Northern Counties to have looked into."

"I'm sure they did just that, sir, and they failed. Just as we did — on the particular patterns I've mentioned. But we probed a little further."

"Go on," said Anderson, sitting back.

"The days on which deaths occurred are: one on each of the fifth, sixth, seventh, ninth, thirteenth, and fifteenth. Two on the eleventh, and — if you count the actress who was found dead on the twenty-first after being missing for a week — three on the fourteenth."

"No pattern there. Just a fair scattering, it seems to me. Or am I being bloody obtuse?"

Masters handed over the paper. "Perhaps you would care to look at this, sir."

Month	d	h	m	Victim	Date of Death
January	13	07	09	Pop Singer	14
February	12	02	39	Actress	21 (14?)
March	13	21	14	Beauty Queen	15
April	12	13	15	Councillor	14
May	12	02	01	Athlete	13
June	10	11	55	Tennis Player	11
July	9	19	59	Swimmer	9
August	8	03	01	Journalist	11
September	6	10	59	Solicitor	7
October	5	19	35	Deaconess	5
November	4	05	47	Doctor	6
December	3	18	08	?	?

Anderson spent just long enough to read the sheet of paper before looking up and saying: "Those on the left are almanack figures, I suspect."

"Dates and times of the full moon each month this year to be precise, sir. The figures on the right are the dates of the murders. We think that the two dates in each case correspond very closely indeed. If we accept that the actress was killed on the fourteenth of February, all murder dates, with the exception of that of the journalist, fall within forty-eight hours of the dates of the full moon, and even the exception is within seventy-two hours."

"I don't believe it, George," exploded Anderson. "You of all people asking hard-headed men like those in Northern Counties to believe that the man they are looking for is a madman affected by the full moon."

Masters shrugged. "You've got the dates in front of you, sir."

"But it's . . . it's rubbish, man. Old wives' tales. The mooncalf! The loony! If we put this forward we shall be a laughing stock."

"Do you then propose to withhold that table when you report to NC, sir?"

Anderson expired in dismay. "You're sure you've got all these figures right, George?"

"Checked and rechecked," said Green. "I felt much the same way as you, sir, when George first started on that particular bit of tarradiddle."

"But?"

"You know George, sir. He set out to prove or disprove the moon theory. I think you'd better hear what he learned."

Anderson looked across at Masters, who grinned and said: "I consulted a number of authorities, sir. Psychiatrists and ordinary medical consultants."

"And what did they say?"

"They were mostly a bit long-winded on the subject, but the gist of their opinion is that there is no specific evidence to support the belief that the full moon affects the behaviour of people in general."

"Ah! I thought so. It's all tripe."

"Not quite, sir. All agreed that the old wives' tale was not completely without foundation because observations in specific

14

individuals seem to support it."

"You're joking."

"No, sir. Everybody — all animals — have periodic cycles. That is proven. A woman's sexual cycle is a case in point. Not tied to the phases of the moon, of course, but we all have biological rhythms which have been proved to be related to day and night. Now it appears likely that in addition to the short-term rhythms, if I can describe them that way, we also have rhythms related to longer periods."

"Such as lunar months?"

"Just so, sir. There has been a deal of observation in animals which, apparently, do behave peculiarly at the full moon. Not all of them, perhaps, but enough to keep the ball of investigation rolling. And the consensus among all those I consulted was that though there is no absolute proof that every member of the human race is affected by the moon, it is a fact that some individuals are."

"I still find it hard to believe," said Anderson, shaking his head.

"I have written the evidence up for the report, sir. You can, of course, discard it if you wish."

"But you would prefer me to tell Northern Counties they are looking for somebody affected by the full moon."

Masters shook his head.

"No?"

"No, sir."

"Then what is all this blarney about phases of the moon? You've spent the last ten minutes telling me I can't disregard it."

"I think you would be wise not to cast it aside, sir."

"In words of one syllable, George, tell me why."

"I have suggested in the report, sir, that the murderer has used the dates of each full moon as the days on which to pick his victims. He could have used a pin on the calendar just as easily to choose his times. But I think he is a man who prides himself on his cunning. I think he is choosing his victims on the dates of the full moons in the hope that the police will eventually discover the connection and assume they are looking for a true loony."

"Why pick his dates at all?"

"Because there are triumphs such as we have discussed every

15

single day of the year, sir. He can't kill every twenty-four hours. It amuses him, probably, to see which woman is unlucky enough to have some little private success on the days he has earmarked in his almanack."

"I think I understand, George. I'll decide whether to mention this moon business when I've thought it over."

"Mention it, sir," urged Green. "Don't think it over. If you do, you may come to the wrong decision, with nasty results."

"Nasty results, Bill? How come?"

"According to George's table, the next victim will be chosen on the third of December. If you have had that warning and haven't mentioned it to the Northern Counties . . . " Green shrugged. "You may not be able to prevent the murder, but at least you'll have given them the hint to take what steps they can to see it doesn't happen."

Anderson digested this for a moment. Then he asked: "Do you both honestly believe that the next victim will be chosen because of some triumph of hers on the third of December, and that she will be dead by the fifth?"

"Yes, sir, I do," said Green.

"George?"

"Emphatically yes, sir. I do believe that."

"Then I shall use your report in its entirety, gentlemen. Thank you for what you have done."

The Northern Counties police accepted the written opinion from the AC (Crime) with a deal of scepticism, as had been foreseen. There was one senior officer, however, who expressed great satisfaction with the work of Masters and his team. He was Detective Chief Superintendent Matthew Cleveland who, under his own Chief Constable and ACC, had been largely responsible for co-ordinating the investigations of the various Divisional detectives.

At the meeting called to discuss the opinion, copies of which had been circulated for reading before the discussion, he stood virtually alone in championing the acceptance of the Yard conclusions.

"I can't stomach all this moon business," said one burly

superintendent.

"Why not?"

"Because everybody knows that moon-madness is a load of rubbish."

"What of it?"

"What of it? You want us to deploy our men on looking for a mooncalf?"

"The Yard opinion doesn't suggest that you should. Nor do I."

"So what good is it, this . . . " He waved his copy of the report. "This . . . this nonsense from the Met? I knew we should never have involved them."

"So you didn't bother to read it, is that it?" asked Cleveland.

"I read it, sir."

"Then you will know that the Met said, specifically, that the murderer was using the date of the full moon each month simply as the day on which to pick his next victim. There is no hint that the man himself is loony."

"I still don't like it."

"Why not? Can you disregard the correlation of the dates in their table?"

"Well . . . "

"Either you can or you cannot. Are their figures wrong? Have you checked for yourself that their moon tables are correct or not? Are you saying the dates of the murders are wrong?"

"I think the link is too far-fetched for us to accept."

"Or to consider, even?"

"Yes."

The Chief Constable intervened. "Matt," he said to Cleveland, "I think myself that those figures are just a coincidence. They just happen to correlate."

"I'll believe them, sir," said another DS, "if the Yard's fortune-telling department comes up trumps. They've said we'll get another on December the third. I mean, seeing the future! We all know the top boys in the Met live in cloud-cuckoo land, but I've never heard of them going in for telling the future before. It's the sort of . . . well, I suppose the right word is moonshine . . . one gets from the booths at Blackpool and Bridlington."

"And you are willing to risk another killing on the third of December without doing anything about it?"

"Be fair, Matt," said the ACC. "Even if we believed this prognostication, what could we do? It's the twenty-seventh of November now. Six days in which to prevent an unknown crime being committed anywhere within three or four thousand square miles?"

Cleveland replied: "We may achieve nothing, but we can try. We could get local papers to print warnings. Broadcast warnings, even."

"Saying what?"

"That anybody who achieves anything out of the ordinary on that day should take particular care."

There was a general hubbub of dissent. When it had died down, the Chief Constable asked: "So you believe in what the Yard calls its triumph theory, do you, Matt?"

"I believe in proven facts, sir."

"And you think the Yard has proved this theory?"

"Yes, sir, I do. At least it is something they have come up with that we haven't."

"I agree with your last statement, Matt."

"Thank you, sir."

"Only because it is too fanciful for us ever to have considered it."

"Are you saying, sir, that as policemen we shouldn't consider everything?"

"I'm saying we should keep our feet on the ground. That means considering every theory that is realistic. Not whimsical stuff like this."

"So you intend that we should disregard the triumph theory, too, sir?"

"I do. And for the best of practical reasons." The Chief Constable sat back, the buttons of his uniform jacket straining in their holes. "Let us examine this business about triumphs, as the Yard has insisted on calling them. Let us turn this question on its head by taking any small group of people on any day in the year. My own family for instance, yesterday." He sat forward in his chair. "My wife won a prize yesterday for baking a cherry cake in a cookery competition run in connection with her flower society's chrysanthemum show. My son came home and told us the director of the department had given him a two-hundred-and-fifty-pound merit award for some sales scheme he has thought up. My elder daughter, the married one, saw her name in the list of prize winners for the competition crossword for a week last Saturday. She gets a five-quid book token. And my younger daughter, not to be outdone, was told yesterday she had been selected for the New Year concerts." He looked round. "The Yard would call those triumphs. I don't. I call them everyday happenings. Some of the little things that go to make up everyday life. Now, gentlemen, I ask you. Had yesterday been the third of December, and being aware of this bee in the Met's bonnet, would I have been expected to say to my missus, 'Don't bake a cherry cake today, dear, in case you win the thirty-bob prize'? Or should I have said to my son, 'If your bosses attempt to give you a pay rise, bonus or merit award today, ask them to keep it till next week'? Or my married daughter, should she have rung up the paper and said, 'I did your prize crossword ten days ago. If mine is one of the first correct answers out of the hat, please don't announce it before December the fourth'? And finally, my young lass who has set her heart on getting into that orchestra. What would I tell her? 'If they offer you a place in the first fiddles and the date is December the third, refuse it'?" He shook his head. "I don't think so, gentlemen. To say anything like that would have been madness. To warn them that these little ordinary, everyday happenings could be dangerous would be futile, because if they avoided the things I had warned them against, something else of a like nature could have occurred.

"Let us look at our murder victims. A solicitor. Every day there are solicitors winning cases. Every day there are councillors pushing through controversial proposals, as those of us who sometimes have to attend such meetings can confirm. And, thank God, every day there are doctors performing miracles.

"Now, gentlemen, if we were to start warning the general public against little successes on December the third, we'd not only put the wind up ninety per cent of the population, but we'd have to close courts, hospitals, cancel council meetings, sports meetings, ads on TV, and tell the papers not to print any successful scoops or announce winners in any competitions at any function whatsoever." He looked at DCS Cleveland. "Have you stopped to think how many possible triumphs, as the Met calls them, there could be in the Northern Counties on any given day? Thousands. Probably tens of thousands of successes as small as passing an exam or winning a point in a magistrates' court." He looked about him. "To take any action whatsoever over this is impractical, even if we were sold on the Met's theory. However, everything the AC Crime sent us is not valueless. I am prepared to accept the conclusion he has reached about there being one murderer at large. I think we'd all agree that if there were eleven, we'd have got some of them by now. And I like the statistical backing he has given to that conclusion — the one about the variety of methods used. We were guilty of missing that, and I know some of you gentlemen were saying openly that there were eleven murderers at large. We'll nip that in the bud here and now. The official policy is that we are after one killer. All our efforts will be directed towards that one end. Any questions, gentlemen?"

"Yes, sir," said Cleveland. "Are you going to give the Met your reasons for ignoring their opinions about dates and triumphs?"

"I can't see why I should do that, Matt."

"And if — I say if, because most people here don't believe it will happen — and if, by any remote chance, the twelfth murder does occur within forty-eight hours of the third of next month, what then?"

The Chief Constable grinned. "Don't be a bloody fool, Matt. It's just because there's a one in thirty-one chance of our pal knocking off another victim on the third that I'm not going to tell the Met that their ideas are rubbish. If it happens, and they claim they warned us, we claim that we had their warning very much in mind, but there was nothing we could do about it. Which is the truth. We can't. Practicalities, Matt. Knowing the likely date of a murder, with no idea of the place or the victim, is of no use to us. Not even when some Smart Alec at the Yard has foreseen or guessed the date. So we'll carry on as before, and I'll send my thanks to the AC Crime. Does that satisfy you, Matt?"

"I shall carry out your orders, sir, but it doesn't satisfy me. I have a contact in C Division at the Yard. I spoke to him a couple of days ago, and he mentioned that he had heard one of their murder squads was preparing something for us. Just out of curiosity I asked him who it was."

"And?"

"It was done by DCS George Masters and DCI Bill Green."

The Chief Constable made no reply for a moment. "Two jacks with big reputations, eh? Masters the whizz-kid?"

"Two intensely practical and above-average successful detectives, sir."

"Yes. Yes, I know. But it makes no difference. The best of us can make mistakes." He thought for a moment or two, and then addressed the meeting again. "Gentlemen, you have all heard of the authors of the paper we have been discussing. Now, I'm no respector of persons or reputations, but we've got to think of ourselves in this business. So, to show that we're not fools big enough to ignore what Masters and Green have done for us, even though we think their ideas are as far-fetched as guano from China, I'm going to ask these two Yard men to visit us. Not to do any investigating. Using the excuse that we'd like to talk over their ideas with them. And I'd like them to be up here over the few days covering the third of December. I'll tell you why. They can be up here to see that, if the next murder does take place then, there would be little we could do to prevent it." He grinned. "And if it doesn't take place on the date they've forecast, we'll have the pleasure of seeing them with egg on their faces."

The assembled detectives laughed a little. The Chief Constable got to his feet. "That's all, gentlemen. Matt, will you come along with the ACC to my office. We'll discuss arrangements for getting the Yard men up here."

Anderson handed Masters the letter he had received from the CC Northern Counties. "Read that, George. Bill can read it after you."

"You sound slightly less than pleased, sir."

"To be honest, I don't know how I feel about it. We can discuss it when you've both seen what he has to say."

Masters began to read.

Dear Assistant Commissioner,

I am writing personally to thank you for the written opinion you sent me because I reckon I cannot say in an official letter what I want to tell you about how it has been received up here.

First off, though, I want to thank you for it. I know how long and hard one has to work to get out a document like that, and unless I'm much mistaken there'd be a few pairs of shiny pants at the Yard by the time it was finished.

Now for your opinion itself.

We drink strong ale up here, but I have to tell you that some of my officers have found it hard to swallow what you have said. I distributed copies to every plain-clothes officer from Divisional Inspector up to my DCS and then brought them all in together to discuss it.

They didn't think much of the successes, or triumphs, as you called them. They didn't think that what any of the victims had achieved shortly before their deaths had been anything out of the ordinary. We have a sort of inverted pride up here. We like winners and we like winning. But, as one of my people said about the girl sprinter who died, and I quote him word for word: "She'd never have won that race if Elsie Semple had been running. I say she'd never have won it. Not her. Not if Elsie Semple had been running." In other words, they always attribute success to luck or circumstance, and they can't recognize that the achievements of these girls were anything other than mere chance. As one DI said: "If those are what the Yard calls triumphs, no wonder the teams from the south can't hold a candle to Liverpool and Man United."

The idea of using the full moon to pick dates for crimes struck them as ludicrous. Their logic goes something like this. Nobody who wasn't loony would think of using phases of the moon for their purpose. But everybody knows there's no such thing as a loony in the sense that they are affected by the moon. Therefore the idea is daft. Despite your explanation that the man merely wanted to use something for choosing his dates and had picked

22

the phases of the moon as the way rather than use a pin or his telephone number or something like that, the idea went down like a lead balloon.

All of them accepted your opinion that there is only one murderer, first because they agree they'd have apprehended at least one among so many before now, and they saw sense in the statistical point about the methods employed to kill the women. But they see that as hard fact. They don't like what one called "indefinitiveness". For my people, a spade has to be called a bloody shovel, otherwise it could mean one of those things the kids use for building castles on Scarborough sands.

However, the opinion has fully convinced my DCS. He's called Matthew Cleveland, and he agreed in its favour all through the meeting. And because he's my senior detective, I have to take account of what he says. In addition, we've heard that the chief author of your paper was DCS George Masters. Any jack with his head screwed on right would pay attention to anything a man with his reputation has to say. So here's what I'm going to ask you. Could you send DCS Masters up here for a few days? With his team, of course, but in an unofficial capacity? Just so that DCS Cleveland could talk to him about one or two points and some of the others could have a word or two as well? I'd be grateful if you'd let him come up here on Sunday which is December 1st. Then he could be present to show his ideas are right if what he says might happen on the third or soon after actually does. If it doesn't happen, of course, he could have egg on his face, but if it does, he'll actually be up here in the area to prove his points and perhaps give us a helping hand.

Please ring me if you can send Masters and his team to Nortown, and arrangements will be made for them — and us — to make the most of their time up here.

> Yours sincerely,
> A. Pedder
> Chief Constable

After Masters, Green read the missive slowly, then he handed it back to Anderson.

"What do you think, gentlemen?" asked the AC.

"I'll tell you," replied Green, before Masters could speak. "Throughout the whole of that letter, Pedder never tells you what he thinks himself. It's all about what his officers think. They say this and they say that, but never a word about his own opinion. And that makes me think he believes what we sent him is a load of old cods. It's a polite way of saying so — blaming it all on to his junior officers."

Anderson nodded. "It struck me in much the same way," he confessed.

"And," went on Green, "he disbelieves it so much that he's certain the next murder won't be on the day George has suggested, and he wants him there to kick him in the teeth when it isn't."

Anderson turned to Masters. "I agree with Bill. Pedder is as good as asking you to put your body where your mouth is. I think I should let him know you'll be busy most of next week, don't you?"

Masters smiled. "There's something else the CC has missed out of his letter, sir, and that's any mention of any steps he proposes to take as a result of your passing on our thoughts to him. I am certain that had he proposed to initiate any move whatsoever, he would have said so, probably in the bit where he thanked you. Said how grateful he was for the lead and so on. As it is, there's nothing. Further proof, I suggest, of Bill's opinion that our work is to be totally disregarded as a working theory. The invitation, as well as being an opportunity for them to see me discomfited, is, I suspect, also a challenge of one sort or another. Either to me personally or, as it were, to a Yard team, to see how a practical force works."

Anderson nodded.

"I don't believe in rising to challenges," continued Masters.

"You what?" demanded Green in amazement.

"Not prepared ones, such as we believe this to be. It smacks of taking unnecessary risks, like kids playing that stupid game of Last Across the Road."

"So I'll tell them you're not going, shall I?"

Masters looked across at Green. "Shall we take them on, Bill?"

Green grinned, a thing he rarely did at such times. "I reckon we got more in a week, sitting on our backsides, than the whole of that lot put together got in the best part of a year. Not that that was too difficult, because they got nothing."

"Exactly what I was hoping you would say."

"Exactly? You mean word for word?"

"Just about. They got absolutely nothing in eleven months. I wouldn't have said they were in much of a position to rub our noses in the mud." He turned to Anderson. "They haven't liked what we sent up to them, sir. They've given the excuse that we've been too whimsical for the hard men of the north to accept our theories. I believe that not to be the truth."

"You don't?" asked Anderson. "How do you see it, then, George?"

"They're teetering, sir. They've missed what we saw. And they damn well know it."

"And don't like it," added Green.

"Quite. Now, sir, say we had produced absolutely solid, material evidence for them, they would have been obliged to accept it. As indeed they have accepted Bill's solid statistical analysis and our suggestion, based on probability factors and their own investigative prowess, that there is only one murderer at large. The other bits — the things they describe as airy-fairy suggestions about triumphs and phases of the moon — they are not too sure about. As I said, they are teetering as to whether to accept them or not. They are taking this attitude, not because any of the material we sent them is wrong, or even refutable. They may denigrate it, they may even deny it, but they cannot refute it even though their every instinct is not to accept or believe it. Why? Because it is new to them. They haven't come across such possibilities before. Hard men, as they claim themselves to be, are by nature conservative. So they can't accept what we have said, but neither can they refute it."

"Sitting on the fence," murmured Anderson.

"Sitting there and looking for a sign to tell them which way to jump, sir, hoping like hell that the sign, when it comes, will be a clear indication to jump down on the anti-Yard side." Masters smiled. "The clearest sign they could have, in their opinion, would be the fact that we, the authors of the whimsicality which worries them, had not enough confidence in our ideas to go up and face them, particularly over the crucial period."

"You're saying, George, that if you don't go up there they'll tear up your findings, but if you do go up they will probably hang on to them long enough to prove you right?"

"More or less, sir. Bill and I are confident that we have produced an opinion which is of value. It may not be totally correct in every detail, but the last thing we would do to members of another force, who are up against it and have appealed to us for help, is to send them material we did not consider relevant and valuable."

"I know that," replied Anderson. "But let me get it straight. You are saying that your good ideas have to be sold before they will be either accepted, and consequently made use of by Northern Counties, or not?"

"That's about it," agreed Green.

"And the thing that will sell the goods is your presence to authenticate your strong belief in their value?"

Masters nodded. "I always remember a chat I once had with the director of a big sales force. His was a reputable company, selling first-class goods, many of which are household names and as good as, if not better than, anything in their class. He told me that it cost his company at least ten pounds to put a representative on the doorstep of a potential customer. But the problem then was to get that customer to agree to see the rep, presumably to hear about new lines and so forth. The answer, according to this very successful director, was to spend another fifty pence or a pound on providing the rep with some form of inexpensive gift or small but useful article for the customer personally. A diary, or pen, or road map — that sort of thing. In order not to waste his original ten pounds, he felt obliged to spend that little bit extra with which to woo the person the rep needed to see if he was to sell his goods to that shop or office."

"I get the drift," said Anderson. "Your suggestion is that you should go up there gift-wrapped in order to save the work you put in down here."

"That's it, sir. If you are agreeable and if Bill also agrees with me."

"All the way," growled Green. "I'll even take Mr Pedder a slice of Christmas cake. Doris baked ours last week."

Anderson said, "Make your arrangements, George. I'll write a reply to Pedder. You can take it up with you. I'll butter him up a bit. Tell him that we were honoured by his first request, and that nothing on earth would make us miss the opportunity to come and learn at first-hand how a force, spread over so large an area of the country, combining urban and rural communities and problems, manages their affairs so successfully, etcetera, etcetera. How would that be?"

"First-class, sir. Please remember to include the fact that both Bill and I, genuinely, were impressed by the files they sent us. The reports from the centres they set up at each murder site were very well done. All they fell down on was in not having a sort of supra incident centre to collate the separate collations. I think that is one move I shall suggest to them, should I be asked."

Anderson made a note on his pad. "I'll remember to include your admiration for their paper work. As you say, the suggestion of collation can come from you in person. Anything else?"

"Stress that our visit is to be strictly a non-working one, sir. At all costs they must be left in no doubt that we don't think we are going up there to do their job for them. For our part, we shall make no move, even if invited to do so, without consulting you first."

"Very good point." Anderson made another note. "Anything else? Bill?"

"We seem to have covered the ground, sir. We can't plan ahead. We'll just have to play it off the cuff. Unless . . . "

"Unless what?"

"Unless you like to include a hint that I like a few slices of black pudding for breakfast."

Anderson laughed. "It might be a nice touch," he conceded.

Chapter Two

"WHY ASK US to go up to Nortown on a Sunday, Chief?" asked DS Berger as the big Rover sped up the M1. "Not that I mind, particularly, but Mr Pedder specified it as the day he wanted us to go. When I read his letter, I wondered why."

"I've been wondering about that, too, Chief," said Reed who was driving. "Is there something on we don't know about?"

The afternoon was cold, dry, grey and blustery. The further north they travelled, the windier it became. The inside of the car was a haven of warmth and well-being. Green, in his usual nearside rear seat, was snoozing after his habitual Sunday lunch of roast beef, Yorkshire pudding, roast potatoes and Brussels sprouts, followed by apple pie. He blew slightly through pouted lips as if to indicate he didn't want to be disturbed by, or at least to join in, a question-and-answer session.

"I can give you no very good answer," replied Masters, whose pipe was behaving itself and drawing very well. "I've thought about it, of course, and several things have occurred to me, none of them very satisfactory, I'm afraid."

"Such as what, Chief?"

"As you know, Tuesday is the vital day as far as we are concerned — or rather this first week of December is, if we allow for a lapse of forty-eight or seventy-two hours. I think Mr Pedder had the idea of having us up there among them for the whole of the week, and as today is the first of December, I expect it seemed to him to be a nice tidy sort of date on which to start our visit."

Berger replied: "You think he is tidy-minded, Chief? The sort that would want us to be ready to start whatever it is we have to do at the first moment of the working day on Monday?"

"Possibly. Certainly his Divisional files were tidy, and by that I mean well compiled, cross-referenced and so on. If the attitude of the man at the top percolates down through the whole force under his command, then I should imagine the Chief Constable to be precise, practical and tidy-minded. But that is just guesswork. The only thing I am sure of is that our journey is being undertaken at his request, but we are not going for the purpose of investigating their cases. So I should like you both to remember that we are not going there to offer our help unless specifically asked to do so."

"Just going to talk, Chief, in an advisory capacity?"

"Not even in an advisory capacity. To talk, yes, but only at their instigation. By that I don't mean we should be stand-offish. That would give them a totally false impression. We are there to respond to anything they like to throw at us."

"Meaning we defend our opinions if asked to do so?"

"Defend sounds a little bellicose. Explain would be a better word."

"Will they be gunning for us, Chief? Just because we're from the Met?"

"I think not. I don't anticipate a battle of whatever proportions. But make allowances for their sense of failure in this series of crimes. They are liable to be a little sensitive. They've worked hard and long and got nowhere. Such an experience is calculated to give any man a slightly jaundiced outlook. As a body, Northern Counties will be feeling a bit niggled. I think, however, that individuals among them will be as welcoming towards us as anybody else."

"More so," grunted Green soporifically.

Berger turned in his seat. "I thought you were having your Sunday afternoon nap. I was just going to open my *News of the World* and lay it over your face in the time-honoured fashion of the armchair zizzer."

"Fat chance of a snooze with you lot babbling away," retorted Green, struggling to sit more upright in his corner. "One of God's better inventions is a Sunday afternoon kip, thought up on the seventh day of His creating stint as the reward for an honest week's toil. But if He'd foreseen that three jokers like you would be one of the by-blows of His labours, He'd have made all animals dumb, including humans. Though, come to think of it, He did make quite a lot that way without, unfortunately, depriving them of the ability to make noise."

"Tetchy," said Reed, keeping his eyes on the road. "Everybody feels like nothing on earth after forty winks in a sitting position."

Masters asked: "You made some sort of remark there, Bill. Something about our Northern Counties colleagues giving us a good welcome. Did you mean it, or were you just coming back to earth?"

"I meant it, and I've heard every word you three have said."

"Are you going to tell us why they'll be waiting, open-armed, for us to appear among them?"

Green dragged a crumpled packet of Kensitas from his jacket pocket. As he opened it up, he said: "They're more hospitable in the north than we are down south."

"I've heard so."

"That's why I asked Anderson to include the bit about me liking black pudding for breakfast. That remark will get 'em going."

"You mean we'll actually be served fried blood-pudding with eggs?" demanded Berger.

"Not only that, lad. Penny ducks. . . . "

"What on earth are they?"

Green applied a match to his cigarette. "Up north, they have pork butchers. The genuine article who sell nothing but the products of the pig. I know one place up north where they have what's called a Monkey, Pig and Pie shop. Outside the window, at the top of the pillars, there are actual carvings of a monkey, a pig and a pie. Beautifully done, like in a cathedral, and all gilded."

"Never mind that, what about penny ducks?"

"Well, lad," replied Green, "you'd know them as burgers or some such new-fangled name. In my day they were known as rissoles if you made them at home. Or faggots, perhaps, if you bought them made individually down south. But up north the pork shops didn't make them one at a time. They used to fill a great, straight-sided baking tray with meat. A layer of it, two inches thick. Then, after it was cooked, they'd take a big, pointed knife and divide it up into rectangles about three by two. And you got one of those slabs for a penny."

"Penny ducks?"

"That's it, lad. For a tanner you could feed mum and dad and four kids at teatime. You heated the ducks up in the oven, and ate them with bread. Enough to keep anyone going till the next day."

"And you think we'll be given penny ducks?"

Green nodded. "Highly seasoned," he said. "Nothing better, unless it's scraps hotted up."

"Scraps of what?"

"Pork fat that's been rendered to get all the dripping out. They cut the fat up into one-inch cubes and then bung them into the oven. They come out — after they've been drained — all crisp and golden and only about a quarter their former size."

"And you eat those hot with bread?" asked Berger in disgust.

"Bread and butter, actually. For tea. And don't turn your nose up, lad. I've been to some posh cocktail parties in the Smoke where the hostesses have done exactly the same with bacon rinds. They've baked them dead, till the things just shattered at a touch, and then handed them round as smally eats and the guests have lapped them up. Up north, they don't include the rind."

"Anything else we're likely to be offered by the hospitable Northern Counties people?"

"Scads of things. Apart from such things as tripe, there are chitterlings. Now, there's a dish for you to get your teeth into, but don't have 'em unless you're sure they've been well cleaned."

Berger's face was blank, devoid of any understanding or knowledge of this last delicacy. "Cleaned?" he asked. "You mean it's a sort of shellfish?"

"Shellfish? We're talking about pigs."

"You have to clean them, you said."

"Well you would have to, wouldn't you, chitterlings being what they are."

"And what are they?"

"They're the guts of a pig, lad. The smaller intestines to be precise. They have to be turned inside out and cleaned, of course, before you can fry them to eat. For myself, actually, I prefer a bit of skirt."

"Now what's he on about, Chief?" asked Berger faintly.

31

"The frill, some people call it," said Green.

"Ah, now I'm with you," said Masters. "It's frilly," he explained to Berger. "Much like those cascade things some people wear on the fronts of their shirts."

"What's frilly, Chief?"

"The mesentery."

Berger banged his forehead with the heel of his hand. "Chief!"

"You don't know what the mesentery is? It's part of the chitterlings. Strictly anatomically, it's a fold in the peritonaeum which attaches part of the intestinal canal to the posterior wall of the abdomen. Butchers call them frills because of their appearance, but if you get a good pig's fry, it will have a bit or two of the frill in it, and then it becomes known as skirt, because it is slightly reminiscent of the bottom of a petticoat. Exceedingly tasty. In fact, a great delicacy."

"Quite right," said Green. "Pork butchers up north close on a Monday afternoon. That's when they kill their pigs. On Tuesday mornings the housewives queue up to buy a couple of pounds of pig's fry for their old men's dinners. There's always a bit of skirt in a fry, lad."

"Chief," said Berger. "If that's hospitality, I want to go home."

"Seventeen miles to Nortown, Chief," said Reed.

"Good," said Green. "That means I've got a few minutes left in which to have a snooze." He glared at Berger. "That's if you lot will let me."

"Don't worry," murmured Berger. "I won't say another word till we get there. Pork butchers! I've had them."

The Northern Counties HQ in Nortown was a pillared and porticoed edifice, built by wealthy Victorian mill owners as the town hall of the up-and-coming centre of their industrial successes. But the growing town had soon outstripped this Council House. A new one had to be built, almost next door. Still pillared and porticoed, it contained a ballroom, two court chambers and a wealth of offices for local government officers, besides the council chamber, mayor's parlour and committee rooms. The older building had been bequeathed to the police when Nortown had first set up its own borough force and, subsequently, handed on to become the HQ of the more recently formed Combined Force.

The traffic was light on this cold, windy and, by now, dark Sunday afternoon. There was no difficulty in finding parking space at the kerbside immediately in front of the steps of the HQ building.

"It's a bit gloomy," said Reed.

"Good, solid building," said Green. "None of your breezeblocks and asbestos sheeting about this. Stone, lad. Built to last for ever."

"Millstone grit, I imagine," said Masters, pausing to examine a pillar. "Found below the coal measures round here, and used fairly widely in buildings such as this. If they were to clean it, you'd find the surface lovely."

They went through the heavy, glass swing doors. The desk was to their left. After hearing who they were, the sergeant called the duty inspector from his office.

"Mr Pedder, Mr Braithwaite and Mr Cleveland are waiting for you upstairs, gentlemen."

"Mr Braithwaite?" queried Masters.

"The Assistant CC, sir."

"Thank you. Shall we find our own way up?"

"I'd better take you, sir. It'll save time explaining."

"Lead on then, lad," said Green.

The inspector came round the end of the desk. "I prefer to be called by my name. It's Limbrick."

"What's your first name, son?"

"Harold."

"Okay, Harold, lad. Let's hope there's a pot of tea waiting wherever you're taking us."

There was tea waiting to be made. The electric kettle was filled and ready to be plugged in. A tray on the Chief Constable's desk was covered by a white voile shroud with a blue edging. The cups and whatever else was under it bulged invitingly.

Masters introduced himself and then his colleagues.

"Make yourselves comfortable," said Pedder, "while I boil the water for mashing the tea."

There was a silence after this announcement. It seemed nobody

33

knew how to continue until Green said: "Chief Constable, is your office a no-smoking zone?"

"Nowhere in Nortown has been a smoke-free area for the last two hundred years."

"Thanks. Nice bit of panelling you've got round your walls. I like a bit of good wood. Classy. Adds tone."

"Not bad, is it. Gives us a lot of trouble though. They wanted to varnish it a couple of years back. I had my work cut out to stop 'em."

Masters removed his overcoat and hung it on the stand just inside the door. As he sat down again, he said: "I don't think I thanked you for inviting us, sir."

Pedder turned to him. "You might not be so ready to thank me before you go," he said.

"Why would that be, sir?" asked Masters innocently.

"Don't tell me you didn't read my letter to Mr Anderson."

"I read it, sir. I thought it expressed your point of view admirably."

"You don't mind having your opinions jumped on, then?"

"Why should I — or we, sir? They were merely opinions. You didn't expect us to find anything glaringly obvious that your chaps had missed, did you?"

"No, I didn't." He proceeded to pour boiling water into the pot.

"I thought not. For two reasons. First your files were excellent. Second, if you had thought we'd find anything, you wouldn't have sent them to us."

Pedder put the kettle down and looked keenly at Masters. "I'm not saying you're wrong."

"In that case, sir, there should be no reason for us not to appreciate your invitation, even when our visit comes to an end. Unless, of course, you propose that there should be some form of less-than-amicable competitive spirit promoted between us and that, I feel sure, is not your intention. Nor is it ours."

"I'll say this for you, Masters, you say what you think."

"Not always, sir. I find it politic to suit my attitude to my company. I imagine you could give me points on being outspoken, anyway, so why try to compete with you when, as I have just said, I

34

can see no cause for competitiveness?"

"You've a fair way with words, Masters. Not that I'm surprised. I read that opinion of yours, so I knew what you could do. But not everybody who writes 'em can say 'em to your face."

"I can, so let me put your mind at rest, Mr Pedder. If you can see our faces are red when we leave here, you may be amused, but I shall be extremely happy. So will my three colleagues. Happy because we shall be thankful another woman has not died to prove our theory. Happy, also, for you, that you will not have a twelfth murder to agonize over. Green, Reed, Berger and I are mentally fireproof, whichever way it goes, and whatever the outcome of our prognostication." Masters paused a moment. "I thought I ought to make our feelings clear at the outset, sir, because you had been so kind in your letter as to voice some worry lest the lack of a twelfth tragedy might cause us some discomfiture. With your mind at rest on that score, sir, you need no longer concern yourself over what may or may not happen during the next week."

Pedder stared for a moment without saying a word, then he turned to the tray on the table and lifted away the shroud. "Would anybody care for some plum bread with his tea?"

"Plum bread, sir?" said Berger in bewilderment.

"Yes, sergeant. Never had it?"

"Bread with plums in it, no, sir. Date bread, nut bread, and things like that. But not plums, sir."

Pedder looked hard at him. "Haven't you ever heard of plum cake, son?"

"Is that what we call fruit cake, sir? With currants and sultanas?"

"That's right. Plum cake. And this is plum bread. Just like plum cake but made with yeast instead of egg. You cut it in slices and butter it. Here, taste a bit." He offered the plate to Berger who took a slice and bit into it. Pedder waited for the verdict. "This is good, sir. Really good."

"Glad you like it. Here make yourself useful and hand it round while I pour the tea."

As the Chief Constable handed a cup to Masters, he said: "I didn't answer you just then George. I'm gunna call you George, by

35

the way. I didn't answer you because though what you said was sassy, I liked the way you said it. But I'll answer now — with a question. How can a chap like you, a practical cop with both feet on the ground, dream up airy-fairy fantasies like those opinions you sent us?"

"Have you checked what I said, sir?"

"Matthew Cleveland has."

"Has he faulted them in any way?"

"Dates and things like that, no. But the notion, George, the notion. How could we work on those ideas? We have a saying up here when something's impossible to do, we say it's as hard as trying to poke smoke up a cat's backside with a knitting needle. And that's what you are more or less suggesting we try to do. We just can't keep track of every competition, event or everyday happening where somebody might score a small personal triumph."

"I agree with that, sir."

"You do?"

"Of course. But the document was not meant for you to act on just like that. I put the theories forward for your chaps to think about."

"How do you mean?"

"Is there an overall pattern to these jobs? I don't just mean the choice of dates or the method of choosing the victims. I mean, is there a reason behind them? Are they being committed for some specific purpose which, however trivial it may seem to us, has assumed hideous proportions in the killer's mind?"

"I don't get you."

"The man must have some form of motivation. You can, of course, just write him off as a psychopath, but more often than not psychopaths are motivated by something, even if it's only a persecution complex."

Pedder rubbed his chin with a heavy, podgy hand. "Go on. You're interesting me."

"Look again at each murder. There were several of the murders where, I gathered from your reports, the man had something of a struggle with his victim. Two of them were the swimmer and the

36

doctor. Now I would guess that a young woman long-distance swimmer in full training would be quite a handful to grapple with, so I should begin to wonder about the age and strength of the killer. What the doctor's physique was like, I don't know, but while we are discussing her, I would suggest that somebody on the investigating team should ask a question which I had expected to see in the reports."

"But which wasn't there?"

Masters shook his head. "The woman doctor was called out at night. For whom would she turn out?"

"A patient of course. One of her own or her partners'."

"So you know the murderer is a patient of that group practice?"

"How can you say that? She went out on a call and was waylaid."

"You've checked there was a genuine call?"

"She had four partners. She was on duty that night. She was there to attend any one of about fifteen thousand patients registered with the practice. She took the call herself. We know that because all calls are routed through the surgery to the quack on duty. But she wouldn't be in a position to know if the call was genuine — to recognize the voice or whatever. And she didn't go to the surgery to pick up the patient's records, so we don't know who called her or where she was supposed to be going."

"There was no note of any address on her pad in the car?"

"Nothing like that. We found her pad, but it was clean."

"Which suggests somebody had ripped the top sheet off?"

"That was our opinion."

"So you've interviewed all the fifteen thousand patients to check which one of them called her out that night?"

"We're not stupid," said Pedder heavily.

"Meaning you did. With what result?"

"Everybody denies making a call at the relevant times. There were some who tried to call her but got no reply. We've satisfied ourselves they were genuine calls, and their timing helped us to decide she was lured out and killed before two in the morning."

Masters nodded. "So somebody masqueraded as a patient. A youngish man, one presumes."

37

"That's right."

"Then the question I would ask is how would that youngish man know that the woman doctor he wanted to kill would be on duty that night and not one of her colleagues — possibly a male?"

Pedder glared at Masters for a moment or two. "What's your answer to your own question?"

"Youngish men are not usually conversant with the duty rosters of doctors, the times of surgeries and so on. Least of all healthy males, as we must assume our man to be. Women know these things better than men because they have to enlist medical help for their families so much more often. I'm disregarding elderly, unfit men, of course.

"Now, my belief is that if most men wouldn't have that information about the habits of doctors in their own home areas, how much less likely are they to have it in an area away from their own stamping ground?"

"You're as good as saying that the killer is from the catchment area of that particular practice."

"Either that, or he got the information he needed from somebody in that area — perhaps even from the practice itself, in which case somebody spoke to him. And you can narrow the time down. He hadn't got much of it to play with between the announcement of the doctor's exam successes and her murder."

Pedder regarded Masters speculatively. "You're a clever man, George. You were determined to make me accept the fact that your triumph theory is important. And here you are using it to support a logically developed argument which I can't shoot down."

"You asked us to come up and talk with you, sir, presumably to see if we could substantiate our opinions in any way. That is all I've tried to do."

"And I suppose you have other little suggestions up your sleeve which you didn't bother to put on paper?"

"It would be a long job, sir, writing out all the little things that can occur to one in a long and protracted job like this. Besides, they come out better in a chat."

Pedder grunted. "I'm not asking you to take over, George . . . "

"I think you would be making a mistake were you to do so."

38

"Hear me out."

"Sorry."

"But I'd like you to spend a lot of time with Matthew. He's sold on your opinions already. If you can make him free of a few more thoughts such as you've been baffling me with, he'd be more than grateful."

"If that is what you'd like us to do, sir, we shall co-operate gladly."

"And one more thing."

"What's that?"

"You've now made me as nervous as hell about next Tuesday. Before you came I was laughing it off. Now I'm not so sure."

"I shall not attempt to calm your feelings by telling you to forget it, sir. You'll understand why. But I will say that there is very little I think you can do in the way of preventing it. Unfortunately we'll all have to wait for the blow to fall before we'll be able to grapple with it."

"And you think then we'll be able to bottom it?"

"We can't guarantee it, but after Mr Cleveland has spoken to us at length and then, perhaps, acted on some of our suggestions, I think we'll get somewhere near a result."

"You sound pretty sure of yourself."

"Such was not my intention, sir, but I can see no mileage in anticipating failure. In fact, I refuse to do so and, I suspect, so do you."

"You're right there. Now, come on and have a slice of plum bread before those others have scoffed it all. And another cup of tea, and while you're having it we'll talk about a few arrangements we've made for you."

When Pedder was seated once more in his chair, he called the meeting to order.

"I've been neglecting some of you this last half-hour," he said apologetically, "but I wanted a gas with Mr Masters, and what he's had to say leads me to believe we can do business. But that'll be for the daytime and Matt Cleveland will make arrangements for conversations at all levels.

"When we invite guests, we like to do them proud. We're

hospitable people up here. . . ."

"Chitterlings," said Berger to Reed in a loud whisper.

"What's that you said, Sergeant? Chitterlings? We're not that hospitable. You won't be lashed up with all the greatest delicacies like chitterlings, caviare and such, but we'll entertain you. We've booked you in at the Station Hotel here. It's a bit old-fashioned, but good. The only thing you'll have to watch out for is the waiter who rushes to spread your napkin on your lap. I've not quite decided whether he thinks I don't know what the damn thing's for or whether he's trying to touch me up, so forestall him if you're at all sensitive that way.

"We've got some sort of entertainment for you every night. Tonight, for instance, we're having a drinks party here in our mess. I've invited all the jacks involved in this case to come and meet you four and to have an informal gas about things. In case you've been wondering, that's why I wanted you to come up here today, because they'll be coming in from all the divisions and I didn't want to drag them in during the working week."

Green asked: "What's their attitude going to be like, sir? Will some of them be a bit anti, or will their natural courtesy overcome the big laugh they're expecting to get?"

"Natural courtesy? I like that. There'll be no natural courtesy, Mr Green. They'll take you as they find you."

"Expecting to find us as soft as Joe Soap?"

"Highly likely. Are you feeling windy?"

"Do I look as if I am?"

Pedder laughed. "I reckon you'll give as good as you'll take." He spoke to them all. "Time's getting on. The lads will be gathering by eight o'clock, George. If you and yours will make it across here as soon as you've had dinner, that'll be fine. You can make it on foot. It's no more than a lock of perches down the road. It'll save drinking and driving."

"We're looking forward to the party, sir."

"My name's Alf," said Pedder. "You and Green can call me that. It'll save all this sir business which you seem to chuck in at every touch and turn. To keep me in my place, I reckon. You sergeants will obey the rules. Only because of discipline."

"Fine by us, Alf," said Green. "I'm Bill to everybody except George's missus and she calls me William."

"Right. We'll discuss further arrangements later. Matt, will you take our friends along to the Station Hotel? Show them the mess as you go." He turned to Masters. "It's the old council chamber. The chairman's bench makes a good bar."

As soon as Cleveland had seen them into the hotel, Masters said: "Right. It's a quarter to seven. I want everybody in my room, bathed and changed, by seven o'clock. We've a lot of talking to do."

"Why not the bar, Chief?"

"Because I want everybody to be clear-headed when we meet this crowd tonight. We'll stick to water at dinner. You'll be able to get enough free booze at the locals' expense later in the evening."

"See you on the ice," mumbled Green and lumbered towards the lift.

As soon as they were all gathered in his room, Masters said: "Pedder is playing the old game of divide and conquer. He's going to split us up on the pretence that we shall cover more ground that way. You two sergeants will find yourselves being given the third degree by a number of Divisional DIs. The DCI and myself will be cast in the role of clay pigeons for the Supers to fire at. We've got to take a common line, so take it all in."

Masters then recounted in detail his conversation with Pedder. When he got to the end, he said: "That ties in one of our theories and gives them something to think about. And for tonight, you will concentrate on the woman doctor. Draw your opposite numbers out as to how her killer could have learned she would be on duty."

"Stress he must have been a local from her area, Chief?"

"Not exclusively. There are lots of other possibilities. Apart from questioning local chronic patients who would know the movements of all the doctors, their private phone numbers and so forth, make the locals say whether they looked for possibilities in the practice Ansafone if there is one. Make them say whether they've done anything about other possible callers to the surgery that day. They won't have done so, because it's our line of thinking and consequently new to them. So you'll have them at a disadvantage.

"In this connection let me remind you of callers at a surgery. Drug reps, equipment reps and, these days, computer reps. Then there are members of the surgery staff. Have they told anybody about the rota? Is there a regular rota displayed in the waiting room? Were there any casual patients that day? If you think about it, you can probably come up with scores of ways the killer could have known that the doctor was on duty."

"Chief," said Berger, "I know a way."

"Let's hear it, lad," encouraged Green.

"Our local practice uses the garage near us for petrol. The one I use. I know, and the people at the garage know, that the doctor who's to be on duty that night always comes in to fill up about tea time. It's a ritual with them. A sort of standing order of the practice."

Masters said nothing for a moment and then: "We're not drinking tonight, Sergeant Berger. But the next time we find ourselves together at a bar, remind me I owe you one for that idea. I don't say it is the right one, but I have a feeling it's very close to the mark. What do you think, Bill?"

"It smells good to me. I mean, for petrol you could read Polo Mints. She might go into the local sweetie shop to arm herself with something to suck to help keep her awake in the small hours when she's driving around. But it's the same idea. Anybody present at the time of buying — petrol or mints — could get the information that the lass was on duty by the simplest bit of questioning."

"Use it," commanded Masters. He got to his feet. "Time to eat now. We'll continue this over dinner."

Masters made more points. "Stress the fact that the killer cannot be a weakling. Stress also that he seems to be an unmarried man or a travelling representative.

"I'll go into that last. He gets about far and wide at all times, day and night. That's difficult for a normally married man. Reps, however, are away on their own most nights, so there's no wife about to grow suspicious."

"Tie in with reps calling on doctors, Chief?"

"If you like, without being too specific. Let our friends do a bit of putting two and two together for themselves. In fact, don't be specific at all, or you could get a kick in the teeth, later. But urge every one of them to go through his own case or cases, treating it like we've treated the doctor business. Don't be drawn into arguments about our opinions, and make sure that we'll be pleased rather than otherwise if there is no murder this week. That will draw some stings."

The conversation went on in like vein until Masters was satisfied each member of his team was well enough briefed to be able to hold his own in the battle of words that lay ahead. Finally, he said: "We've been sitting here longer than we should have done, but I'd rather be ten minutes late for the party than that any of us should find himself surrounded and at a loss. Drink sparingly, please. We can always have one when we get back here. In fact, we'll take it as read that we shall meet in my room later."

As Masters had foreseen, it was all well laid on. Pedder led him round the various groups of detectives, Braithwaite shepherded Green, and Cleveland took charge of the sergeants. The ice was thick. Masters got the impression that before his team's arrival on the scene, fresh orders had been issued to the locals. "Don't go for them like a bull at a gate, lads. There's something in what they've been saying after all." Deprived of one sort of ammunition, and not yet provided with another, the locals seemed in something of a quandary and in some doubt as to how to deal with the visitors.

"My name's King," said a DI to Green, "and there's summat I want to ask you. Would you like another of the same before we begin?"

"I'm quite happy as I am at the moment, Mr King. Or shall I call you Fred?"

"Fred'll do. It's about those dates. The moon thing."

"What about them?"

"I want to know how it is your lot came up with them and ours didn't."

"How do you mean?"

"Four of you work for a week. There's nearly four hundred of us been working for a year. You get something we didn't. Why?"

"Have you ever had all eleven files in front of you at once, Fred?"

"I haven't, but they have had them here at HQ. And a computer to help them find the answers."

Green accepted a cigarette and a light. "The point is, Fred, that you can only get out of a computer what you put in. So when somebody asked your computer to find some sort of pattern to the dates of the killings, it said there was no sort of correlation. Which there isn't as far as it can tell unless somebody has first fed it with the figures relating to the phases of the moon. And I don't suppose anybody other than an astronomer would ever do that to any computer."

"You mean the Yard computer had been programmed that way?"

"No, mate, it hadn't. It was a case of the human brain beating all these new-fangled contraptions. George Masters found the relationship."

"I've heard he's got a brain on him like a computer."

"Then you've heard wrong."

"He hasn't? But if he can come up with answers like that, he's a bit out of the ordinary, I'd have said."

"But not like a computer. He's too creative. Some people say he's a great lateral thinker, others that he can take mental leaps in the dark, that he's got a crossword-puzzle mind, and so on. But he hasn't any of those things. He's just developed the ability to concentrate his mind and to think of literally one problem at a time, to the exclusion of everything else, for as long as it takes him to come up with a solution or possibly several solutions.

"He can do it sitting in a car, walking the streets, lying awake in bed, anywhere. I've often said he's jammy, but he isn't. He makes his own luck. As I say, he can come up with two or three alternative and possible solutions, but he won't know which is the right one until some little thing happens to identify it as the right one. Then he romps home. As I said, I've called him jammy, because those little things seem to happen for him. Actually, mate, they happen for all of us. He's the only one who recognizes their importance as often as not."

44

Fred King held out his hand for Green's glass, and this time the Yard man surrendered it. When King returned, their conversation turned to other things and Green became the centre of a group discussing everything in the world but the eleven unsolved murders.

"Minor triumphs," said Masters, half sitting on a table and addressing DS Benjie Daley.

"Their significance," replied Daley. "Look here, Mr Masters, I've got my DCI and my Divisional DI alongside me right now. Sandy Finch and Ashley Head. You met them when you first arrived at the party."

"I remember," replied Masters. "Good evening once again, gentlemen."

"We want to get to the bottom of this triumph business," said Daley.

"Right enough," said Finch, "because Ashley and I reckon we've taken that into account in our investigations, and quite frankly, Mr Masters, we reckon it doesn't work."

"May I ask which of the victims you have been concerned with, gentlemen?"

"Two of them. The beauty queen and the town councillor," replied Daley.

"And I can tell you," said Finch forcefully, "we covered the ground to see whose backs had been put up by the councillor getting her bit of nonsense through the council. Some people were going to suffer by it. We knew that. We combed through the lot to find those who held a grudge because of it. And then we went to town on them."

"But nothing came of it, obviously."

"Same with the beauty queen," said Head. "Wherever there's a do where these girls chill their beef in public to get a bit of a cheque and a sash to keep them warm, there's a lot of noses put out of joint. I came across the usual cattiness, but I didn't come any-where near getting a lead on her murder."

"So you see, George," said Daley, "we beat you to your theory. We investigated those triumphs and they're meaningless in our view."

"Now listen, all of you," said Masters. "I spent hours and hours on your files and I was most impressed by your reports. So I am not trying to suggest that you fell down in your investigations concerning people who might wish to ease grudges by killing any of those women."

"You're not? So you agree your triumph theory is a non-starter, at least in our two cases."

Masters shook his head. "There are two sides to every coin. More to some."

"Meaning?"

"There are two ways of approaching the triumph theory. You exhausted one approach. In the opinion we sent up here, we suggested the second approach might lead to gold because, when we applied it, we found similarities in all cases."

"I don't understand that at all," said Finch.

"Nor me." Head was slightly belligerent.

Masters spoke quietly and patiently. "We will use your two cases as examples. The beauty queen first. She, presumably, was chosen by the usual panel of judges. She perhaps won the contest by the narrowest of margins. If one of the judges had, perhaps, reversed just one pair of names on his or her list, the girl who won might have been placed second or even third."

The three local detectives nodded and murmured their understanding of this obvious point.

Masters went on: "So, gentlemen, if the girl who won had come second, there are two questions to be answered. The first, would there have been a murder at all? The second, would the girl who is now dead still be alive, while the one who beat her and is still alive have been the one to be killed?"

Daley grimaced while thinking. Head frowned. Finch opened his mouth as if to speak, but uttered no sound. Masters waited a moment or two for an answer.

"I'm beginning to get this," said Daley at last. "What you're saying is that it didn't matter who came first in the contest, whichever girl won would have got the chop."

"Don't you agree it is a possibility?" asked Masters.

"It is," agreed Daley, "because, well, because it is there as a possibility."

"So," said Masters, "it is not the death of one particular girl you are investigating, but the death of the winner of the beauty contest. And there is a difference, gentlemen. The victim could have been Miss White, Miss Black or Miss Brown. Those who disliked the panel's choice would be different in each case. Our man went for the winner, whoever she happened to be. So, had the marks been slightly different, your victim would have been different."

Finch said: "You're saying the death had nothing to do with the girl herself, other than the fact she was lucky enough to win the title."

"Or unlucky enough, depending on how you look at it," murmured Head.

Masters nodded. "Taken in isolation, that one example might well be of no value at all. But I'll ask you, Mr Head, whether your woman councillor would be dead had she not succeeded in getting her proposal accepted. What do you think?"

"By both your theory and ours, she would still be alive, sir. According to us, if she'd failed she wouldn't have made enemies — not by that particular bit of legislation, at any rate — and by yours because if she hadn't pushed it through she wouldn't have had a personal triumph."

"So you agree that in both cases the triumph idea could have some merit?"

"It looks like it."

"My job is not to convince you of anything," said Masters, "but merely to chat with you and answer questions if possible. However, as I have caused you at least to consider that a second approach exists, could I suggest you look at some of the other nine cases in the same light? Just to satisfy yourselves that a second, similar approach is possible in each case?"

"That little actress," said Finch. "I'd seen her once or twice in plays. Quite good, she was. Her agent must have got her that part in the TV ad. What if he hadn't, Mr Masters? It could have gone to a girl from anywhere outside our area. How would the killer have managed then?"

"You wouldn't have had a dead actress," replied Masters.

"Some other woman who achieved something on that day, within your area, would have been killed. The same rules apply. Your actress wasn't killed as a person, she was killed as an achiever."

Head grunted. "I've got the point, Mr Masters. Ordinary women, living ordinary lives and not winning anything, are perfectly safe. Is that it?"

"I believe so, Mr Head. And that proposition may well help you to find a motive for the murders."

Pedder cornered Braithwaite for a quiet chat.

"He's a clever bastard, that Masters, Stan."

"What's he said or done now?"

"I've been wandering around, listening in to the groups as they chat to those four."

"And?"

"They're word perfect. He's got 'em rehearsed. They're all toeing exactly the same line, with their own little variations of course. Even the two sergeants, they've got it all off pat."

"I'd noticed they were holding their own. I thought a bit of top-weight might make them a bit unsure of themselves, but they're not. They're standing up well under fire."

"The point is, Stan, Masters didn't know we'd laid on this little party. Nor what the idea behind it was. So he couldn't have briefed his lads that thoroughly before he got up here."

"No way he could have known what line we'd be taking, Alf. Not beforehand, that is."

"Which means that between them leaving my office at half-past six and getting back here by half-past eight they've changed, had dinner, and had a dress rehearsal for the show they've put on tonight."

"And they're word perfect, you reckon?"

"Not only in their own parts, Stan. They know everybody's words."

"Are you making a point, Alf?"

"Yes. We could learn a lot from them."

"You're not serious, Alf."

"I am. Teamwork, Stan. Teamwork at the drop of a hat and of a very high order. Like it or not, that's what we need — what every

48

force needs — when it comes to God-awful problems like these eleven murders." He raised his eyes to heaven. "I overheard that sergeant, the one called Reed, explaining to a veteran DS old enough to be his father that a modern, successful jack like Masters now carries round with him, in addition to his murder bag, a library of reference books including, besides Martindale and toxicology books, a current *Whitaker's Almanack* just so that when he has a bright idea like this one about the moon he can look up the dates of the phases. Now I ask you, Stan, can you see any of our chaps ever consulting an almanack?"

"Not even Old Moore's, Alf."

Pedder shook his head. "They're a bloody revelation to me, this lot, I can tell you."

"Not what you expected then?"

"Not by a long chalk. I don't know what I did actually expect, but I suppose I expected Masters to wear suede shoes instead of highly polished brown brogues. Shows how mistaken one can be."

"Meaning we could have been wrong about these murders, Alf?"

"Not wrong exactly, Stan. Even Masters says the stuff we've got is impeccable. We just haven't got it all. We're short on ideas or concepts, and I agree with Masters when he says that if we were more of a team, not working quite so much in divisional pockets, we'd spark more ideas off each other and so bring home the bacon."

"Matt's DCS. He should draw it together."

"He does, Stan, he does. And to do him credit he stood up for the Yard's opinions, remember. But Matt works in isolation. It all comes up to him here at HQ. But he's just one man, virtually speaking. If he misses out on his co-ordination, there's nobody with him to discuss it with. Not on the level that's needed, anyway. I'd give quite a lot to have Judder Masters up here."

Braithwaite nodded, and then grinned. "You've not called him Judder to his face, have you?"

"Not yet," replied Pedder, "but it'll slip out. When I was a kid, every lad christened George was Judder to his mates and the habit's stuck."

"Same with me," said Braithwaite. "In fact my brother's always known as Judder. Even his missus calls him it."

After a short debriefing meeting in his room, Masters sent his team off to their beds, satisfied that they had kept the flag flying high.

The next morning at breakfast he told them what had been laid on by Braithwaite, who seemed to be in charge of such arrangements.

"It's divide and conquer again, I'm afraid. You two . . . " he nodded towards the sergeants, " . . . are being taken to a division each day. You'll go together. I have no doubt about your ability to cope, so I shall not attempt to brief you again. The big thing is to listen, and only to answer when appealed to directly. And keep your replies brief and along party lines."

"No suggestions at all, Chief?"

"Play it naturally. If there are any suggestions on a par with the one about the garage, give them the benefit. That's all I want to say about that. You will take the car, because I don't want you stranded or delayed by the locals. They'll be generous, so drink sparingly, if at all. It may even be their idea of a joke to get you squiffy. Don't let them. Drink as much tea and coffee as you like, but be back here by five at the latest and don't let them detain you."

"Stay strictly sober, lads," counselled Green. "They'd breathalyse you as leave as look at you. Just for laughs. Don't give 'em the chance."

"The DCI and I will manage on foot," resumed Masters, "as we shall be at HQ here. But I should add that they've laid on some form of entertainment for us every night."

"Like what, Chief?"

"Old-time music hall tonight. The local Christmas performance of *Messiah* tomorrow night. Some form of cabaret on Wednesday and we're all dining with Mr and Mrs Pedder on Thursday. That's the lot. We'll have a session at six tonight. As we're only going to a theatre after dinner we'll be able to have a drink together, I hope. I seem to remember I owe Berger one."

"First round on you, then," said Green, removing the rind from a fried circle of black pudding. "I wish they'd taken this off before they cooked it."

"They can't," said Masters. "It would break up in the pan if they did."

Green grunted and cut a chunk from the end of a sausage.

Chapter Three

THE FIRST TUESDAY of December and Masters, despite his self-control, was nervous. He sensed, in every limb, an expectancy of tragedy. At least that is how he identified it to himself. He had tried to think through the alternatives. The prospect of failure in the matter of his prognostication for this day did not, he felt sure, worry him in the slightest. The idea that he could be made to look foolish he dismissed. He had already drawn the sting from that one and, he confessed to himself, he had had egg on his face many times before. He toyed with the idea that his wife Wanda and son Michael might be in some sort of trouble and so made an early call to his home to reassure himself on that score and to dispel the idea that some degree of extra-sensory perception was working overtime between himself and his loved ones. He considered the possibility that he was sickening for something, but discarded the idea when he discovered at breakfast time that his appetite was so unimpaired that he ate almost as heartily as Green.

As soon as the sergeants had left them to go about their visits arranged for that day, he turned to Green.

"Bill, I've got the jim-jams."

"Collywobbles?" asked Green sympathetically. "The beer up here's strong. The locals tell me that it keeps them as regular as spring medicine. You had a couple of pints last night."

"Nothing like that."

"What then? You had a good breakfast. That didn't upset you, did it?"

"No. I thoroughly enjoyed my meal."

"In that case, all I hope is it's not catching, whatever it is."

"From which I am, I suppose, to gather that you are feeling one hundred per cent fit and chirpy with it."

Green looked at Masters for a moment. "Actually you're not."

"I'm not what?"

"To gather I'm on top of the world."

"Ah!"

"I thought it was just me. But if you say you've got the jim-jams . . . look, George, I think you're tired. You've had a heavy year, starting with three months off sick with hepatitis. You've had two or three big cases since, and now this caper. You worked till all hours on those files, you wrote that long-winded opinion and then you've rushed up here on a Sunday, without any sort of weekend break, listened to Pedder, attended his party, held briefing sessions for us, chat shows for the locals, attended their tribal theatre gathering last night and so on. It's not stopped for long enough."

"You could be right, Bill."

"I know I'm right, because I'm feeling tired myself. I wasn't off sick for three months, I know, but I balance that out with my old age. So if I'm feeling tired, so are you. And I'm going to tell Braithwaite that we want to stop at lunchtime so's we can get in a bit of kip this afternoon before going to hear this *Messiah* thing tonight. Right, chum?"

"A very good idea, Bill. A siesta. Just the ticket."

"Leave it to me to arrange. Actually, I don't think they'll mind a break from us. We must be a damn nuisance to them by now, and they'll welcome the chance to get on with some routine work. We could cut out the *Messiah*, too, if you'd rather."

"I think not, Bill. Matthew Cleveland has a contact at the Yard, and when it was decided that we should come up here he took the trouble to ring his pal in an effort to find out what would interest us. He was told that I like good singing, so they made a special effort to get the seats for tonight's performance. I wouldn't like to appear boorish in the face of such kindness. Besides, I really would like to hear the work. You know that rack in the foyer where there are handbills for local events? They had some for this show, so I helped myself to a copy. The soloists are top-liners."

"Oh yes? Would I know about any of them?"

"Margaret Whitehead, the soprano?"

Green shook his head and then changed his reply. "We heard her a few weeks ago on a record in 'Your Hundred Best Tunes'."

"Very likely. Then there's Nancy Festival, contralto."

"Even I know about her," said Green. "She's a worldwide celebrity, isn't she?"

"Without equal in most people's view."

"What's she doing coming here, then? I'd have thought she had no need to go anywhere but London, New York, Milan and big centres like that."

"She sings in all the big places, of course, but I suspect that even the greatest will occasionally come out to the provinces for major concerts. The Nortown Philharmonic Choir is pretty well known. Not quite on a par with the Huddersfield and Glasgow people, perhaps, mainly because they are not nearly so long-established and because they've never gone in for household names among conductors. But they're good enough to attract Whitehead, Festival, with Darren as tenor. I don't know the bass, James Capper, but if he's in company like that he should be able to sing 'The trumpet shall sound' well enough to bring a lump even to your throat, Bill. And talking of trumpets, they've imported a chap called Maxwell Mawby as the instrumental soloist."

"Quite a line up, then. Just up your alley."

Masters nodded. "I'm looking forward to it."

DCS Matthew Cleveland drove Masters and Green back to the Station Hotel at lunchtime by way of the Central Hall where *Messiah* was to be sung that evening. The detour was ostensibly to show them where to come and where to park in the Freemen's Square with its central clock tower. As they went, Cleveland said: "You'll not get dinner at the Station Hotel tonight as the performance begins at seven-thirty and they don't start to serve till then."

"I've got it sussed out," said Green. "They'll supply us with a plate of sandwiches somewhere about half-past six, and we can have a light supper if we like to order it for when we get back. They put up a sort of chicken salad picnic in a confectioner's box with half a bottle of vino and a tuppenny custard each."

"My missus," said Cleveland, "wondered if the four of you would like to come back with us afterwards. She'll be with me tonight, and she thought we could all go back and have a bite at our place. It might save you the bother of arranging your picnic and she'd like it."

"We shall certainly come in that case," said Masters. "But I hope Mrs Cleveland won't go to too much trouble. Four of us, rather late at night, is a pretty tall order for a woman who is going out for the evening herself."

"Philippa suggested it herself, George, and believe you me, she's not the sort to suggest doing something she doesn't want to do. She's heard a lot about you four these last few days and she said she'd like to meet you if it could be arranged."

"We're already looking forward to it," said Green. "Tell her she can include us in."

Cleveland dropped them at the hotel, but refused to join them for a drink. "To be honest," he said, "you two taking a few hours off gives me a chance to do a bit of catching up and thinking about what we've been discussing."

After the local man had left them, Green took charge. He ushered Masters into the dining-room and ordered a bottle of wine with lunch — to aid sleep. Then, when the meal was over, he hurried Masters upstairs. "Get into your pit and snore your head off, George. I'm going to get the old head down myself, but I'll be knocking on your door at half-past five expecting to wake you up out of a deep sleep. So get to it."

Masters smiled. "Thanks, Bill."

"Still got the jim-jams?"

"Yes. An indescribable feeling. Mental unease."

"Expectancy, that's what it is," grunted Green. "It's the day. The feeling will be gone tomorrow."

A few minutes later Masters was in bed and, contrary to his own expectations, was soon asleep.

The full moon, though not yet riding high, was already surrounded by a yellow storm halo. The low patches of cloud, driven by the north-east wind that had been increasing in intensity for the past three days, whipped rapidly across its face like so many crêpe-de-Chine scarves flicked by an *ingénue* of yesterday pretending an insouciance she neither felt nor possessed.

The chill wind, gestated over distant frozen wastes, buffeted the dark buildings of the mean little street, gloomy as a candlelit cellar, dark-walled and shadow-filled. It was playing silly winds: pole-vaulting over roofs, screaming abuse at chimney stacks, whirling wrapping papers high in the air and piling the dry gutter grit into dirty grey barkhans. It was gate-crashing, too: finding cracks in the ill-fitting woodwork of old window frames, it was strumming jew's-harp melodies with loose edges of wallpaper; sliding gleefully down chimneys, it was puffing smoke out into small sitting-rooms, causing eyes to smart; everywhere it was infiltrating in mean draughts so that grannies, crouched by their hearths, drew shawls closer round their thin shoulders while younger, more active folk struggled to plug gaps with tightly folded sheets of newspaper.

This mean, deserted street was Market Street, Nortown. The inhabitants of the houses had already immured themselves against the night. The small terrace houses were full of noise from radios, tapes and televisions, and none of those who lived there was showing the slightest interest in what was about to take place almost on their doorsteps. They were, apparently, unaware of anything outside their own walls except the discord of the wind storm.

The clock in the tower in Freemen's Square which had been shown to Masters at lunchtime, a hundred yards from Market Street, struck seven, the notes first loud, then faint, as the gusting wind toyed with this new plaything. As if on cue, a switch in the foyer of the biggest building in Market Street was flicked down. Lights blazed, illuminating the front of the vast Central Hall. Through the glass of the doors, on an old-fashioned easel, could now be seen a large, hand-lettered poster:

Tuesday, Wednesday, Thursday
December 3rd, 4th, 5th
at 7.30 p.m.

The Nortown Philharmonic Choir

accompanied by the Nortown Orchestra

presents

MESSIAH

by George Frederick Handel

Conducted by Rodney Butcher, LRAM, ARCM, ARCO

Soloists:		
	Margaret Whitehead	Soprano
	Nancy Festival	Contralto
	Desmond Darren	Tenor
	James Capper	Bass
	Maxwell Mawby	Trumpet

The Central Hall, Market Street

Admission £2.50, £2.00, £1.50,
bookable at The Music Shop, Goldhawk Road, Nortown
Phone No. 3906 1206

At the moment the lights went on, Masters and his team were preparing to set out for the Central Hall. So were many others.

A mile away, in a new semi on a recently erected housing estate, Robert Frame and Ena, his wife of seven months, were putting on their coats before braving the elements. They had two seats for this first performance.

Robert was a professed atheist, an active left-wing socialist and a would-be intellectual. Fortunately for him he was still sensitive to the good things in life as lived in Nortown. So sensitive, in fact, that eighteen months earlier he had fallen in love with Ena, a pretty, God-fearing member of the Pennine Road Chapel choir. He was still so much in love with her that though he never accompanied her to chapel services, he made no objection to her continued and regular attendance. So great was her influence over him that she could, occasionally, persuade him to forget his atheism and assist at those functions which, under the generic name of efforts, were held to raise funds for the furtherance of the propagation of the gospel or to repair the chapel roof.

In a moment of weakness, one evening a fortnight before, when Ena was standing naked before him, all warm and cuddly after her bath, he had consented to attend tonight's performance of *Messiah*.

At the time it had seemed little enough to agree to as a quid pro quo for the delights before him. Now he was regretting his promise. His principles and the inclement weather bolstered his protests as Ena straightened her coat collar in front of the hall-stand mirror.

"Some entertainment this is going to be." His voice was grumpy because, apart from an innate reluctance to patronize oratorio, he knew that for the space of three long hours he would be denied the pleasure of smoking his own hand-rolled fags. That, he realized, would be penance enough without listening to what he mentally described as a load of biblical caterwauling.

"It'll be lovely. You'll enjoy it." Ena's voice was enthusiastic and placating at one and the same time. "Once it starts you'll be pleased you came."

"I've heard it before. Bits of it at any rate. That Hallelujah thing."

"The Hallelujah Chorus. Don't forget we shall probably have to stand up when they sing that." She turned and kissed him on the end of his long, rather thin nose. "As a mark of respect."

"Respect? Who for? You know what this show's about, don't you? It's just so much classical pop for the culture vultures."

"Oh, Bob, it's not. It's nice."

"That's what I meant. Nice! A prestige disco for the status conscious. All the nobs in Nortown parading to show how much they appreciate what they call good music."

"It's not like that at all, really it isn't. People like the arias and choruses because they know them."

He opened the front door. "That's even worse. You're saying it's a singalong in fur coats. A sentimental wallow for those who like to hear only what they already know. Nothing atonal, no discords, only sweet stuff. And I bet they go because they know it'll be played how it always used to be played in their young days. Not hotted up." He hurried out to the little car. "I'll bet they think of them as golden days, forgetting that half the country was going hungry then."

"You're being unfair, Bob."

He slammed his door and started up. "Am I? You ask 'em. They'll fill you full of crap about when all their world was young and life was as rosy as . . . " He eased on to the road.

"As rosy as what?"

"Hell, I don't know. What is rosy?"

She answered him quietly. "Our life's rosy, Bob."

He grunted assent and then, quite surprisingly, said, "As rosy as an apple polished for a harvest festival. There, you see, you've got me on this chapel kick now."

She hugged his left arm. "I remember how you polished those apples for me to take to the harvest festival. They looked lovely piled up in a little pyramid in front of the rostrum."

Frame was human enough to feel a thrill of gratitude for having pleased her so much that his polishing the apples was still remembered after three months. The prospect of sitting through a performance of *Messiah* didn't seem quite so bad now, but he still had serious doubts about the artful nature of a religion which, by battening on an atheist's love for his wife, could cause that same atheist, in some measure, to contribute to its own insidious success. His thoughts were darkened by the discord in his mind.

Simultaneously, Sid Carrot and his wife, Elsie, were bickering. They were joint caretakers at the Central Hall, and it was they who had switched on the lights in the foyer.

Sid, a tall, lugubrious man, was in his shirt sleeves and braces. Elsie in a smock. She stood over him as he stooped to lift the bolt at the bottom of the big swing doors. "You'd better getter jacket on before they start arriving, you Sid. There'll be the Alderman here." She was, as her husband knew, referring to Alderman Herbert Wrigley, the chairman of trustees for the hall and so, in a sense, their employer. Like most women, Elsie was careful of appearances when she thought such care would pay dividends.

"I don't care what you say, I'm not staying here all night to listen to that lot a second time in one day. Not when I've got the same again Wensdy and Thursdy nights." He straightened his back very slowly, not because he was in any pain but because it was in his nature to do everything slowly. He sniffed derisively at the bolt as if to show he had bested it in some way, then he opened and closed his mouth, slowly, as if anticipating the taste of beer.

"Don't you try to fool me, Sid Carrot. How can you have heard it once already today?" Elsie's voice was harsh and unmusical, with a break on each vowel, as if the vehemence of her feeling were too great to be sustained by her vocal chords. It gave a hectoring note to what was, after all, her normal tone of voice when addressing her husband, whether at work or indulging in connubial bliss. So there was no objection from Sid who proceeded to explain his former statement.

"I had a bellyful this afternoon listening to rehearsal."

"Get out of it. That was only some of the band and the principals as they call them."

"Know it all, don't you? Band? It's an orchestra. An' them principals is soloists. They y'are, it says so on the placard. I tell you, Else, they had one of the men singers up on the stage with an Adam's apple as big as a blooming conker. It went up an' down like a chunk of fat pork on a bit of string as is being swallowed and brought back time an' again. Just like a seasick landlubber greasing the ways for his next throw-up."

"Thanks very much. Choice, I must say."

"He kept howling 'Come for tea, Come for tea', to row after row of empty seats. Reminded me of one of them touts they used to have outside the caffs in Skegness, shouting the odds about meat and two veg on a rainy Bank Monday when there was nobody about to hear 'im."

"'Comfort ye'! You wet week. 'Comfort ye'! Not 'come for tea'." The pride of superior knowledge made Elsie's vowels crack more than ever.

"I get all the comfort I want from a pint of half an' half in The Red Duster, and if I want music I can listen to the lad on the piano singing 'Ramona'."

Elsie nodded her understanding. She was one of the last of the old breed of working-class wives who believed that her man deserved his pint of an evening even if as idle as her Sid. So she made no move to forbid the trip so broadly hinted at. She only laid down conditions.

"There's the cups to be got out for tea at the interval and the urn to be filled and lit before you go. And I'll want you back here in good time to put the lights out and lock up. I'm not wandering round this place by myself in the dark. It gives me the creeps."

Elsie was not normally afraid of the dark, but the Central Hall was a big place with lots of subsidiary rooms besides the concert auditorium with its dressing-rooms and kitchen. Sid, however, was not prepared to pander to the frailties of women without having the last word.

"Don't be so daft," he said. "I'll bet you give the Hall the creeps, whether it's dark or not. I know you do me."

"Meaning what?" They moved from the foyer down a side aisle of the auditorium towards the back-stage area.

"Ne' mind. That bastard Rodney Butcher, did I tell you about him this after?"

"He was here conducting, I know that. Pansy, he is."

"I won't forget that piano being delivered this after. That blind chap came to tune it."

"He's ever so clever, being blind."

"Mr Rodney blooming Butcher said he wanted it at concert pitch, whatever that is. The blind tuner said that's what he'd got it at. Half a tone above the ordinary I think he said. That bastard Butcher said it wasn't and laid down the law about himself having perfect pitch so he could tell when a joanna was out and never mind your tuning forks.

"Sweet as a nut that blind bloke had it. Trilling up and down the scales as if he could see as well as me what he was doing. Butcher swore burnt down as it was wrong. So Mister Blind said okay, he'd take her up a semitone if that's what Butcher was insisting on. Butcher said he was insisting and then the fun began. 'The strings won't take it,' said Mister Blind. 'They'll snap if I turn the key.' 'They'll take it,' said Butcher, who thinks he knows it all."

Sid stopped by the urn. "You know, Else, I reckon I was wrong for not clouting Butcher when the first string snapped and caught Mister Blind slap between the eyes. It cut him. There was a line of blood. Then he said quietly, 'Do you want to go on, or are you satisfied? 'Cos if you want more you can do it yourself and see what a job you'll make of it with your perfect pitch'."

"What happened?" demanded Elsie.

"It was left as Mister Blind said. He put in a new string and some of them soloists came in to rehearse. 'Sorry,' said Mister blooming Butcher, greasy as a tin of vaseline, 'but the joanna's only at ordinary pitch.' But that toff of a tenor, the one with the Adam's apple, said, just right to add a bit of brightness to the singing. And that rotten bastard, Butcher, never said a word about it being due to that blind tuner."

Things continued to happen.

Maxwell Mawby, the trumpeter, had played at the Central Hall in Nortown on so many occasions that he was completely familiar with the building. Unbeknown to Sid and Elsie, he had let himself in at the small back door they regarded as their private entrance. He knew the subsidiary room he needed. In his evening dress with white tie, he ensconced himself in the ill-lit and dusty back-stage storeroom.

The reason why he had arrived early and secreted himself in this place was because he needed living heat for his trumpet, and in this dusty cupboard was a spluttering gas fire, the only one in the building. He needed it to give warmth to his blunderbuss of an instrument which he had stood on its flared bell close to the blue flames. Warmth made it sound loud and true.

But there was a second reason for Mawby's wish for solitude. He was feeling very depressed: a frustrated artist.

Mawby was, in fact, a man of infinite creation, but as yet he was unrecognized and unsung. His mood was very much in tune with his shabby surroundings, the broken chairs, dilapidated tables, dusty curtains and worn-out rolls of carpet.

Without a doubt, Mawby was recognized as a virtuoso of the brass. He knew that everybody who heard him later that evening would be stirred by his playing. It would be difficult for them to imagine that a human being capable of producing his clarion call of angels could experience the baser human emotions. But as he mused in his depressing surroundings, his thoughts were solely concerned with George Frederick Handel.

Mawby hated the very name of Handel. Every melody he had ever written — in Mawby's opinion — was so like its predecessor that the modern signature tune could be called his offspring, so clearly was his signature impressed on every composition. Mawby was wondering by what means Handel had climbed where he could not follow. After all, Mawby, too, had composed operas, oratorios and sacred pieces, but nobody would listen to and applaud them. Why? Mawby reckoned it was just because he hadn't yet composed his *Messiah*, *Saul*, *Samson* and *Judas Maccabeus*.

But Handel had been acknowledged as the greatest for more than 200 years. Couldn't anybody realize that reputations such as that are made only to be superseded by those who follow after? All Mawby had managed to achieve was some parochial renown as a trumpeter, which was laughable, because the trumpet was only his second instrument. His first was the piano.

Mawby mused on his lack of success as a pianist. His ability, he reckoned, had been swamped by a multitude of lesser tinklers and his compositions ignored while bobsters who hotted up former maestros were fêted and made rich by people as undiscerning as those who, later that evening, would listen to him enhancing, in perfect performance, not his own reputation, but that of Handel.

As he suffered these mental agonies, Mawby, from time to time, moved his instrument a quarter turn before the flames. He also kept an eye on the time. He noted it was ten past seven when a face peered round the door momentarily and then disappeared without a word.

Other people were now arriving at the Central Hall.

Fred and Jessie Croft, for instance. They pushed open one of the heavy main doors and staggered into the haven of the foyer. As the door closed behind them, the sound of the gale died appreciably.

Jessie had been obliged to hold her tongue for some minutes because the wind would have filled her lungs with cold air had she opened her lips, and also because she was out of puff through struggling against so strong a hurricane. The silence had been a penance because she was as great a talker as husband Fred was taciturn.

"Fred!" There was dismay, even distress, in her tone.

The harsh light of the foyer showed Jessie Croft to be — at a guess — fifty-five. But Jessie's age scale was of elastic so overstretched that she would admit to no more than thirty-seven despite the fact that she had two offspring already married and

63

demonstrably fecund. Husband Fred was as grey and lean as Cleopatra's needle which, seeing he had purported to be, for many years, a pillar of the chapel and of rectitude, was not an inapt description.

"Fred!"

Fred still did not reply. Taciturn, and despite the fact that he was here to enjoy the most famous of sacred presentations, he was not in the mood for conversation. But then, he rarely was.

"Fred!" Jessie's voice was now a controlled hiss because they were no longer alone in the foyer. "Are you deaf? I might as well talk to a brick wall as ask you a question."

Fred disliked inexactitude. It stirred him to words. "You haven't asked me a question yet, so why should I waste good breath in trying to answer what I haven't been asked? I've always told you that keeping your counsel pays bigger dividends than wagging your tongue."

"Your mind's never off money. Who's interested in dividends?"

This was heresy in Fred's eyes. He couldn't let this remark pass without comment.

"You, for one. To buy that fur coat and pay for permanent waves. Though why you bother beats me. It's nothing but a waste of time and money."

"So that's what you think. A waste of money! Last time you told me it was playing with the devil."

"And so it is. It achieves nothing. At the moment you look like the original fuzzy-wuzzy."

That hurt. It stung Jessie to anger.

"And who's fault is that, Fred Croft? If you'd brought the car to the door instead of making me walk from Freemen's Square in all that wind it would have been all right."

So even the wind was causing dissension. The prospect of an uplifting spiritual occasion was not enough to overcome the despair felt by this woman who knew her appearance to have been spoiled despite all her previous care and attention. For Fred was right. His Jessie looked a fright even though she had used a headscarf in a vain attempt to protect her artificial waves, unsubtly

64

tinted in the hope of regaining the colour of yesteryear and, when she had set out, semi-frozen by a gum tragacanth spray into a still-life semblance of a turbulent sea momentarily transfixed.

Fred, divesting himself of his heavy, clerical grey Crombie coat had, by this time, thought up a profound reply to his loved one's accusation.

"Don't be so daft. Freemen's Square is the car park, isn't it? With petrol the price it is, why should I waste it driving first here and then there? And in any case, I'd have had to walk back. You've got a comb in that handbag of yours. Use it."

Succinct to the point of rudeness. So often the hallmark of the Nortown self-made man. Visitors to the town, such as Masters and Green, were usually quick to notice there were many cast in Fred's mould: the say-what-you-mean-and-mean-what-you-say species.

But Jessie was not prepared to let the matter drop. She was, by now — to use a favourite expression of her own — worked up. "A gentleman," she hissed, and emphasized it by repetition. "A gentleman would have dropped me here without being asked. I wish I could teach you how to behave proper."

Anger had affected her grammar adversely. It also niggled Fred.

"Behaviour is as behaviour does, woman."

"You're nothing but a mean old grump, Fred Croft."

A pillar of the chapel and of rectitude escorting his lady to a wallow in spiritual bliss. Anybody who had overheard their conversation would have found it hard to believe that once he had wooed and won her. Perhaps there was some truth in the rumour current in Nortown that it was she who had proposed the match and had then taken his usual ensuing silence to mean consent. If so, Fred's favourite aphorism about least said being soonest mended was palpably untrue — at least in his case.

The audience streamed in, but the performance was not due to start for some time. A performance in which 150 voices would be lifted up to the greater glory of God and more than 30 in-strumentalists would play to the same end. Seven hundred and sixty-three people were expected to listen to the incomparable music either attentively or quietly occupied with their own thoughts. Whichever it was to be, Rodney Butcher knew that they would all have him to thank for it.

Rodney Butcher was the conductor of the Nortown Philharmonic Choir, and the object of Sid Carrot's wrath over the tuning of the piano. Butcher had given some thought to timing his arrival nicely. To be too early would be infra dig, for in his own estimation, at least, he would be the most important person in the hall. His parents, who arrived with him, were naturally of the same opinion. They, too, thought that it would be wrong for Rodney to be backstage too early. The great arrive late. And it would have been a mistake for him to have used the stage door. He needed to enter by the foyer and make a majestic journey the length of the auditorium in full view of those who had already arrived.

But — and it was a big but — there were important professional soloists engaged for the performance. Rodney must not miss the opportunity to hobnob with these famous ones who would, while on stage, be so dependent on him for so much. So Butcher allowed himself 20 minutes in which to queen it in the principals' dressing-rooms.

Few people who knew him would have thought it unfair to suggest that he would queen it backstage. He walked with a mince, he was forty-three and unmarried, he was tall and knock-kneed, and he had a far from handsome face, pale and long. Of late he had grown a moustache, a luxuriant droop, trained downwards towards the full, wet lips. It was the same dun colour as the lank hair held greasily back from the skull-like forehead which bulged high and wide above rimless spectacles.

Opinions about Rodney's character varied as much as they did about his musical ability. But he, himself, had no doubts concerning the latter as he passed through the foyer, self-importantly edging his way through the gathering throng, leading with a bent right arm under which was grasped the conductor's score.

At exactly the same time as Butcher arrived to make an entry at the front of the house, Margaret Whitehead, the soprano soloist, was entering the hall by the stage door. She had been brought to the Central Hall by Jack and Norah Jagger, who were her host and hostess for these three days. The Nortown Philharmonic Choir committee was not prepared to spend money on hotel expenses when it could cajole local families of some standing to entertain visiting soloists. A penny saved was a penny made.

And many of the pennies that were made on tickets bought by this audience could be directly attributed to the presence of Miss Whitehead. To most of those present all the soloists, with the exception of Capper, were household names, made so by countless radio programmes devoted to hundreds of best tunes and discs destined for divers desert islands. But Margaret Whitehead was held in special affection. Many of the audience had come to hear her sing 'I know that my Redeemer liveth'. When she rose to her feet for this aria she would personify an old and trusted friend to many of her listeners. They had heard her sing it many times and had never tired of doing so. Her voice, justly renowned for its clarity and girlish innocence — a worthy achievement on her part as she was rising fifty — would draw them towards her in spirit just as if she had opened her arms in welcome and each of them her eager lover.

Not everybody, of course, was prepared to fall down and worship at her shrine. Among the members of the chorus who were now congregating by the dozen backstage was Alice Mundy. Alice was, herself, an amateur soprano soloist whose voice had withstood the acid test of innumerable oratorios in Moab chapels the length and breadth of the country. She was small and sharp-featured and though sheathed from top to toe in the uniform virginal white of the Philharmonic Choir, she had long ago lost her virginity and with it those qualities which even the most un-maidenlike of her sex so often retain despite their loss. Alice had lost love for all but herself. She had lost hope, too, of ever achieving her musical ambitions; but chiefly she had lost what little charity of mind and soul she had been endowed with when born.

Tonight her rival — for as a soprano soloist Alice regarded Miss Whitehead as a rival — was the object of her jealous scorn and scurrilous scandal. "She's ugly. Her face would stop a double-decker. It would, straight."

Another choir member close by replied: "I know her looks are a bit unfortunate . . . "

"Unfortunate? They're a calamity. It's a well-known fact her husband had to be paid to marry her."

"Go on! How do you know?"

"And even then he was doubtful. He said so. He didn't know whether her voice would compensate for her looks."

"He still married her."

"Yes, he did. And he's regretted it ever since. You know what I heard?"

"No. What?"

Alice's voice dropped to low confidentiality.

"They've never slept together."

"Now I know you're making it all up. She's got a son. . . . "

"Maybe she has." Alice smiled maliciously. "But only because her husband has managed — only now and then, of course — to accept the fact that all cats look grey in the dark."

There was still some time to go before the performers would be asked to flood on to the stage. In the foyer, stewards dressed in dinner jackets were attempting to hurry all who wished to linger for a gossip to seats which, by now, were almost inevitably in the middle of well-filled rows. This was causing so much movement and noise that the auditorium resembled a cross between an exposed ant heap and a wasps' nest where not even the half-hearted apologies and forced smiles passing between those who were being disturbed and those who, in brushing past, were perpetrating outrages against the person, could dispel the hurt, outrage and dissension so caused.

Bob Frame and his Ena had been installed for some minutes.

"Look out, love, here's another lot. Bumping and boring. Why is it that those who come latest always have the sharpest elbows?"

"It's known as Murphy's Law, I think, Bob. Anyway, some Irish name. It stipulates that a dropped hammer shall always fall where it will do most damage."

"Up you get again, love. I've never known anywhere quite like these halls . . . ouch!"

"Quiet, Bob. You're not really hurt, are you? No, he's all right, really, Mrs Syme."

"All right? That woman's handbag caught me in the . . . "

"No, Mrs Syme. You just touched Bob in the . . . well, in a tender spot as you might say." Ena turned to her husband. "Smile, Bob, smile. She's our supervisor at work."

"What? That old co . . . cor, strewth! She's coming back again."

While the dissension was growing like an evil thing between men and their wives, strangers, friends and even enemies, the confusion was further confounded by the stewardesses. They were all young, personable girls, clad in long evening gowns and carrying Dorothy bags on their wrists to hold the coins wrung from those who agreed to buy programmes. Each girl had a squared-up bundle of the folders cradled lovingly between one bare forearm and one breast which, under the pressure so induced, was revealing more of its talcum-powdered roundness than modesty had intended. Some of the matrons were outraged by this display. Their thoughts were typified by Mrs Norah Jagger, hostess to Miss Whitehead.

Mrs Jagger, followed by husband Jack, and having seen Miss Whitehead safely to the stage door, was about to plough her way along Row D to seat 14. She was doing as much unthinking damage on the way as a heavy tank in a vineyard. This was partly because of her anger at seeing that the stewardess selling programmes to the few rows near her seat was pretty Cissy Spring, and partly due to the actions of her husband.

Fast little hussy, thought Norah. I might have known if it was Cissy Spring she'd be showing all she'd got. And Jack's no better, ogling her. . . . "Oh, so sorry, Mrs Hallet, my bag's caught up in your . . . ah! now it's free." . . . And what she's got are so big I'll gamble she wears . . . "Mister Dann, how nice to see you. Jack's just coming." No, he isn't. He's still fussing with that girl, and she's bending so far forwards I can see . . . no, she doesn't wear pads after all. She doesn't wear anything underneath. Her mother ought to make her wear a coatee. It's disgusting what these young girls . . . "Hello, Minny, am I next to you? How nice! What a pretty dress, my dear. That seaweed-green colour does suit you and I do so like that high-necked military effect. So becoming."

Husband Jack was not hurrying over the business of buying a ten-pence programme. He was dawdling almost as if he knew what Norah was thinking, and that amused him. It caused him to smile at the thought that Norah would have weighed him up and found him wanting — mistakenly, as he well knew, because for years he had pulled the wool over her eyes.

Little Cissy Spring! Not so little now, by jove. You don't know it, my dear — nor does anybody else except your mother, besides myself, that is — that I'm your father. It's really laughable to suppose that old Bert Spring could have sired a beauty like you when he looks like nothing so much as a pug-dog's daddy. I can't tell you, of course, but you, little Cissy, are my beautiful indiscretion.

Secrets such as this, even when closely guarded as this one had been over the years, do not make for harmony. Like murder, they will out, or at least their effect will be felt in various ways. Now, Jack's paternal interest in his natural daughter was fostering misunderstanding in Norah's scrawny bosom. Her face, stiff as an icicle under its layers of make-up, showed — in addition to her displeasure — that she was a frightened woman. Frightened that her Jack who, at one time, before marriage, had had a reputation as a womanizer, should revert to type. Frightened that Jack should look at a younger woman lest the two should cultivate an affinity. Already she was mistaking the natural attraction of consanguinity for something much more dangerous to her own position. She was blind, of course. Blind with jealousy and almost literally blind not to see the close facial resemblance between handsome Jack and lovely Cissy. She was also lacking in imagination — fortunately for Jack — because no spark in her mind led her to suspect the true relationship between her husband and his daughter, yet she was obsessed by the belief that should the opportunity arise for extra-marital bliss with Cissy, Jack would seize the chance.

So, more discord over unwarranted jealousy. Norah couldn't help hissing in Jack's ear when he took his seat beside her, "That girl's a trollop, and you're no better. Carrying on like that in public."

"Like what?"

"You know. Looking at her."

"Of course I was looking at her." His voice became slightly menacing as he continued. This was no surprise to Norah, and

70

confirmed her worst fears. "Don't call her a trollop. I asked for change for a pound. I wasn't getting an eyeful down the front of her dress like you're insinuating, but I'll tell you this. I like her. I like her face, her voice, her manner. Like them. Nothing more. And do you know why? Because I like to think that any daughter of mine — a daughter you couldn't or wouldn't bear me — would be just like her in every respect. So let's have no more of it, Norah. One word — one single word — of condemnation or criticism of Cissy Spring and you will have condemned yourself."

Norah had had it easy over the years as venomous tongues do have it easy over easy-going natures like Jack's. Now the worm had turned, but because she had never had to do so, Norah had not learned when it was wiser to say nothing.

"Condemned? What sort of a word do you think that is to use to your wife over a chit of a girl?"

"I'd keep my voice down if I were you, Norah. People are beginning to stare. But condemned I said and condemned I mean."

"You've gone mad, Jack Jagger. Condemned? What to, may I ask?"

"Life without me, that's what to. I swear to you, Norah, that silence as far as Cissy is concerned is the safest course for you. One word, and you'll break the link. It's pretty weak now. Time and your tongue have corrupted it as surely as rust does iron."

Norah did not take this lying down. It was not in her nature to do so. She returned to the attack.

"Well, I never! You mean to say you would leave me for that . . . that . . . ?"

"Careful, Norah! One word, I said, so watch it. And just so's you don't get the wrong idea, I won't be leaving you *for* Cissy, but *because* of her, or rather your criticism of her. Do I make myself clear? Or do you want to go on and pursue a subject that can be buried and forgotten if you'll only keep your mouth shut?"

Norah was understandably angry and bewildered. She didn't understand. She never would. But she was possessed of enough sense to realize that if Jack had, for the first time ever, spoken to her in this way, her best tactics were to keep quiet as he had demanded, and to nurse her suspicions and anger in silence. So, where another woman might have got up and left him, she remained sitting beside Jack, seething with rage against — not surprisingly — beautiful Cissy Spring who was completely blameless, and not against her handsome Jack who had, unbeknown to her, been unfaithful on countless occasions.

The atmosphere surrounding their two seats was electric with discord. One wrong word could have caused an explosion.

By now it was late enough for the really important people to be arriving. Among these were Alderman Herbert Wrigley, chairman of the trustees of the Central Hall, and his wife Flo.

Wrigley was an obese man. There were those in Nortown who said that it was obesity which had kept him from being conscripted during the war. Perhaps that was the real reason and not the conscientious objection he had made on a secretive trip to a Spalding tribunal in 1940. At any rate, despite food shortages he had remained obese throughout the war which he had spent in the Nortown ration office, rising quite quickly, due to the departure of other men for the armed services, to the rank of supervisor. In other words, he was the boss, for several years, of the office that issued every ration book, points card and clothing coupon in Nortown. The more charitable suggested that was the reason he did not lose weight in lean times. The less charitable pointed out that Wrigley made a lot of new, wealthy friends during the war, and their shadows had never grown less, either. They further pointed out that, at the outbreak of war, Wrigley had been an office clerk earning exactly two pounds a week, yet on nothing more munificent — ostensibly — than a mediocre government wage for a few years, he had been able to buy out the largest wholesale grocer in Nortown long before rationing ended in the 'fifties. Not that Wrigley had resigned from the ration office. He had stayed on there till the bitter end, but by that time he had bought out three retail grocery shops, among them the Fortnum and Mason of Nortown.

Flo Wrigley had also worked in the ration office. That is where Herbert had met her. Again the less charitable had some comment to make on the union. In broad terms this was that Wrigley would never have looked at her a second time, let alone married her, had he not been obliged to do so. Quite simply, the obligation was founded, not on the fact that Flo was with child, but on the bedrock of blackmail. In short, Flo had discovered the funny business with the ration cards and had demanded marriage as the price of silence. Nor had she ever produced offspring.

Now, Wrigley was an alderman of Nortown. An alderman of long standing. He and Flo were another of the couples who were entertaining a soloist. Their guest was Desmond Darren, the tenor. Wrigley would have preferred to welcome the bass, because he himself had been something of a bass with a large, fruity voice which he had employed largely in the rendering of Negro Spirituals. But the bass for this performance, James Capper, was not nearly so well known as Darren, so the tenor had been chosen.

Like Butcher a minute or two earlier, Wrigley had decided that the proper entrance for the Chairman of Trustees with a famous guest in tow was via the foyer and the auditorium. Darren, dressed in white tie and tails discreetly hidden by a heavy coat with upturned collar, had seen the auditorium in the afternoon, but it looked far grander now, fully lit and peopled. He expressed his surprise at finding so fine a concert hall in Nortown. Wrigley was fully prepared to dwell on the history and merits of the building of which he was inordinately proud. He halted, with Darren alongside him, and Flo a pace behind, in the middle of the main centre aisle.

"Some years back, we — that is, me and a few like-minded colleagues — decided that it was high time we solved a problem that we reckoned was hampering the cultural development of Nortown. You've no doubt heard, Mr Darren, that we're very cultural people here in Nortown?"

"The mere fact that you are promoting oratorio on such a scale as this for three nights speaks for itself, Alderman."

"Quite right. I don't want anybody to run away with the idea that we miss out on owt round here. 'Cos we see to it that we don't. All this singing and dancing and suchlike carryings-on have to be catered for. And they are catered for in Nortown, thanks to me — and a few like-minded colleagues."

"I assure you, Alderman, that I have never supposed otherwise."

Flo felt it was time to remind them of her presence. "We've got everything round here, haven't we, Herbert? Herbert sees to that, don't you, Herbert?"

"That's right, Flo. When owt's needed, owt's got."

"Even, it seems, items as big as this magnificent concert hall, Alderman."

"Aye, the Central Hall. Mark you, we've got a tidy town hall an' all. But the big room there's got a ballroom floor and the seating's no good for listening to chaps like you for hours on end — if you get my meaning."

Flo came in again. "So Herbert — and a few like-minded colleagues — decided on permanent upholstered seats, a gallery, and that big stage with rising rows of seats. And an organ and seven smaller rooms for smaller functions all under same roof, didn't you, Herbert?"

"Aye, lass, we did. And we did the right thing by building on a cheap old site in this little side street. We saved a lot of brass, an' all. No need for a car park with Freemen's Square so near. No need for expensive land for gardens and seats and the like. Every farthing we had went into the hall itself."

"Very, very commendable," said Darren, unaware that Wrigley had omitted to mention that he, and those colleagues he had rightly claimed as like-minded, were, in truth, a power-seeking, political caucus, parochially active and willing — for their own ends — to impose a five-pence rate for five years on the people of Nortown in order to build this extravaganza for minority use. He did not confess to having no qualms that the elderly, the hard-pressed, the young married couples striving hard to make ends meet, and the near-bankrupt shopkeepers were all having to dig deeper into pockets already pitifully pillaged by the rapacity of the city fathers. Nor did he add that nine tenths of the citizens of Nortown would never see inside this place built with their money, in Wrigley's name: that there had been fierce opposition to the scheme from the outset which, though ineffectual at first, was now the cause of rising dissension because the hall could not pay for its own upkeep.

As Desmond Darren made his way backstage, and Alice Mundy was still spreading spiteful gossip about a more gifted woman, the victim of her malicious tongue was preparing to fight a battle she had fought many times before. Stage fright. Alone in the lady principals' dressing-room she was doing her utmost to quell the rising tide of fear. Deep breathing first to get possession of herself, and then an inelegant manoeuvre. Leaning forward so that her trunk was at right angles to her thighs and legs, she walked slowly, singing quietly, non-stop, the single syllable me-me-me. Me-me-me, until the saliva ran from her lips. Me-me-me, until her voice fell forwards in her head to behind the top of her nose so that the resonance improved to the point where the smallest whispered headtone would be heard throughout the auditorium. This mechanical preparation always helped, even though the floor was dribbled on and her make-up would need attention.

At this moment, the largest limousine from the largest car-hire firm in Nortown drew into the kerb outside the main doors. Out stepped six people. Four women and two men. One woman, in evening dress and long fur coat waved a cheerful goodbye and disappeared down the side entrance that led to the stage door. It was Nancy Festival, arriving with her hostess.

The hostess was Mrs Sarah Fenny. A widow, she was the mother of the other four, and perhaps, for those who knew her, the most complete person they had ever met. She was the mother of strong men, clever men, the mother of personable daughters, clever daughters, gentle women. Two sons, two daughters who, with Sarah at their head, seemed to hold life and the world in the palms of their hands to enrich them. These young people, totally immersed in living, had yet found time to escort their mother to the performance to give her pleasure. Thoughtful of her welfare, they had hired a limousine that would bring her right to the door.

Mrs Fenny's white hair, a well-cared-for halo, perfect in its simplicity of style, was uncovered. Mrs Fenny knew how to dress for an evening affair. Not like many of the women in the audience who were using the occasion to parade their best hats. Sarah, fair and round of face, was perhaps the one person in the hall who knew instinctively the right thing to wear — the right colour, right material and right style — to suit her individuality. For Mrs Fenny was a true artist with probably more artistry in her embroidery needle than most of those who were to make the music she had come to hear.

Her entry was a progess. Flanked and ushered like a queen, her daughters her ladies-in-waiting, her sons her supporters, her presence had an effect on those about her so that they fell away from her path, ceased talking, murmured appreciatively or returned her gentle smile which was bestowed as a gesture of thanks as well as of recognition. Hers was personality personified, so strongly felt by others, that one could have been forgiven for thinking that it was for Mrs Sarah Fenny and her children that Handel had composed his greatest work 200 years in advance of their time on earth, to allow it to mature, like good wine, until it should be needed in the auditorium of the Central Hall, Nortown on this night.

As the Fenny family neared their seats, Cissy Spring came towards them with her programmes. She was blushing. Her lovely young face was now even lovelier with pleasure and — possibly — embarrassment.

"Good evening, Mrs Fenny, would you like a programme?"

"Thank you, my dear. I know your face. You're Cissy Spring. You look charming. That colour suits you so well, and your hair is very pretty."

"Oh, thank you, Mrs Fenny. Do you really think so?"

"Certainly I do." Mrs Fenny turned to one of her daughters. "Jane, you should ask Cissy where she got that charming dress."

"It really is nice," said Jane. "What I like is the . . . "

"Not now, please," said David Fenny. "Cissy, could we have five programmes, please?"

"Five? Five did you say, David?" Cissy was blushing more than ever, but her eyes were shining with pleasure.

"Yes, please. You know, it's a long time since I saw you at the Hamiltons' party. I only had one dance with you and . . . what is it Peter?"

"Let the young lady get on with her job. We're blocking the

76

gangway. If you want to talk, do it later."

"Thanks for the tip. May I see you in the interval, Cissy?"

"I'd like that. In the foyer? And, David . . . don't forget your change."

A moment or two later, they had reached their seats. Sarah asked, "Are we all settled?" and then turned to her elder son. "David, she's a very nice girl."

"And very obviously stuck on David, isn't she, Juanita?" asked Jane of her sister.

"Absolutely gaga over him." Juanita smiled at David. "But in such an open, honest way that I should think half the people here could tell it just by looking at her. I like that."

"I've only ever spoken to her once before."

"And she's remembered you ever since," said Peter. "Lucky chap."

"Don't break her heart, David," said his mother. "The hearts of young girls in love break very easily and even though they mend just as quickly, it can be painful at the time."

David smiled. "Somehow, I think she'd break mine before I broke hers."

"Do I scent incipient romance?" demanded Juanita.

"David could do worse," said his brother.

"In that case," said Sarah, "why not ask her to come to supper afterwards, David? If she cares for ham salad and hock, that is, and doesn't mind meeting Nancy Festival."

As Juanita had been clever enough to suggest, there were others in the auditorium who had noticed Cissy and David talking together and the obvious interest Cissy had in the elder Fenny son. Two of them, of course, were Norah Jagger and husband Jack.

Norah knew that to make any remark about the girl would be dangerous. But the embargo on words did not apply to thoughts. Cissy Spring is at it again. This time she's buttonholed that nice-looking Fenny boy. She'll make eyes at anything that wears trousers. I hope he isn't being taken in by her, the little hussy. Still, it's an ill wind. Now she's found somebody younger to make eyes at, she might leave Jack alone, though I can see he's still watching her like a cat watching a mouse and almost licking his lips over her.

77

It's disgusting.

Norah was quite right about Jack watching Cissy. But he was not, as she seemed to think, watching his daughter lasciviously. His parental interest had been aroused by Cissy's encounter with the Fenny family. Unwilling to bring the subject of Cissy up again, he, too, said nothing. But, like Norah, he had his thoughts.

From the way Cissy is chatting to the Fennys, and David in particular, I wouldn't be surprised if there was something going on between those two. And if there is, I for one am not going to feel sorry. David Fenny, or his brother Peter, is just about the best catch for any girl round here. And they look fine together. Even the Fenny girls can't put Cissy in the shade, and that's saying something, because Juanita is reckoned to be the most beautiful girl in Nortown, though I can't see that she beats her sister by much. But then, Sarah Fenny! What a woman! She's the only person I've ever known who's been liked equally well by both sexes of all ages. And when you consider how many rivals Fenny had before he married her, that's saying a lot. You go right ahead, Cissy, lass. If you can marry into that lot — and if you want to — you'll be doing all right for yourself. And it's no more than you deserve.

Meanwhile there was Nancy Festival who, having just arrived with the Fennys, was making her way down to the stage door entrance.

Where two, if not three, of the other soloists were national celebrities, Nancy Festival, the contralto, was an international singing star of great repute. She was acknowledged as a supreme interpreter of great works, an enhancer of many of them, an entrancer of audiences, an inspiration in oratorio and a charmer in ballads. And this great, great woman, still young, had started her career some years ago here in Nortown. She was not a native of the borough. It was just that the Nortown Philharmonic Choir were the first people ever to engage her as a fully-fledged professional soloist. She had made her début here, in this hall, singing in their annual performance of *Messiah* .

The people of Nortown loved her. They had recognized the talent that was there from the outset, and while others were havering during the first two or three years of this great career, they engaged her to come and come again. Their enthusiasm gradually spread countrywide, and those older, more experienced professionals who were invited to sing with her, or to conduct the works in which she appeared, began to realize, too, that they were in the presence of an exceptional artist, and said so. The Ibbs and Tillet list itself began to applaud her, and eminent soloists began to hope for engagements in her company, just to bathe in reflected glory. All except, that is, for one or two contraltos who, outshone, had seen their bookings fall and were often obliged to accept offers which had first been refused by Nancy Festival.

Nancy had a special place in her heart for Nortown where, as an unknown, she had earned her first fee and where she had first met Mrs Fenny and her family. She had been met, that first time, at the station by Mrs Fenny in person. Her hostess on that first visit had become a firm friend to whom she had returned on every subsequent visit. She was accepted as one of the Fenny family, a worthy addition to its numbers.

Because of this, whenever Nortown wished her to return for a performance of *Messiah* and her international tours permitted, Nancy Festival always agreed to appear at — for her — a modest fee. It was her way of expressing gratitude to those who, unwittingly perhaps, but nevertheless wholeheartedly, first set on the ladder of fame the woman who was generally regarded to be the greatest of her kind.

This lovely woman, though no fairer of face than many of those present, was lit by inner fires. It had been said — in Italy — that the face of God Incarnate illuminated her features when she sang. Here, in Nortown, they had no such flights of fancy, but they did recognize that the Almighty had given her what he affords to very few. To his prophets He gave the gift of many tongues. To this one woman He had given an endowment of golden sound so precious that pundits had said that it is never granted in this degree to more than one human at any one time.

They spoke of her voice as an organ, and went on to add that no organ fashioned by the hand of man could produce such liquid melody as that fashioned by the sinuses of Nancy Festival's fine facial bone structure. For Nancy Festival sang with her face, never her throat, and interpreted with her mind. The body played merely a supportive role: that of bellows to produce the breath and to supply the means of controlling it so that the voice could reign supreme.

This was the woman who entered the female principals' dressing-room which she was to share with Margaret Whitehead.

"Margaret, my dear."

Miss Whitehead straightened up from her me-me-me position. "Nancy, darling."

"You're dribbling well enough to play for Manchester United, Maggie."

They were friends, these two, the older and the younger woman. Margaret Whitehead in the grip of nerves, slightly red-faced and dishevelled. Nancy Festival, serene and smiling, but with just that air of seriousness appropriate to the occasion. As Nancy put her two cases — briefcase and travelling vanity case — on the table, she said: "Would you like me to tidy your hair? It's a bit out at the back."

"Would you, Nancy, please? You're always having to do it for me. There isn't much time. . . . "

"All the time in the world, Maggie. A good five minutes, and they can't start without us. Sit down, dear. . . . "

A tap at the door and Rodney Butcher looked in. "The choir is about to go on, ladies. I'm sorry I haven't been able to have a chat, but I had to put James straight on one or two things. He wanted to do the run on the word 'light' in the second and third bars at the top of page forty-five in 'The people that walked'. I really had quite a tussle with him to give just the dotted C sharp to 'light' and to insert a preliminary 'have seen' on the run up to the E and then repeat 'have seen' as normal. Really, quite a tussle."

"You mean he was singing it correctly according to the score, but you want him to sing it differently?"

"I do so like the run on the word 'seen'. Much better than on 'light', don't you think?"

"As I don't have to sing the aria . . . there, Maggie, that's fine. If you'll touch up your lipstick . . . excuse me, Mr Butcher, but we do prefer a little privacy when powdering our noses . . . yes, we'll see you at the interval."

It was at this moment that Detective Chief Superintendent and Mrs Cleveland were moving down the centre aisle, followed by Masters, Green, Reed and Berger. They were making for six empty seats, three in front of three, fortunately on the ends of rows C and D. Cissy Spring approached them, one woman and five big men. The tallest of the men stopped beside her.

"Six programmes please," said Masters. "That is, if you can spare that many."

"Oh, yes, sir. We have enough for three nights."

"Thank you."

The transaction completed, Masters took his seat at the end of row C. To his immediate left was Mrs Cleveland and on her left her husband. Green, too, had chosen to take the end seat, so that he was immediately behind Masters. The two sergeants were behind the Clevelands.

"Nice bit of capurtle selling the programmes," said Berger. "Pretty face and eyes. She looked happy about something."

"Good figure, too," said Reed. "What I could see of it. I wonder what her legs are like?"

Green leaned forward in his seat. "Just right for time, George. The penguins are coming on."

The tenors were filing on from the right as they faced the audience, the basses the left. Well schooled, they came up into sight and climbed the steps leading to the top tiers on each side of the great organ standing high and proud, centre back. The black and white flood cascaded downwards as the rows filled. More basses than tenors, the heavier voices began to fill the seats below the organ as well as those in front of their topmost colleagues. Then the women, all in white. Sopranos after the tenors, contraltos after the basses. This time there were more from the soprano side, so they overlapped the front of the organ in their turn. It was all very orderly. Then came the members of the orchestra, who were to occupy the greater portion of the stage itself.

"You enjoy this sort of music, I believe, Mr Masters?" said Mrs Cleveland.

"Immensely. Should I close my eyes, please don't think I am getting bored and have gone to sleep."

"You prefer to concentrate just on listening?"

"To the choruses, never to the soloists."

"Why is that?"

"I find a lot of the faces of members of choirs too earnest. They glue their eyes on the conductor and have a habit of leaning in his direction. When this happens and they've all got their mouths open wide, I am reminded of a nest full of hungry chicks, beaks open, waiting for a parent bird to drop food in. I find that distracting. Soloists are very different. They are usually expressive and they are not so dependent on the conductor. In fact, very often, if not always, he has to watch and follow them."

"I can see you are a connoisseur. Ah! The orchestra is starting to tune up. All those little pingy notes. So unobtrusive I sometimes wonder how the musicians manage to hear them."

Masters smiled his agreement with this comment and then turned his attention to the stage. The hubbub of conversation died as — from the doors that the choir had used — came Margaret Whitehead followed by Desmond Darren to take their two chairs in front of the orchestra on the soprano side, while Nancy Festival led James Capper in on the contralto side. Last of all came Rodney Butcher to take the railed rostrum.

"Now for it," whispered Green.

Chapter Four

NANCY FESTIVAL WAS trying to think of anything but her forth-coming performance.

I'm delighted with this dress. The accordion pleats seem to be hiding the bulges I'm putting on fast at the tops of my thighs. Nancy, my girl, you may be on a diet, but you're not . . . heavens, the basses and the orchestra seem to be on top of me. And talking about basses, Jimmy Capper doesn't seem too happy. I hope that silly fool, Butcher, hasn't upset him too much. But then, Jimmy never does seem very happy when I'm beside him. I think I must frighten him. Perhaps if I hold his hand as we take our bow it will reassure him. There, what a podgy little hot hand it is, but he looks grateful. And slightly surprised. I believe he's thinking I'm not as demure as I should be, and perhaps just a little bit fast. What fun if he really does think that. Ah, Nancy, my girl, a pretty bow to the audience. That's it. Turn, and another bow to the orchestra and choir, keeping in time with Jimmy. I do believe he likes holding my hand. I can see I shall have to watch him, but he is quite sweet — all cuddly — even if his voice is a bit woolly, poor lamb.

Now, the audience. I must see . . . no! The Queen! I like the anthem first. It gives me a chance for a pipe-opener, if only those drums would stop and we could get on with it. Ah! Elgar's setting. Well, I can do my stuff with that all right.

Excellent. This choir can certainly pump it out. All sit. There! Jimmy's dropped a paper from his score. Ah, yes. It's the note he's made about breaking up that run. Though why put it on paper and not mark the score. Perhaps because it's only a temporary alteration. Now, the audience. I must find Mrs Fenny. I want her lovely face to sing to. . . .

Margaret Whitehead's problems were mainly due to nerves. Her thoughts were chaotic.

I'm in agony. My diaphragm support is killing me. And they've given me so little room here. An upright chair with potted ferns behind and nothing in front but a foot of stage to stand on when singing. It's always the same. I can't be the only one to get so nervous that I can't sit comfortably for more than two hours on a hard chair full in view of a large audience. Not without fidgeting at least. Still, I shall be a bit better when I get started. In *Messiah* the tenor comes off best. Just this short overture that man Butcher is gathering the musicians for. Not long to sit and think before his first recit and aria. He can clear his throat immediately while I sit here suffering from a dry mouth and yet with a string of saliva in my throat that I can't get rid of.

Nerves! Damn them, I'm literally shaking. No matter how often I appear I'm nearly driven to distraction by nerves. They say — the ones who always know everything — that without nerves to screw one up to concert pitch one can never give more than a merely competent performance, and that only nerves tautened to breaking point can give the fine edge of perfection that makes the good great or the indifferent better. Nancy never seems to suffer from nerves. She's great without them. Heaven knows what she would achieve if she were to suffer like I do.

These were the mental battles Margaret Whitehead was obliged to fight every time she appeared on stage in a testing role. She had often asked herself why she did it. Had anybody suggested it was for the money, she would have been shocked and hurt. She sang because she knew she must. Her talent was not sold, but simply rewarded by an inner sense of great achievement as much as by adulation and money. And who could deny her these things? Alice Mundy, perhaps?

But with the overture now under way, the eyes of many of the audience were on the long back of Rodney Butcher, earnestly encouraging, with an overlong white baton, instrumentalists who had forgotten more about *Messiah* than their conductor had ever known.

Even Sarah Fenny, the kindest of women, but a woman of vast common sense and the mother of fine sons, could not resist a critical musing on Rodney Butcher.

He's a silly ass! A day's work wouldn't do him any harm. And a wife would help — if one could be found to take him on. He's undernourished, or at least he looks it. Too tall and thin, with legs too weak to hold him upright. He plaits them at the knees. With an evening shirt and white tie on he reminds me of a donkey peering over a whitewashed wall. My goodness, I wish he were more of a man. But there, I don't suppose the poor thing can help it if his hormones are all wrong.

And Jack Jagger, unacknowledged father of pretty Cissy Spring, and much given to judging others by his own standards, was also musing unkindly on Rodney Butcher.

He's like a jelly. If old Larry Butcher had put him to work and allowed him to go out with lasses he'd be different. Whoever heard of letting a lad — a real lad, that is — leave school to study music at home? Not that he's got any further than any other kid learning the rudiments of music in half-hour piano lessons from some local teacher on Saturday mornings and being sent in for the elementary grade examinations. And he's lived off old Larry, I know that, even if he does claim to make a living from the few pupils he's got who can afford to pay the fees he feels he's worth. And this sort of thing he's doing now! I wonder how many musical societies he's joined to get himself appointed honorary conductor — as long as they'll pay honorariums?

Larry Butcher and his wife Liza were present, as they would be on all three nights, to watch their son. They were sitting in the middle of row F, in complimentary seats. Jack Jagger would have been surprised to hear Larry's thoughts, but not those of Liza who was preening herself in reflected glory.

Larry was feeling depressed.

I'm getting on. In fact, I feel right old tonight. And there's our Rodney, up there, conducting. Conducting what? Lord, I wish I'd not listened to our Liza years ago and had sent him out to do a job of work. In a year or two's time I'm not going to be able to support him, genius or not. And he's becoming more expensive to keep with every day that passes. That new evening suit he's wearing cost me more than I could afford. But his mother insisted on it. Midnight-blue, indeed! What our Rodney wants is a pair of midnight-blue overalls and a job in a rolling mill. Then he'd know what's what. And a woman wouldn't come amiss to him — that's if he knew what to do and didn't get a fit of artistic temperament at the crucial moment when the tempo quickened.

Liza Butcher had a very different point of view. For her, Rodney was everything — her boy, her pride, her joy, her love, her life. She, too, was thinking of him as she sat there, eyes glued to his every movement.

Those chrysanthemums dad grew for Rodney's early concerts aren't good enough for that suit. He should have had a carnation, poor lamb. But they come expensive and Larry wouldn't order one for the boy. Home-grown chrysanthemums, indeed! If I'd known, I'd have got him an orchid. He's worth it all, and more, standing there, controlling those famous singers, that big chorus and orchestra. His movements are artistic. Yes, that's it. Artistic. He uses his baton like a great artist applying the final touches to a wonderful painting. I'll tell Larry he has to hire the Wigmore Hall again for Rodney to give another London recital. It wasn't the poor lamb's fault that so few came to hear him that last time. So embarrassing for the boy — only seven and us turning up. No wonder his playing was disappointing. He was so disappointed himself. And I'm sure this orchestra won't give him credit this time, either. They're not watching him closely enough, except that violinist, Frances Barnes. She's got her eye on him in more ways than one. I'll soon put a stop to that.

Liza Butcher was a large, ungainly, ill-favoured woman bereft of the kindness that shines through and so often beautifies the natures of even the least fair of human creatures. Her failing was that she craved the love which she had never made the effort to deserve. By an unfortunate paradox, she had sought to shower the love she herself did not receive and therefore hadn't got at her disposal, on her far from manly son. Her love was a sort of foolish concentration of uncritical devotion which, had it been more thinly spread over husband and friends, would, like any wise investment, have yielded dividends in love returned, and would not have ruined the son she adored.

Liza had made sure no other woman had ever entered his life

86

except to make sycophantic mouthings in praise of his musical talent. These had usually come from elderly women, long past caring about the delights of bodily love. Young women turn to earthier things, but none, save one, had ever been able to envisage Rodney in passionate embrace. But Liza, her eye sharpened by covetous possession, had identified that one as Frances Barnes, a poor thing who was incapable of distinguishing love of music from love for man. This was the threat this mother feared might lure Rodney from parental hearth and home and maybe into nuptial bed where, if rumour was right, his performance on the delicate instrument of love would be even less virtuoso-like than had been his performance on the piano in the Wigmore Hall.

But Frances Barnes knew nothing of Liza's thoughts. Poor Frances, playing second fiddle in the orchestra, was one of those girls born to play second fiddle every night.

The end of the overture, and the tenor had got to his feet. Masters sat back to enjoy Darren's opening recitative and aria. It was uplifting with every note true and every word as clear as a bell. Masters, attentive, was aware that Mrs Cleveland had glanced his way, presumably to see if there was any reaction showing on his face. He pretended not to notice. He preferred to listen to Darren.

And then, after the choir had sung 'The glory of the Lord' chorus, James Capper rose to his feet.

Masters was still interested but not as thrilled by this voice. Nancy Festival, sitting on the stage, was probably thinking substantially what he was thinking.

Poor Jimmy. His voice is too heavy for him to manage. Too broad for him to control. The runs are his downfall. He's like a skier doing a slalom. He's getting round the course, but he's hitting every marker stick on the way. He can't point every note clearly because the value of each is too short and so the movement is too quick for him to move his voice with exactitude. The result is rather like a tape laid over the general run of the pattern instead of a cotton joining each peg. But if he were to avoid Handel, perhaps he would be happier. I think I ought to suggest to him — if I can find a really nice way of saying it — that he should choose his repertoire with a great deal of care.

The choir again.

Then Nancy Festival. Recit, air and chorus.

Masters had heard Miss Festival sing in broadcasts many times and twice before in the flesh. Where he had closed his eyes when the choir sang, excellent though it was, he opened them to watch the contralto sing. He was interested, very interested, in her ability to become one with her audience. Other soloists, first-class singers, were sometimes, he felt, a little aloof on the concert platform. They gave him the impression that they looked slightly upwards, over the heads of those in the body of the hall, to some spot high on the back wall or balcony. Detached, perhaps too self-absorbed, or perhaps too immersed in the music for its own sake as exemplified by their holding some slightly exaggerated, unnatural stance while waiting for the accompaniment to end some time after they had finished singing. He appreciated that no singer should detract from these final bars or distract the audience by unnecessary movement at such a time, but he had often wished that more warmth could be shown.

Masters, though passionately fond of such good singing, knew little of the technique. For instance, he was not aware that some singers look slightly upwards, not out of aloofness, but because mechanically they could raise the brightness of tone by looking — and thinking — upwards. Miss Festival was different. He, quite rightly, accredited her with warmth and friendliness. He failed to realize that this, too, was to some degree due to technique.

One of her first thoughts on coming on stage had been to seek out Mrs Fenny, sitting just one or two rows back and, therefore, recognizable from the stage. Had Sarah Fenny not been there — as, indeed, she would not be on the two succeeding nights — Nancy Festival would have looked for, and chosen, another pleasant, sympathetic or motherly face. This was part of her technique. She never attempted to sing to a full audience, but just to one person within that audience. Having chosen somebody, she concentrated on pleasing that person. She sang directly to her. On this night she sang directly to Sarah Fenny. Never taking her eyes from Mrs Fenny, Nancy sought, by the sheer beauty and skill of her singing, to charm her chosen one. Miss Festival knew that, by putting all her heart and soul into achieving this one objective, she

88

would have succeeded in delighting her whole audience.

This was her technique, based simply on the feeling that she needed to personalize her singing so much, that just to sing to an impersonal audience would not be enough.

This night she had chosen Mrs Fenny. Small wonder. They were friends, almost like mother and daughter. Perhaps it was deep calling unto deep. The two most gifted women present had found each other. From Sarah Fenny, Nancy Festival knew she would receive the inspiration necessary to raise her performance to those heights which only she could reach. And from Nancy Festival, Sarah Fenny — and hence every member of the audience — would receive a personal, uplifting performance sung, as it were, for her and her alone.

Had he known of this, Masters would have approved, while finding it remarkable that even the finest solo singing was not necessarily the effort of just one person, but of the sympathetic co-operation between two: the inspirer and the inspired, a combination which elevated both and produced the warmth and friendliness which he so much appreciated.

The performance continued until the 'Pastoral Symphony' had been played, and then the soprano, Margaret Whitehead, rose to sing for the first time. It had been a long wait for her. She took time to compose herself before glancing at Butcher to signal that she was ready for the recit.

Those few moments taken to prepare herself, had been cause enough for Alice Mundy mentally to denigrate her jealously.

Stuck up thing! Just look at the way she holds the score. By opposite corners down in front of her stomach. Closed, just to show she knows it all and doesn't have to look at the words and music like everybody else. And that frock! Pink, at her age! So unsuitable for a woman like her. I'll bet half the men in the audience can see the outline of her corselette through it. And she's not getting on top of those high notes. She's under them the whole time. I could do better myself, but nobody will pay me a fat fee for doing a better job than her.

Spiteful Alice Mundy had not sense enough to realize that Margaret Whitehead's apparently studied pose with score aslant across her body had a purpose. Miss Whitehead, like many women her age, was growing slightly thicker round the middle, with muscles enlarged by many years of constant breathing exercises. So the score was held strategically, to hide from public gaze, the movements of her diaphragm from which came the power to reach and hold the headtones which rang so clearly round the huge hall, even when merely whispered by the great voice. Artists, like Margaret, who strove for and achieved perfection, were aware that distractions such as a visibly moving diaphragm, inadequately cloaked by an evening gown, were liable to become a focus of attention, depriving both audience and singer of absolute concentration.

The criticism that Margaret Whitehead was not reaching her high notes was simply untrue. What Alice Mundy had again not realized was that the acoustics of the Central Hall, though good, were not perfect. The audience heard perfect singing, but those sitting behind the soloist — like Alice Mundy, deep in the mass of the choir — tended to get an impression of flatness of tone, particularly on high notes. In this case, the criticism was totally unjustified. Margaret Whitehead sang well and true.

But even so, for Masters, and indeed for most if not all of the audience, the highlights of the performance were the contralto solos. 'He shall feed His flock' and 'He was despised' seemed to mesmerize all who listened.

Eventually the interval. Not coinciding with Handel's three-part break-up of his oratorio, but taken after the chorus of 'Lift up your heads, O ye gates'. The conductor and soloists left the stage and after them the orchestra and choir filed away for the refreshment provided by Mr and Mrs Carrot.

Green got to his feet and stretched his limbs. "What do you think to that, Bill?" asked Masters, also rising.

Green took a moment or two to reply.

"You know me, George. I'm not like you about all this opera and stuff. Perhaps it's because I've never sat down and really listened to it. But I'll tell you this, I've nearly had tears in my eyes once or twice tonight."

"So you're going to stay for the second half?"

"Might as well," mumbled Green. "There's a special trumpeter coming on, isn't there? I mean apart from the two in the orchestra who had a bit of a battue in that 'Glory to God' chorus."

Mrs Cleveland left them with a vague murmur about having a word with a friend. Cleveland joined the four Yard men. "The gents is on the right of the foyer if you want it."

"Thanks. There isn't a bar, is there?"

"Not even a cup of tea, I'm afraid."

"Not to worry. Can we have a fag in the foyer, or is that taboo, too?"

"A lot of chaps will be out there for a quick drag."

"In that case, we can kill two birds with one stone." Green led the way back through the auditorium.

They were standing in a group, when Green asked Masters: "Still got the jim-jams, George? Or has this little lot settled you down?"

"Was he ill?" asked Cleveland.

"Not ill exactly. He threw a mental wobbly this morning."

Cleveland stared hard at Masters. "Are you subject to . . . I mean . . . ?"

Masters laughed. "No, I'm not a nut case, nor do I get fits of depression."

Cleveland's face cleared of its anxiety. "What's Bill on about, then?"

"I woke up this morning with an odd feeling."

"That something was going to happen, you mean?"

"Exactly that. I put it down to the fact that today is the third of December."

"The day on which you forecast something might happen."

"That's it. Fortunately, as far as we know, nothing has happened."

"HQ knows where I am," said Cleveland. "We'll get a message here if there's anything to report."

"Good. But let's hope the performance won't be interrupted."

"Time to get back, Chief," said Reed. "They're moving in."

"Thank you. Shall we go, gentlemen?"

The second half lived up to the promise of the first. Green enjoyed the familiar 'Hallelujah Chorus' and appreciated Maxwell

Mawby's playing in support of James Capper in 'The trumpet shall sound'. But the highlight of this latter portion was, without a doubt, Margaret Whitehead's singing of 'I know that my Redeemer liveth'. So clear-cut and innocent that the audience appreciation could literally be felt as she sang. But for Masters there was a big disappointment. In the Nortown version of *Messiah* there was no music for contralto after 'The trumpet shall sound'. As so often happens, the alto recit. 'Then shall be brought to pass', and the alto and tenor duet which follows it in the score were omitted, together with the next chorus and the final soprano aria. So Nancy Festival was not required on stage for this second, shorter part.

The choir was in great voice in the last chorus, 'Worthy is the Lamb'. They and the orchestra came together to a majestic end after the multifold Amens. Butcher turned to the audience and bowed, and then signalled to his orchestra and choir to stand. There was clapping, but the soloists were obviously waiting for Nancy Festival to join them to take their bow. She appeared at the back entrance to the stage and James Capper threaded his way back through the orchestra to escort her forward.

The applause had already started, but some of the audience held back until Capper had passed the contralto in front of him. It was then, when all four soloists were before them, that the audience really showed their appreciation. The applause rose in volume. The four principals bowed and bowed again. As they stood there, the audience began to get to its feet, just a few at first and then the whole throng. Desmond Darren, straight-faced and very self-controlled, Margaret Whitehead, faintly flushed and a little self-conscious at so great a reception, James Capper, grinning broadly at this his greatest ever share of applause, and Nancy Festival, serene and smiling gently. When the clapping was at its height the contralto half-turned, as though looking for her chair, but then, before she could find it, she collapsed. Nancy Festival crumpled slowly to the ground, despite the efforts of James Capper to hold her.

Silence.

Masters was going up the aisle at a run. As if sensing what Masters feared, Green, Reed and Berger were after him as soon as they could extricate themselves from between the seats. Cleveland, impeded by the fact that his wife was between him and the aisle, was somewhat behind the four Yard men.

There was a short flight of side stairs which Masters took in two bounds.

"Back, please," he ordered. "Police."

Nobody demurred. Had they done so, Green and the sergeants were there to enforce his command. Masters knelt for a brief moment beside Nancy Festival, seeking vainly for a pulse at neck and wrist.

"Ask if there's a doctor here, Bill."

Green cupped his hands about his mouth and put the question in stentorian tones.

There was an immediate response from two different areas of the hall. As both doctors hurried forward, Masters rose to his feet and said to Cleveland: "I'm fairly sure she's dead, Matt. It's your case."

"What do you suggest, George?"

"That you put one of my sergeants at each back exit to the stage to prevent the choir and orchestra getting out to the dressing-rooms. Remember she was alone throughout the second half of the show, so you'll want to nose about out there."

"Audience?"

"I think I should let them go, but don't let any of them come back here."

The first of the doctors said quietly. "No sign of life." Masters overheard him as he was instructing Reed and Berger to take up their positions to see that nobody left the stage. Then he turned to Green. "Bill, would you take Miss Whitehead backstage to show you Miss Festival's dressing-room?"

Green grunted his acquiescence and started to force his way past the conductor's rostrum.

"She's dead, right enough," said the second doctor.

"Thank you, gentlemen. If you wouldn't mind standing by for just a moment." Cleveland turned to Masters. "I've got to find a phone, George. Would you mind telling the audience to go and the choir to stay?"

"Do you need to keep the choir particularly? All their names and

93

addresses will be known to their committee, and you really have no reason to keep them."

"No reason?" demanded Cleveland.

"You may have simply a natural death on your hands, not a murder."

Cleveland stared hard at him. "You know in your guts that isn't true, George. We may not know how she died, but I'll bet a thousand quid she didn't die naturally."

"So would I. But betting's not good enough grounds for keeping a couple of hundred people here."

"You said yourself we don't want them rampaging backstage."

In the end, at Masters' suggestion, the sergeants let six women and six men from the choir go at a time. They were asked to touch nothing except their own garments and to leave quickly so that the next six could be released.

"As you leave the stage, ladies and gentlemen," said Masters as he told them what was to happen, "I would like any one of you who saw anybody whom you didn't recognize as a member of the choir or the orchestra, or anybody who was dressed wrongly, behind the scenes tonight, to give his or her name to the plain-clothes sergeant at your exit door. Anything or anybody suspicious, inside or out."

"May we know why?" asked one portly gentleman in heavy horn-rimmed spectacles. "Miss Festival is obviously dead, otherwise you would not have covered her face with your coat. But she died, she wasn't killed. We saw her die, with nobody near her. She was in perfectly good health and then she . . . well, had a heart attack, I suppose. So why all this . . . this holding us back and your suggesting we might have seen something suspicious?"

"I am taking precautions, sir. Just in case things are not quite so straightforward as you seem to think. I shall be sure after Miss Festival's body has been examined, not before. Better be safe than sorry, sir, and anyway, you will all be away in about ten minutes, I expect."

Cleveland was back before all the members of the choir and orchestra had gone. By this time the orchestra, too, were herding towards the stage exits, so Masters had been able to move the chairs and music stands back to give plenty of space round the collapsed body.

"Everybody is on the way. Chief Constable, forensic, ambulance, a dozen CID men and half a dozen uniformed constables under a sergeant."

"Good. I see Mrs Cleveland is still sitting in the hall. Perhaps you should have a word with her."

"I'll do that, and I'll lock the front doors."

"To keep out reporters? You're unlucky. There was one here to report on the performance. I've told him to sit down and keep quiet and not to go near a phone. Fortunately he is only the music and drama man, and he hasn't got a camera with him, but by now he'll have scribbled out an eye-witness account."

"I'll deal with him, too," grated Cleveland. "I'll tell him we suspect a heart attack and he'd better get his copy in fast. There's been no mention of foul play, has there?"

"Not directly, but I'm afraid I may have given him a hint by telling the choir and orchestra to mention anything they saw backstage which was out of the ordinary."

"Does he know who you are?"

"No."

"Then I can get rid of him without any trouble. Hang on here, if you will."

Cleveland had given the car keys to his wife and sent her home and dealt with the young reporter before the Nortown squads started to arrive.

"I'll leave you to it, Matt," said Masters, taking his coat from the body. "God, what a waste. A woman like that. . . ."

"No you don't," said Cleveland.

"Don't what?"

"Just push off and leave me to it."

Masters put an arm into the sleeve of his coat. "It's your business, Matt, not mine. I'll collect my people. We'll be with Bill Green backstage for a bit if he's found anything. After that, I suppose we ought to see Miss Whitehead gets home."

"Don't go without letting me know."

"If that's what you want."

"Pedder will definitely want to see you."

"I'll make sure he has a chance to speak to me."

Reed and Berger joined Masters as he went through to the female soloists' dressing-room. Both looked grave. "This one isn't going to be easy, Chief."

"It's not our pigeon. At least, not yet."

"You think it will be?"

"I really couldn't say. Before we can join in, Mr Anderson will have to give his permission. If Mr Pedder asks for our help and the AC agrees, then we shall have to do what we can."

"After singing like that tonight," said Berger. "It's more than murder, Chief, it's . . . "

"We don't know that she didn't die from natural causes. There may be no need to treat it as anything but an ordinary death. The forensic people will decide."

"Pull the other one, Chief."

Obviously Green heard their voices in the passage. A door opened and he put his head out.

"In here, George."

They trooped in. It was a bare, sparsely furnished room with a bench backed by make-up mirrors and three or four chairs, a coat stand with a variety of hangers, a movable screen, a small table and a wardrobe cupboard. The walls were cream washed, the floor covered in dark-brown carpet tiles. Dark-green curtains covered the small window. On the table were a briefcase, a vanity case and two empty tea cups. Despite the warmth from the central heating radiator, Miss Whitehead had put on a heavy coat. She was sitting on one of the chairs close to the table, her flat, zipped music case on the floor beside her.

"I asked you to come in here, Miss Whitehead, just to get you out of the mêlée on the stage. Not to keep you for any reason. Now that things have quietened down I expect you would like to get away."

"I would, rather. I expect Mr and Mrs Jagger — my hosts while I'm here — will be waiting for me in their car."

"Outside the hall?"

"They said he would walk to the car park and then come back here for me. They expected me to be ready to go by then. They will

96

probably be frozen by now."

"Please stay where you are for the moment. Sergeant Berger will go to see if Mr Jagger is there. If he is, you can then go. But we wouldn't like you to stand around in the cold."

"And if he's not there?"

"You will have the pleasure of being taken home in a police car. An unmarked one, driven by Sergeant Berger."

Miss Whitehead managed to smile, despite her obvious distress. "In that case, I think I hope Mr Jagger has left me stranded."

Berger left them.

"During the short time we have got, Miss Whitehead, may I ask whether you have been able to tell Mr Green anything you feel we should know?"

"The dear man has not questioned me, and quite frankly I can't recall anything to tell you. Nancy was her usual happy self before the performance and during the interval when I last saw her. She said she was going to read some lurid corset-stripper while we slaved away on stage and that she would see me after the final chorus. Mr Green has, poor man, studiously tried to avoid giving me the impression that Nancy died anything but a natural death, but I fear his efforts have not allayed my fears."

"We shall know how she died after the doctors have examined her, but her collapse was so sudden and so unexpected that we have had to play safe. I know young people do sometimes suffer fatal heart attacks but they are, fortunately, so rare as to be suspect until confirmed. Consequently, as there were five policemen in the audience, we immediately took the view that we should consider this an unnatural death until proved wrong. If we are wrong, the precautions we have taken will have caused no harm. If we are right . . . " He spread his hands. "We shall have been justified in our actions."

"Of course. Poor Nancy. She was the nicest person and her voice . . . " Miss Whitehead was now near to tears. "It had no equal, Mr Masters. The rest of us, as you must have guessed, were just also-rans beside her."

Reed, unexpectedly, said: "If you others were also-rans, ma'am, I don't mind listening to a few of you coming in a few paces behind the favourite. I'm no music buff, but you brought a lump to my throat tonight more than once."

"How very nice of you to say so."

Berger came in. "Mr and Mrs Jagger are there, sir. I said I'd escort Miss Whitehead out to the car because the whole circus has arrived. It's like Piccadilly out there."

"Thank you. Are you ready Miss Whitehead? Just one word. I don't know what is happening about the other two performances, but I feel sure that if things are as we fear, one of the investigating officers will want to talk to you tomorrow, so please don't leave Nortown before we let you know."

"We shall be singing again tomorrow night, I feel sure. A replacement will be found, I expect."

"In that case, make sure you have a good night's sleep. Get Mr Jagger to give you a strong nightcap."

"I'll do just that. Goodnight, everybody."

As soon as Berger had escorted her away, Masters turned to Green. "Anything, Bill?"

"Could be. Look at this."

The vanity case, squared up, black leather, fourteen by ten and four inches deep, held closed by two sliding clip fasteners was not for make-up but for carrying syringes and throat sprays.

"I've not touched them. Miss Whitehead said they were for Miss Festival's throat. Four sprays. That long tube has that widened out bit — that's called an expansion chamber. The short thing is for the nose apparently. The big one is a skin spray. The different coloured holders differentiate between the aerosols."

"Small," said Reed. "Like the sprays asthmatics use."

"And," said Green, "no label on them to say what they're for."

"George!" The bellow came from the passageway. Masters hurriedly closed the lid of the case and stepped to the door. "In here, sir."

Pedder, with Cleveland in attendance.

"First guess from the quacks, murder," said Pedder heavily. "Poisoned somehow. They're preparing to take her away."

Masters nodded. "That's what I was afraid of, sir."

"Afraid of?" Pedder pushed the cups and cases aside and half sat on the table. "All right, George. You told us it would happen on the third of December. You said it would be connected with a triumph, and Matt here tells me she was getting a standing ovation when it happened."

Masters nodded, but said nothing.

"It seems you were right about everything, and us sceptics up here were wrong. Now you've got to help us bottom the thing and get our hands on the bloody maniac that's doing these murders."

"My instructions, sir, were to put myself at your disposal only if you made a specific request to Mr Anderson for me to do so."

"He'll agree, won't he?"

"I feel sure he will if you care to call him and make the request, sir."

"Alf. Not sir."

"He won't mind being disturbed at his home. After all, it is not yet half-past eleven. I can give you his home number."

"Let's have it, then. I'll do it from HQ as Matt says the phone here is dicey. I want to say you'll take over. All right?"

"I would prefer to work alongside Matt. There are so many local connotations here that he would be necessary."

"Matt?"

"I won't mind working with him, for him or anyhow else, Alf. We've got a chance to nail the bastard this time, and I'm not going to let questions of who's boss get in the way." He turned to Masters. "Anything you say, George. Count me in."

"That's settled then," said Pedder. "Get to it, gentlemen."

"Now what, George?" asked Cleveland.

"Two things, Matt. First, could you arrange for the dregs in these cups and the contents of these aerosol sprays to be analysed? After they've been dusted for prints, of course."

"We can do that for you. What's number two job?"

"Do you think Mrs Cleveland will still have some of that supper left lying about?"

Cleveland stared at him for a long moment and then burst out laughing. "Give me a couple of minutes. I'll give her a ring, and then arrange for these goods to be collected. I'll leave a couple of men in the building overnight once they've taken the body away."

"It's gone, sir," said Berger. "I saw them carry out the shell after seeing Miss Whitehead away. Just a minute or so ago."

"George," said Green. "Her next of kin. They should be informed."

"Being done," said Cleveland. "I told my DCI to find out who it is and then to deal with it on my behalf. Anything else, or can I go and phone my missus?"

After Cleveland had left them, Green said: "You're playing this pretty casually, George."

"Am I? In what way, Bill?"

"This supper. Don't get me wrong. I'm all for it. My belly's beginning to think my throat's been cut. But I reckon Pedder would be a bit put out if he knew you hadn't got your nose to the grindstone."

"He will know. At least, after he's spoken to Anderson, he'll try to get hold of me to tell me that all has been agreed. Well, he won't find me here. Why should he? There's nothing and nobody here for us to investigate. We've sent the cups and sprays for analysis, and I'm certainly not going to start knocking people up at this time of night to interrogate them. And, just to cap it, Bill, when he can't get hold of me here or at the hotel, it's a pound to a penny he'll ring Matt's house."

"Where you will be, having supper."

"Where I shall be in conference with my team members and the senior of our local colleagues. If Mrs Cleveland likes to offer us a sandwich while we're there, working . . . "

Green produced a crumpled packet of Kensitas. "I know it says Nosmo King in here, but I haven't had a fag since the interval. And to show I'm good-natured, I'll even offer you lads one."

The sergeants both reached out to help themselves.

"I said one," growled Green. "Between you, not each."

"We know," replied Reed, lighting all three cigarettes. "But look at how many you've saved while sitting there listening to music and not being allowed to have a crafty drag."

Cleveland travelled with them in the Yard car to direct Reed to the house on the outskirts where the DSC lived.

Philippa Cleveland may not have had much time to prepare for their coming, but the sight that met their eyes when they entered the sitting-room caused Green to exclaim: "Now that's something like. Philippa, love, you've saved my bacon. I've been telling this lot there's nothing like northern hospitality and they haven't really believed me. Now perhaps they will, seeing what you've got here."

"I thought it would be nicer to eat in here because there's a good fire still going, so I just moved a table in and put a cloth on. The food was all ready, you see. And we'll be able to sit down and be comfy here."

"Have a drink first," urged Cleveland. "I've got a bottle of malt. Anybody can't drink that?"

"I'll just have coffee," said Philippa. "Whisky is wasted on me." She turned to Masters. "That poor girl. Dead, after singing like that. Sit down everybody and get warm. I've got the fire in a blaze. And she had a very nice frock on. All those accordion pleats. I was saying to Matt I'd like one just like that for the Mayor's Ball." She looked about her as if to make sure Masters and Green were safely ensconced in the big armchairs and that Reed and Berger were comfortable in the smaller fireside ones. "That's right. Matt and I can use the settee. Was it as cold as this in London when you left?"

"Not quite as windy," replied Reed.

"And now you've come up here to one of our gales! I was saying to Matt we hadn't provided a very warm welcome for you and he said some people had tried but hadn't got very far. I didn't know what he meant, but I hope you're comfortable at the Station Hotel."

"Very comfortable, thank you," said Reed.

"That's good, because you're all very clever, aren't you? Matt says you've all got second sight."

Masters laughed. "Matt is very kind, Philippa."

"So he should be if you've come all the way up here to help him. He doesn't tell me much about his work, but I know all these girls getting murdered has worried him ever so much. And now Nancy Festival. He says she's one of the same lot, though how he knows beats me."

"What beats you, Phil?" asked Cleveland, backing through the doorway with a tray in his hands.

"How you know so quickly that Nancy Festival has been killed by the man who's killed the other eleven. Are you guessing, or what?"

"Not guessing," said her husband, handing a glass of whisky to Masters and offering the water jug. "George here told us it was going to happen."

"He what? You mean he knew?"

"More or less."

"Then why didn't you stop it? I mean, if you knew and you actually let somebody kill that poor girl. . . . "

"It wasn't quite like that." Cleveland proceeded to serve Green, Reed and Berger while he explained to his wife. "George worked it out that another girl would be killed on the third of December. But he didn't know who and he didn't know where. So we couldn't prevent it. You see, dear, these four gentlemen saw a sort of pattern in the dates of the murders over the past eleven months."

"Which you didn't discover?"

"Which we didn't discover and which most people up here weren't too sure about. But that's by the way. George reckoned that if they were right the woman who was next on the killer's list would be one who achieved something big today. Like Nancy Festival's triumph in the Central Hall tonight. And then, if he stuck to his former pattern, the killer would murder her within the next forty-eight hours."

"You worked all that out?" Philippa asked Green.

"Not me. George."

"No wonder Matt said he had second sight."

"Second sight?" asked Masters grimly. "Bill, I've been a purblind idiot."

"Now what?" demanded Green. "You foresaw this lot. You've been like a cat on hot bricks all day, sensing it was coming. What more could you have done?"

"A lot. I told you I'd got the jim-jams, but I couldn't tell you why. God knows I tried to find the reason for the feeling. But I couldn't, and I ought to have."

They were all looking at him without thinking of interrupting him. "Don't you see, Bill? Matt has just said either today or within forty-eight hours. What's forty-eight hours?"

"Two days," replied Green quietly.

"Just so. Today, Tuesday. Two more days will be Wednesday and Thursday. And what have we been doing tonight? Listening to a performance of *Messiah* which is being put on on Tuesday, Wednesday and Thursday. It was that leaflet about it that I picked up in the hotel last night. It was all there, in black and white and I didn't cotton on. I ought to have done. My mind wouldn't focus properly. I woke up this morning sensing — no, expecting, tragedy — and I couldn't account for it. But the clue was there, Bill. I must have realized it while I was asleep: dreamed it, if you like, but the fact escaped me when I woke up, leaving only the feeling of unease. I tell you I should have foreseen that the murder would be connected with this three-day event. Not necessarily that it would be Nancy Festival who would be killed but that someone connected with that show would be the victim."

There was a moment or two of silence after he had finished speaking, then Green said: "You may be right, George, but I'm not going to say you are, or even that you should have foreseen what you've just told us. In the event it may have turned out that way, but what could we have done to forestall it? Surrounded that place with cops? Then what would have happened? Nothing. And again tomorrow and Thursday? Ask Matt here what the result of that would have been?"

Matt shook his head. "Disaster," he said. "I hate to put it this way, but somebody had to die to prove your theory, George, because I reckon we need that theory, now it's been proved beyond doubt, to get our man."

"To hell with theories," said Masters.

"If we'd somehow prevented what happened tonight, George, nobody would have believed what you've given us, and another lass, and another would get the chop. One every month until we nail this bastard. Now we ought to be able to get him."

Masters looked up. "You're right, I suppose, Matt. Sorry for the temperamental display, but I don't like to think of my own mind playing me tricks."

Cleveland grinned. "Probably, now you've shown it who's master, it'll start helping you to solve this business properly. Sorry for the pun, but you get my meaning."

Reed got to his feet. "If past form is anything to go by, I reckon the Chief has got it half sussed-out already. Shall I pass the pork pie round, Mrs Cleveland?"

Philippa jumped to her feet. "Oh, yes, please. What am I thinking about. There's pork pie, cold beef and pickles or sandwiches. Please help yourselves. Matt, pass the plates round. You men must be ravenous. Don't worry about me, I had a snack as soon as I got home, thinking you wouldn't be coming. Bread and butter anybody?"

It was nearly two o'clock when they left the house to return to the hotel. Berger, who had had only one drink, was driving. Reed, in the nearside front seat, turned as the car gathered way. "I noticed, Chief, that you never said another word about this case after we started supper."

"It was supposed to be a party."

"Rubbish," said Green. "After what happened in the hall? You weren't at a party, George, you were on duty. You deliberately kept off the subject. You even clamped down on Philly Cleveland when she tried to sound you out about something. That means you had a reason for keeping quiet about the case. And that in turn means you had something to keep quiet about."

"I hope Matt Cleveland didn't come to the same conclusion."

"He's not had to put up with you for all these years like we have."

"Good."

"So what's it all about? Or aren't you going to tell us?"

"I'm going to tell you what I've been thinking about. Something Matt said caused it. He said if Nancy Festival hadn't died, there'd be another girl killed, and another. One every month, just as during the past year."

"That seemed a logical statement to me."

"Highly logical until one asks oneself, what if our idea about there being a reason for these killings is correct?"

"A definite purpose, you mean?"

"Yes. What if that definite purpose was the killing of Nancy Festival?"

"You what?"

"What if she was intended to be the final victim? The big job for which all the others were only preliminary skirmishes?"

"This is what you've been considering for the past couple of hours while scoffing brawn and Wensleydale cheese sandwiches?"

"Lancashire."

"What about it?"

"Lancashire cheese."

"Never mind that. What have you come up with?"

"Nothing, actually, but the idea intrigues me. If you three would care to think about it before falling asleep, you might come up with something."

"Count me out, Chief," said Reed. "You two had a kip this afternoon. As soon as I hit the pillow it will be bye-byes for me."

"And me," grunted Berger.

"They've got no professional enthusiasm, George," said Green. "No constabulary pride or investigative drive. Now, when I was a young sergeant . . ."

"And goodnight to you, too," murmured Berger.

Chapter Five

THE NEXT MORNING when the four Yard men went downstairs
for breakfast, they found the dining-room almost empty. Only
two or three very early risers had beaten them to it.

Green studied the menu. "What I find wanting in this pub," he
said, "is the kipper before you have breakfast proper."

"What are you on about?" demanded Reed. "It's printed there
as large as life. Scotch kippers."

"As an alternative, lad, not as a prelude to the mixed grill dish. I
like a starter at breakfast time."

"There's stewed prunes, fruit juice, porridge and seventeen
kinds of cereal to choose from as a prelude. What more do you
want?"

"I've heard it said there's more goodness in a cereal carton than
in its contents. If it wasn't for the sugar and milk you'd be getting a
negative quantity of nutrition by eating them."

The discussion was cut short by Green signalling to the deputy
head waiter on early duty.

"Can I help you, sir?" The man was approaching middle age,
and courteous.

"Do you, by any chance, have such a thing as a penny duck I
could have with my bacon and eggs?"

"I'm very sorry, sir, but we don't actually serve penny ducks in
the hotel. However, the breakfast chef is a Scot, sir. From Dundee
to be precise. He is in the habit of making what he calls Lorgne
sausage. He has a special dish, very long and narrow with rounded
corners for pressing the meat in, sir. He seasons and spices it
judiciously and there is no skin. When turned out of the dish, it is
cut in half-inch-thick slices for frying. It is a close approximation to
the penny duck, sir, but fried, as I mentioned, instead of being
oven-baked and requiring to be reheated before serving. Chef

makes it for himself and many of the staff enjoy a couple of slices with breakfast. Myself among them. Would you care to try the Lorgne sausage for yourself, sir?"

"You can recommend it?"

"Highly, sir."

"Right, I'll try it."

"With your usual Victorian grill, sir?"

"What else?"

"I don't know how you do it," said Reed. "You were eating at two this morning and here you are, five and a half hours later, going in for mixed grills."

"Pass the coffee pot, lad and stop waffling. What's getting up early got to do with it, anyway? It's what's to come that matters. There'll be a big day ahead of us and I want a proper foundation to sustain me. Look at his nibs, for instance. He's eating, not talking, because he knows we've got it all to do, as they say in the television sports programmes."

"He's not talking because he's reading a newspaper, or trying to."

"Don't split hairs lad. You can read and eat at the same time, but you can't talk and scoff at once."

"Some people can."

"Meaning?"

"You've just made a piece of buttered toast disappear while you've been gabbing on."

"Training, lad. When you've had as much experience as I have of missing meals in the course of duty you'll have learned a few of the tricks of the trade."

"Do you want me to polish your medals?"

"No need, lad. They never tarnish. Ah! Here comes the connor."

The deputy head waiter himself carried the large oval platter across to the table and set it before Green.

"I hope you enjoy it, sir."

"Don't worry, I shall."

"There's just one thing, sir."

"What's that?"

"I don't know whether I should mention this to you. It may not be the proper place."

"Don't be shy. I shall keep all my biting for my breakfast."

"It's about the tragedy last night, sir. You gentlemen are policemen . . . "

Masters lowered his paper.

"Please go on, Mr . . . er . . . "

"Cope, sir. Being on early turn this week, I was at home last night when Ginny came in. Ginny is my daughter, sir, and she sings in the Philharmonic Choir. A soprano. Of course, she's only young. Just twenty . . . "

"Please tell us what happened, Mr Cope."

"Nothing happened, actually, sir, but when Ginny got home she was naturally full of how Miss Festival had died on stage. Our girl told her mother and me everything about it and how they had been let off stage in dribs and drabs by some policemen who were there, and from her description of the officers, I thought I recognized you gentlemen."

"We were there," admitted Masters.

"Ginny was very upset, sir. A young girl faced with a sudden death . . . you can imagine the reaction, sir."

"Of course."

"Ginny got a bit worked up, sir, and said some things about an older woman in the choir who had been going on all night about Miss Whitehead. Spiteful, Ginny said it was. About how ugly she was and how she was no better a singer than this older woman herself and how she was singing flat. Ginny didn't like it at all, and then when Miss Festival died . . . well, sir, somehow Ginny got things a bit jumbled up in her mind and seemed to be connecting all that hatred and spite with the tragedy. That's all, sir. Perhaps I shouldn't have mentioned it to you, but Ginny was in a real state about it, and I thought if I could just tell you . . . "

"You were quite right to do so, Mr Cope. I am grateful to you for having the thoughtfulness to come and tell us. Do you happen to remember the name of the older woman Ginny was talking about?"

"Her name, sir, is Mrs Alice Mundy. But I hope you won't involve Ginny . . . please don't let people think she came to you telling tales."

"Don't worry, chum," said Green. "Your daughter won't be mentioned. I take it this Mundy woman was going on to other people, and not just your Ginny?"

"To everybody who would listen, or so I understand, sir."

"Fair enough. Nobody will be able to pin anything on your Ginny. And don't tell your lass you told us, then she won't get frightened. And you can be sure we shall keep this to ourselves. Mr Masters, here, is leading the investigation, so you've come right to the top."

"Thank you, sir. Now, if you'll excuse me, there are more people coming in for breakfast."

"Carry on, chum. And thanks."

Green tackled his breakfast. Berger said: "This opens up a new line of thought, Chief."

"Such as?"

Berger sat back in his chair. "What if the killer was after Miss Whitehead and not Miss Festival? Or, alternatively, that he was after either of them, no matter which?"

"Could be," said Reed. "And not just because we've heard that this Mundy dame was coming the old acid. It's a possibility all the way along the line. The killer doesn't seem to have been all that particular as to the actual personal identity of his victims in the past, only on their achievements. And both those women were achievers of a high order."

"Rubbish," said Green, forking a piece of Lorgne sausage.

"If you don't like it after all the fuss you made to get it," said Reed, "just push it to one end of the platter and leave it."

Green glowered at him.

"You heard what his nibs said on the way home last night."

"He simply asked us to consider the possibility of Nancy Festival being the last victim and the reason for the previous eleven. To consider it, not to exclude every other line of thought."

"It's still rubbish," said Green.

"Tell us why?"

"I can't," said Green, smiling seraphically. "I'm busy eating, remember?"

"Chief?" appealed Reed.

"I certainly didn't mean you to exclude all other possibilities as you so rightly say. I suggest that as it is Berger's theory, with your corollary, the two of you work it out. See where it fits and where it doesn't and then decide whether it is still tenable. Pass the coffee, please. I'll have another cup while we're waiting for the DCI."

They went straight from the hotel to Cleveland's office in the HQ building. The Nortown DCS was working at his desk.

"One or two things, George. The forensic reports, both from the pathologist and the analysts, will be here at lunchtime. Call that one o'clock at the earliest."

"Good. We had better come back here at that time. We shall need a chat session then, in any case."

"I had some of my people out asking questions in Market Street after we left there last night. One young chap, coming home late, said he saw a man rush down the alleyway at the side of the Central Hall just before seven o'clock. He knows the time, because he lives close by and that's when he went out. He didn't see the face. Just the figure hunched up in a very dark coat and carrying a biggish case."

"We shall have to try to trace the man as we go along, but if all that was seen of him was what you've just said, it could prove difficult. But it is a lead. Anything else, Matt?"

"The CC phoned in to say he couldn't reach you last night, but he has cleared it officially with the Yard for you to be here. But I warn you, he's got over being congratulatory about you being proved right last night. Now he's had time to sleep on it he can see the difficulties even being right has raised, and he's going on about seeing whether you're as practical a cop as you are a theorist. He's expecting rabbits to be pulled out of hats, or maybe he isn't. Whichever it is, he's put you on trial, George."

Masters grinned. "I expected as much. We must not forget he's a worried man, too."

"Nice of you to see it that way."

"What other way is there? You needn't tell him so, Matt, but I feel fairly confident we'll pull it off together. There's no point in expecting failure, is there?"

"No. So what do we do? Pedder left me in no doubt that you're to be the boss."

"I've thought it over, Matt, and this is how it strikes me. We're in for a very big stint of interviewing, so I propose to have three parties. I'd like you to take Sergeant Reed with you, while Bill Green takes Sergeant Berger. To go with Bill I'd like you to provide somebody as guide — DC or WPC — anybody you can spare. And the same for me. You and Reed use your car, Bill and Berger can use ours, so I'd be grateful if whoever you assign to me could be a driver with a car. Can do?"

"That's easily fixed. I'd like you to have a DS — just to give him the experience of working with you. Bill can have a DC. Excuse me a moment while I lay that on."

"Send the DS along with Bill, please Matt. He'll talk to Berger better than to me. I'll have the DC."

"Anything you say. When do we go?"

"The sooner the better. Ten minutes' time."

When Cleveland put down the phone, Masters continued. "Matt, I want these interviews to be in depth. Every word, every movement, every time is going to be vital. And you'll have to be able to repeat them — you and Reed — word for word at our debriefing sessions, so though you won't want to take shorthand notes or anything like them which might destroy informality or cause people to watch their words too closely, please note salient points after each interview if you need to. My own people know how I work, so they will be doing the same.

"Now, Matt, I want you to concentrate on Miss Whitehead this morning. I don't propose to tell you how to go about it, but there may well be subsidiary interviews arising out of the main one. In fact, Reed has the name of another woman I'd like you to talk to.

"Bill, you and Berger concentrate on the Central Hall. There must be caretakers there. You've heard Matt's report about the dark figure. Everything, please, including the physical possibilities of entry or hiding on the premises and so on. But I don't have to tell you.

"I shall call on Miss Festival's hostess. But to get to know who she is, I shall first call on Butcher, the conductor. Your man will be able to discover where he lives, I take it, Matt?"

"He'll get it. DC York his name is. He's got a head on his shoulders."

"Excellent. We will meet back here at half-past twelve for reports so that everybody will be kept completely in the picture. Soon after that we should have the medical facts. This afternoon's work will depend on what we learn then. That's all, gentlemen, thank you."

As they were preparing to leave, there was a knock at the door. Cleveland introduced Sergeant Sibley and DC York.

"These two are to be fully briefed," said Masters. "They are to be part of our team and I want as many ears to the ground as possible."

"Along here, sir," said DC York. "Number seventeen. The side we're on."

They were old houses, built, Masters guessed, some short time before the First World War. The bigger, more solid, original semis, with long front gardens sloping up to brick-bayed windows with stone sills and porches with round stone pillars on each side. The type of house that was now being sought after as having a little more character and a lot more staying power than their modern counterparts. There were several with brass plates at the gates, too distant to be read from the car. Masters guessed at dentists, solicitors and the like, but thought he might perhaps have been mistaken when York drew into the kerb. Number seventeen had a brass plate a foot square which proclaimed that Rodney Butcher, LRAM etc., taught music theory and pianoforte playing within.

Pleasant enough, thought Masters. The road good and wide, but not overburdened with traffic. Plenty of greenery about, with a goodly amount of autumn leaves still left uncollected in heaps in sheltered spots. No signs of tumbledown or dilapidated property, but yet no signs of the freshness of paint, outside lamps and the other touches which one associates with young property owners. The area gave the impression of being frozen in perpetual middle age, rather grey and weary in this cold, windy weather.

No garage or carriage drive. A single iron gate giving on to a narrow path paved, chessboard fashion, in alternate black and red quarry tiles. Masters walked up to the door. Ordinary green was the way in which he categorized the paint. He rang the bell, noting that the brass of it had been cleaned so frequently that the paint round about had been bleached and discoloured by the metal polish.

Liza Butcher arrived to answer the door in a washed out full-length fore-and-aft apron and a mob-cap. Masters guessed she was the sort of woman who habitually wore these garments for her housework: that she had lost sight of — or even had never known — that when doing daily chores a woman can continue to look attractive in the oldest of clothes, providing she takes a modicum of care to do so. His wife, Wanda, always managed it, and Doris Green, nearly as old as this woman, was always in well-washed, neatly-pressed garments with shoes cleaned. Liza Butcher had on lisle stockings with holes in and slopped-out, down-at-heel old shoes which had never seen polish for years.

"Police," said Masters, showing his card. "I am Detective Chief Superintendent Masters, and this is Detective Constable York. I should like to speak to Mr Rodney Butcher, please."

"You can't. Not yet."

"He already has a visitor? A pupil perhaps?"

"No, he's not up yet. This business has prostrated him. He's staying in bed this morning. I've rung his pupils to put them off."

"Please ask him to come down."

"I couldn't do that. The poor lamb is too overcome."

"Mrs Butcher, please understand that I intend to speak to your son now. If you point out to him that unless I can talk to him here I shall require him to accompany me to the police station for questioning, I think he will consider it better to get out of bed, put a dressing gown on and present himself as fast as his legs can carry him. Alternatively, I will go up to his room if you wish."

"I'll call him."

"I think we had better come in, don't you? You won't want all the neighbours wondering what is happening."

She stood back to let them enter and then paddled up the stairs, leaving them in the hallway which, with a pot of paint and a bit of goodwill, could have been turned into as bright and cheerful a specimen of its kind as could be found. Obviously Rodney was not one for attempting home-decorating. Probably he felt it might somehow damage his pianist's hands. Masters, sensitive to atmosphere, got the impression that its inmates had depressed this house: that with a cheerful couple and laughing children it would recover to become a happy, welcoming home. Now it cowered under dreary paint, faded khaki wallpaper and dark-oak linoleum.

"He's coming. I had to wake the poor lamb."

Butcher came downstairs, his long body clad in conventional blue and white pyjamas over which he was wearing an elderly fawn mohair dressing gown. Masters noted that the coloured cord with which the edges were piped had come adrift in several places. The face was pale and washed-out; the uncombed hair stood on end in a lacklustre mop.

He came to a halt on the return stair at the bottom of the flight.

"Mr Butcher, I suppose your mother has told you who we are. You have no doubt guessed the purpose of our visit for yourself. We are investigating the death of Miss Nancy Festival. As the conductor of last night's performance you will be in a position to tell us certain things we wish to know. However, as you do not appear, as yet, to be in a fit state to answer my questions, I shall content myself with asking just one at the moment. I shall then leave to give you time to get yourself ready to receive us later in the morning. Your mother has told me that you have put off your pupils for today, so there is no reason why you should not be ready for us when we return."

"I shall have to arrange a replacement soloist for tonight."

"You propose to give a performance tonight?"

"Of course."

"The replacement will be contacted by phone, will she not?"

"Er — yes."

"Then I shall expect to find you here when I return. Your afternoon will be free for any rehearsal you may feel you need with the new contralto, as I expect it is unlikely she can reach Nortown before then."

"She may have to be a local singer."

"So much the better. She can do her private practice at home this morning and be ready to rehearse with you after lunch. Now my one question. Please tell me the name and address of Miss Festival's hostess."

"Mrs Fenny. The Arbour, Nidderdale Avenue. It's a big house, standing alone, painted cream and green."

"Thank you, Mr Butcher. I shall call there and then come back to see you."

"You are commendably early, Mr Masters," said Sarah Fenny. "I had half-expected you to call late last night."

"I did not do so for several reasons, ma'am. I was not absolutely sure then that Miss Festival had died from anything other than natural causes, so though I was present when she collapsed and took a certain number of precautions at the time, I had no valid reason for treating her death as one needing criminal investigation. As well as that, I prefer not to knock on doors in the dead of night unless it is absolutely necessary to do so. The public as a whole takes a poor view of such visits and the recipients of the calls are never at their best and totally ready to co-operate."

"Please come into the sitting-room." She led them from the large square hall into the pleasantest of rooms. There were two sofas set at right angles to the marble fireplace where a log fire blazed comfortingly. The large room also contained a number of arm-chairs and occasional tables. A number of gold-framed originals graced the plaster-panelled walls. Not opulent, thought Masters, but distinctly well-to-do and, above all, tasteful.

"Please sit down. Near the fire if you would like to."

She sat opposite to them.

"Mr Masters, I don't know what happened to Nancy last night, except that she collapsed and died. A moment or two ago you informed me she had not died naturally. That suggests that there was foul play, because I am convinced Nancy would never have taken her own life and we were present ourselves to see that no accident occurred."

"Quite right, ma'am. We haven't yet had the forensic reports, but the immediate medical opinion was that she was poisoned. I need hardly add, I think, that that was my first impression, too."

"Naturally I was watching very closely all that went on last night. From your demeanour — the way you rushed forward to get to her — I got the impression that you had almost expected the tragedy."

Masters paused before replying.

"Had I expected Miss Festival to die, ma'am, I would have moved heaven and earth to prevent it."

"I am sure you are a sincere man, Mr Masters, but I was keenly interested in events and I would have said you were not surprised when Nancy collapsed. In fact, Mr Masters, you were so quick off the mark that you did not pause for a split second to overcome any surprise you would ordinarily have had. Expectancy or lack of surprise, whichever you wish, was there. I saw it and I sensed it. Yet you deny both."

"Certainly I do, ma'am, otherwise I should not have been sitting in the audience enjoying the performance."

"Forgive me for harping on this, but your presence at the Central Hall could just as easily be an indication that you were expecting trouble there last night."

"Mrs Fenny, ever since last night I have been cursing myself for not foreseeing the possibility of tragedy at the performance."

"Which would seem to suggest that it should have been possible to foresee events and forestall them. You failed to do that."

"I am not clairvoyant."

"I would never suggest you were, but you have admitted to cursing yourself for not foreseeing Nancy's death. I would say you were not the type of man to indulge in useless recrimination of himself. This means that, even without benefit of clairvoyance, you feel you should have been able to foretell what was to happen. Why didn't you do so?"

Masters got to his feet. "I have no wish to be evasive, Mrs Fenny, but I could have wished that your mind was not so penetrative." He stood with his back to the fire, a tall, grave man, and gazed down at this woman who had so clearly divined his recent thoughts and actions.

"If I have made you uncomfortable, Mr Masters, I apologize."

"Not uncomfortable, ma'am. But you have disconcerted me slightly. Not personally, but professionally."

"You will have to explain that more fully if I am to understand it."

"I would like you to understand. Hear the story for yourself."

"Thank you."

"Ever since last January, in this police area, there has been a woman killed at the rate of one a month."

She inclined her head to show she was aware of this fact.

"I am not an officer of the local force."

"You are not? Then why are you here?"

"I am from Scotland Yard, ma'am. A week or two ago, I was asked to read and look very hard at the Northern Counties police files concerning the deaths of eleven women. The local police had worked hard and long to apprehend the killer, but despite their thoroughness they had been unable to get any lead to help them."

"I am aware there has been some public disquiet at their failure. I must add that I do not subscribe to the feeling though I would, of course, prefer a success story."

"In desperation the files were sent to the Yard to see if fresh minds could find something, no matter how small, which might help. My team and I — four of us altogether — were given the job. As I said, this was only a week or two ago, so I am a relative newcomer to these cases. I come from the south and don't know the terrain up here, and I have never worked with your local force before.

"That, however, is by the way. Computers had failed to find any pattern or common denominators which the officers themselves had not seen. Then we had a bit of luck. I will not go into the details, but we did find a pattern or a hint of one. What I mean by that is that our beliefs had to be proved before they could be fully accepted as a working theory."

"You mean some people were sceptical?"

"Our ideas were a little far-fetched," said Masters modestly. "There were, basically, two of them. One concerned the timing of the murders and one the choice of victims."

"Are you saying the killer actually chose his victims. That there was nothing haphazard about it?"

"To a certain degree, ma'am. The victims had one thing in common. They were women who had succeeded in something on the vital days. I called them triumphs. One girl had won a tennis tournament, another had just swum Morecambe Bay."

"And Nancy Festival? Was her performance and reception last night a triumph?" asked Sarah Fenny quietly.

"Could it have been anything else, ma'am?"

"Please continue, Mr Masters."

"According to my theory, the next murder would be due on the third of December or within the forty-eight hours following it."

Sarah Fenny gasped. "The third? Yesterday."

"Yes, ma'am. But I couldn't have known where in the thousands of square miles that go to make up Northern Counties area the murder would be done. Nor could I say which woman would achieve a triumph, nor yet what means would be used to kill her.

"But I was conscious of the date yesterday, believe me. I was praying I was wrong, but I felt a strong sense of foreboding. And then last evening I attended the performance of *Messiah*. When I saw and heard the reception given to Miss Festival, the one word that leapt into my mind was triumph. So because I was uneasy and I then had encountered triumph, I was more than halfway to knowing, subconsciously, that Miss Festival was to be the victim. When she collapsed I was, as you saw, as ready to go as a sprinter in his blocks." He looked down at her. "But I couldn't have known the killer had already struck, ma'am. Had he not done so, we could have protected her and saved her life.

"Now you know it all. I have answered your questions and, I hope, exonerated myself in your eyes."

Sarah Fenny looked up at him. "Thank you, Mr Masters. I am sorry to have catechized you, but I am pleased to have heard what you have told me."

Masters resumed his seat. "And now, ma'am, I hope you will talk to me about Miss Festival."

"Please answer me one — no, two — more questions first. Are you in charge of this case, Mr Masters?"

"Your local Chief Constable asked my superiors at the Yard, late last night, for my services. I took charge from the moment agreement was given."

"And will you get your man, Mr Masters?"

"Such is my intention, ma'am."

"Thank you. Now I had better tell you about my relationship with Nancy.

"I am a widow, Mr Masters, with two sons and two daughters, all as yet unmarried. Nancy Festival was like a third daughter in the house and, as she was somewhat older than my girls, became a very dear friend. We all of us looked forward to her visits here both when she came to sing and, as sometimes happened, she felt like a break from her very busy professional life."

"I had not realized the mutual involvement between you and Miss Festival. I can see now why you must feel her death very deeply."

"We shall miss her. Are missing her already."

"All the members of your family?"

"All of them."

"Were any of them with you last evening?"

"All four."

Masters smiled. "That must have made you feel very proud, Mrs Fenny. So often nowadays children do not keep company with their parents, but you had two sons, two daughters and the incomparable Miss Festival with you."

"And had Nancy not died, I should have had yet another on my way home. A very pretty girl whom David was to have brought home for supper. She was selling programmes in the hall."

"I believe I bought my programmes from her. At least the one I'm talking about was twenty-one-ish, fair-headed, white dress. . . . "

"That was Cissy. She didn't come back with us, in the circumstances."

"Your children, Mrs Fenny, are they actually still children?"

"What a pretty compliment, Mr Masters, even to ask whether I might still have young children. No, they are all adult. David, the elder boy, is twenty-seven, a qualified solicitor and secretary of the

119

family firm. Peter is a chartered accountant and is the financial director. One day David will be the managing director. Jane, my elder daughter, is a member of the EEC secretariat and is home for a long leave. Juanita, the younger one, is a pilot. She flies executive jets out of our local airport."

"They sound to be a very fine family, Mrs Fenny. All doing worthwhile jobs and happy in them."

"Extremely happy."

"Was Miss Festival a happy woman?"

"Oh yes."

"Invariably?"

"In her work, with her great gift? What would you expect, Mr Masters?"

Masters smiled. "You didn't answer my question, Mrs Fenny. Had I given you the reply you have just given me, you would have accused me of being evasive."

Mrs Fenny smiled back. "You are investigating a murder which took place last night. What can the vagaries of the victim's moods possibly have to do with it, Mr Masters?"

"The quick answer is that I don't know, Mrs Fenny. But as you are already aware, I work on background information a good deal of my time. I am rarely asked to investigate what for the want of a better word we will call a straightforward killing with obvious means, opportunities and motives. That is why I was asked to scan the local files."

"What you are saying is that you have a reputation for digging slightly deeper than your colleagues."

"That would be one way of putting it, ma'am. But we seem to be straying further and further away from the answer to my question."

"For the past six or seven months, Nancy has been an exceedingly happy woman. She paid us a visit in the summer, just for two or three days, and she was as cheerful as I've ever known her. Since then her letters have been happy ones, and when she arrived yesterday she was in very good form."

"Thank you. But she was unhappy before that?"

"A little. She was in the throes of a divorce earlier in the year.

Most women, I imagine, are affected by the breakup of their marriages. But I recall her saying to me when she came here during the summer that now she was single again — and that is the term she used — she felt much happier."

"Thank you. I realize these breakups don't happen all at once. This one had built up over a long period, had it?"

"I can only judge by Nancy's behaviour when she visited us at intervals, but I think you are right. The trouble lasted for a good many months before the case was heard."

"Thank you. Are her parents alive?"

"Her father only. She was an only child. She thinks a lot of her father. She asked him to live with her earlier this year. They shared a flat in London. I understand that Mr Festival is an excellent housekeeper. He has a woman to help him clean, but he does the cooking himself. He likes it and he's very good at it. Nancy told me yesterday that she had started to diet because she had begun to put on weight due to her father's steak and kidney puddings and raised pies which she found so very tempting. And I can believe her, because Mr Festival had been a baker before he retired."

Masters turned to DC York. "Would you please ask who was informed of Miss Festival's death last night? Make sure it was her father. Ask now, please, if Mrs Fenny will let you use the phone in the hall."

"Of course." Mrs Fenny stood up. "My four are in the morning-room. They decided not to go into work in case you arrived and wished to speak to them. May I ask them to join us?"

Masters, standing, replied that he would be delighted to meet the Fenny family.

David, Peter and Jane came into the sitting-room. Mrs Fenny explained Juanita's temporary absence.

"She's taken the car to the bus stop to pick up Mr Logan, the piano tuner. He's blind, poor man, and though perfectly at home on buses, is not quite so good at finding houses. I always reckoned to have the piano tuned for Nancy, because she did an hour or so's practice in the mornings. Scales usually, but sometimes she would be learning a new work. I forgot all about it until yesterday morning. Then, Mr Logan couldn't come yesterday afternoon because he was tuning the concert grand in the Central Hall, so I asked him to come fairly early today. It would have been all right, I thought, because Nancy wouldn't need the piano here yesterday, as she was going to the hall herself for a short rehearsal. So this morning seemed as if it would do."

"Don't worry, mummy," said Jane.

"I'm not worrying, darling, it just seems so sad. But I'm forgetting my manners." She proceeded to introduce her family to Masters.

"George Masters?" asked David Fenny, the solicitor. "*The* George Masters?"

Masters inclined his head.

"I did some of my training in company law in a London office, Mr Masters. Being engaged on that side of the business I never had any dealings with you, of course, but I heard a great deal about you from friends and colleagues. I must say I'm pleased to hear you are up here to sort this business out."

"Mr Masters has a reputation has he?" said Mrs Fenny, taking her former seat.

"Oh, no," said her son with a grin.

"Meaning, I suppose, that he has."

"The best of," replied David. "And don't you be fooled by him, mama. He's not your ordinary Mr Plod."

"I had never supposed that he was. Still, I have enjoyed our chat, Mr Masters. Whether I have helped you or not remains to be seen."

"No remains about it, ma'am. You have helped."

"Really? I wonder how?"

"I must claim the privilege of silence in front of witnesses."

"Which is as good as telling me to mind my own business, I suppose."

There was a tap at the door and York came in. "It was Mr Festival senior who was informed, sir. He is travelling up by train later this morning. The DCI has arranged for him to be met at the station."

"He must come here," said Mrs Fenny immediately. "Peter, can you collect him?"

Masters intervened. "He will first be required to identify his daughter, ma'am." He turned to York. "Would you please get on to HQ again and ask that they should ring Mr Peter Fenny here as soon as Mr Festival is free from official commitments?"

"Yes, sir." York went back into the hall.

"Are you married, Mr Masters?" asked Jane.

"Why? Have you got designs on the man?" demanded David.

"I am married," said Masters quietly.

"What does your wife do?"

"At the moment she divides her time between looking after our toddler son and me, and voluntary work with an adoption society."

"And before she married you?"

"After university she went into research in the ancient manuscript and old book sections of the museum. She wasn't, of course, the top expert by any means."

"Why do you want to know all this about Mr Masters?" asked Peter.

Jane shrugged prettily. "I was just curious."

Masters got to his feet to leave. While he was saying his goodbyes, York came back. "All fixed, sir. They'll ring Mr Fenny when Mr Festival is free. I said Mr Fenny would go to HQ to pick him up."

"Fine. Thanks," said Peter.

Mrs Fenny accompanied Masters out into the hall to get his coat. While they were there, the front door opened wide and Juanita led in the blind tuner.

"Mr Logan," exclaimed Sarah. "What have you done to yourself?"

The long strip of sticking plaster on Logan's forehead angled down from the hairline to the right eyebrow. Below the dark lenses of the spectacles he was wearing, another strip crossed his cheek down towards the corner of his mouth.

"It happened at the Central Hall, Mrs Fenny."

"Did you have a fall? Or did you bump into something?"

"Neither, actually. I was tuning the piano and that man Butcher told me I wasn't getting it up to concert pitch."

Mrs Fenny turned to Masters. "Rodney Butcher is the conductor. He's a silly ass."

"He's more than that," said Logan bitterly. "He's the sort that won't believe a tuning fork. He ordered me to take it up another semitone. I told him the strings wouldn't take it, but he insisted. Well, I've never seen a piano string break under stress, but I've felt one." He fingered the plaster on his forehead. "If I hadn't already been blind and wearing spectacles, I'd have lost an eye. As it was it broke a lens on that pair and cut me about a bit."

"What did you do?"

"I renewed the string and told him if he wanted it higher he could do it himself. He had the gall to apologize to some of the soloists for it only being at ordinary pitch. But Mr Darren told Butcher he didn't know what he was talking about. And Darren should know, being a tenor. He and the soprano would be the most affected."

"Juanita, darling, take Mr Logan into the drawing-room and see he gets a cup of tea. Tea, mind you. He prefers it to coffee. I'll see Mr Masters out."

"Excuse me, is that the detective?" asked Logan.

"Yes. Detective Chief Superintendent Masters."

"Could I have a word, please?"

"Of course," said Masters.

"I wasn't intending to go to the Central Hall last night, so I hadn't booked a seat. But after that business yesterday afternoon I thought I'd better be there to hear how the piano behaved. There aren't very many seats to be had at the door, so I thought I'd better be early."

"I understand."

"I misjudged it a bit. I sometimes have to wait quite a long time for a bus, but last night I caught one straight away. I was there by a quarter to seven."

"At the hall?"

"Yes. It wasn't open, so I went down the street a bit till I found a bit of a doorway where I could wait out of the wind."

"And?"

"Two men passed me and turned down the side passage to the hall."

124

"Before it opened?"

"Yes. I heard the Freemen's clock strike a few minutes after."

"Were the two men together?"

"Oh, no. The first was about two minutes before the second. The first one had leather-soled shoes. The second one had rubber soles. I could follow their footsteps. They went past me and turned down the passage."

"Thank you."

"You didn't mind me telling you, did you?"

"I'm delighted you did. I'd already heard of one man going down that passage about then. He was carrying a parcel or case of some sort."

"Ah, that's what it was," said Logan. "I'd been wondering. . . ."

"What, exactly?"

"It was definitely a case of some sort and he must have been swinging it to and fro. A case with a handle on those metal bits at the ends that go under the retainers on the case itself. I heard the squeaks and wondered what they were. Of course! I must be going daft."

"Which of the two men had the case?"

"The one with the leather soles — the first one."

"I am more than grateful to you, Mr Logan. Thank you once again." He turned to Mrs Fenny. "Please leave Miss Festival's room as it is ma'am. Constable York will now drive me to see Mr Butcher. He will drop me there and then come back to look over Miss Festival's luggage. Very quickly, just to make sure there is nothing there we should know about. Then you can pack her case for her father to take back should he wish to do so. York will then come back to Mr Butcher's house to pick me up."

"You are going to mention that piano string?"

"Such matters are outside my province as a policeman, Mrs Fenny."

"But plain Mr Masters isn't above mentioning such matters, is he?"

"You never know, ma'am. Perhaps a gentle reference to them might be . . . shall we say, worked in? With a very definite object in mind, of course."

"Shall we say object-lesson, Mr Masters?"

"Why not?"

"If you can spare the time, while you are up here, you must come again. You're a man after my own heart, Mr Masters."

Masters paused with his hand on the door knob. "Do you really mean that, ma'am?"

"Need you ask?"

"I had to, because I should like you to meet the other three in my team, and they you."

"Delighted. When?"

"This evening? After dinner."

"The family will be here, and probably Mr Festival."

"So much the better."

"David warned me to beware of you, Mr Masters. Have you an ulterior motive?"

"At the moment, only a small one. I shall have to have a word with Mr Festival, and I'd rather do it here than in a police office."

"I understand."

"But there's no telling what other motive I may have by the time I get here."

"I'll take my chance with you. Goodbye, Mr Masters."

As York drew away from the front of the Fenny house, Masters asked: "How far out of the direct route between here and Butcher's house is the Central Hall?"

York considered for a moment. "I reckon it would add a good ten minutes to the journey, sir."

"Thank you. Pull in for a moment or two, would you. Where it's convenient."

Masters opened his brief-case. By the time the car drew up he had a sheet of paper and an envelope out. Using the case to lean on he wrote a rapid note and put it in the envelope which he addressed to Green.

"After dropping me," he said, as he nodded to York to drive on, "I want you to go to the Central Hall and deliver this to either DCI Green or DS Berger. Don't let them keep you. Say I've given you express orders to hurry. You heard what I said to Mrs Fenny. I want you to give Miss Festival's belongings and the room a quick once-over. Not forgetting the bathroom. I am sure it will be a mere formality, but I want to know if there are any tablets or medicines or anything out of the ordinary in her kit. It won't take long, because she would be travelling light and I am certain she came by train, so there'll be no car to worry about."

"How can you know that, sir? It wasn't mentioned while I was in the room."

"I think you'll find that singers on Miss Festival's level won't drive long distances on days when they are appearing in the evening. Too tiring, and there's something about the atmosphere in a car that gets at the throat. Too stuffy, too cold, too hot or too windy. Never right."

"Understood, sir."

"And, York, ask one of the Fenny ladies to go up with you to the room. It will give a better impression if one of them were to shake out the underwear."

"Right, sir."

After a few more minutes, York was pulling the car up outside the Butchers' house.

"I won't get back in less than an hour, sir."

"Not to worry. We passed a coffee shop just before we turned the last corner. Look in there for me first. If I'm there, join me. If not, come here."

Sergeant Sibley directed Berger to Freemen's Square. From there the three of them walked the windswept hundred yards to the Central Hall.

"Looks a dump in daylight," said Berger.

"More like a gaol than a concert hall," agreed Sibley. "Slab-sided and no windows to speak of."

"How do we get in?" growled Green, rattling the large, stirrup handles of the front doors.

"Down the side, sir, I should think."

Green grunted and led the way. The passage was perhaps four feet six inches wide, between the new wall of the hall on one side and the grimy, crumbling wall of the property on the other side. So for twenty yards or so, and then the old wall stopped and a sizeable chunk of new hall, built at right angles to the main block, jutted across into a wider space behind the adjoining property. In the wall facing them was the stage door. White letters on the green paint told them so. It was locked, but the path, wider now, followed round the return and then opened up on to a square, concrete yard where a row of four black plastic dustbins broke the cubiform symmetry of the small area. Here was another door. A green but greasy door that appeared to have been pushed open and pulled closed by myriads of dirty hands.

"You can tell that's the caretaker's door," said Green. "I was always taught that cobblers were the worst-shod people in the streets when I was a kid. By the same token caretakers never take care of their own neck of the woods. In you go, gents, and start looking while I just take a bit of a further shufti round the back for broken windows and such like. I'll join you shortly."

"What's he really looking for?" asked Sibley as he and Berger, finding the door open, entered the bare passageway behind it.

"Just what he said, I expect," said Berger. "No fancy stuff with Willy P. Green. He's an experienced down-to-earth jack. If you want flights of fancy you want the Chief."

"I've heard he's a bit of an egghead."

"A bit of a one." Berger lifted his voice and shouted. "Anybody at home?"

It was Elsie who replied. She was busy in the kitchen, washing up the 200 or so cups and saucers used the night before. She pushed her head round the doorpost. "Nobody's allowed in here."

"Where are the policemen on duty then?"

"On duty you call it? Swedging tea all night an' day, that's when they're not snoring their heads off in the most comfortable seats they can find."

"Where are they now?"

"In the hall. Where else? The seats are upholstered in there. Last time I went in there one 'ad 'is number nines up on the back of the seat in front. I told him, I can tell you."

"You're the caretaker, are you?"

"Who's asking?"

"I am," said Green who had come through the door and into the passage. "And I'm from Scotland Yard. So speak up. Are you the caretaker?"

"Me an' my husband. We're joint caretakers."

"Right. Now we've established that, what's your name?"

"Our names are Mr and Mrs Carrot."

"First names?"

"Well, if you must know, it's Sid and Elsie."

"Right, love, let's get down to work."

"Work? Who else works round here 'cept me, I'd like to know. You lot! Work? Asking questions isn't work, it's guessing. And as for Carrot, as like as not he's leaning on a broom somewhere."

"In that case," growled Green, "he won't mind joining us. Where is he?"

"He's supposed," said Elsie, emphasizing the second word, "to be sweeping the stairs to the gallery and doing the gents in the foyer."

"Get him," said Green to Berger. He turned to Elsie. "Where can we talk, love? I'll bet you and your old man have a cubby-hole somewhere where you can brew up in private and Sid can do his pools."

"The staff rest-room," said Elsie with dignity, "is next door and marked private."

"Fine. In there then, and you can make us all a cup of coffee while we talk."

"Tea or nothing," sniffed Elsie. "I don't hold with all this coffee. Tea's always been good enough for us. And no bags, neither."

"Couldn't be better," conceded Green. "You can put the kettle on while we're waiting for Sid."

It was a small room about twelve feet square, with a multi-point gas heater on the wall, obviously there to serve the kitchen and the hand basin provided for staff washing. There was a melamine-topped kitchen table pushed against the wall under the window, with two chairs serving it. Leaning against the side of a wardrobe cupboard was a stack of five or six folding chairs. Odd bits and pieces were scattered about — a cardigan, several newspapers and magazines, a tatty tool box and — on the wall — a calendar advertising real ale.

Sid had an old green pullover tucked into his trousers and braces over the top. On his head he sported an old sweat-stained trilby.

Elsie was mashing the tea in a brown-Betty teapot with water from an electric kettle when he arrived, followed by Berger.

"What's it all about?" he grumbled. "I got work to do."

"Let's all sit," said Green. "Some of those folding chairs will do us."

"If you want sugar," said Elsie, "use the spoon in the jar, but don't put it in the cup after. There's another one for stirring."

Green took them through the events of the previous day almost step by step.

"Now let's get this straight. You opened up the front dead on seven."

"By the electric clock."

"So nobody could have got into the main hall that way before, then?"

"They couldn't have."

"When did you open the stage door?"

"Right after that."

"Was anybody waiting there when you opened up?"

"I looked out. There wasn't anybody."

"So the man who walked down the side alley before then got in at the door at the end of this passage?"

"What man?" asked Sid.

"He couldn't have," said Elsie, "that's our private door."

"Private or not, love, it's still a door, and if it isn't kept locked, somebody can get in. I did this morning."

"They didn't oughter," said Sid. "It's private. No entry except for us."

"But you don't keep it locked?"

"Only at dinner time and at night — when we've finished for the day. Our house is just back there. We're always in an' out. If we locked it somebody would always have to be opening it."

"You haven't both got keys?"

"One key for us. The other's in the office with all the spares."

"I see. So the man who came down the side passage came in at that door. Did you see him?"

"No, we never saw anybody. If we had done we'd have asked him."

"You couldn't have seen anybody, Sid Carrot. You were off to The Red Duster as soon as we'd opened up."

"No I wasn't, woman. I filled those two urns."

"And how long would that take you? Eight gallons? It's no more than four watering cans."

"And lit the gas at a peep like you said."

"You'd got away before I'd got the cups out now, hadn't you?"

"Well, yes."

"It's the only time you do anything quick. When you think there's a drink waiting for you at The Red Duster."

"So you didn't see anybody hanging around who shouldn't have been here?" demanded Green.

"How would we know who should and shouldn't be here?" asked Carrot. "With that choir and orchestra there was over two hundred of 'em. And not the sort we know, either."

"All the men were in dinner suits."

"Maybe," said Elsie. "But they had all sorts on top on a night like last night. Coats, belted macs, duffle coats . . . "

"And nobody with a dark coat on and carrying a parcel?"

"I didn't see anybody with a parcel. They all had books of music. That's all."

Green offered his cigarettes to Sid and Elsie. They both took one. "Who arrived first in the foyer?"

"I wasn't there," said Elsie.

"First?" asked Sid. "Now I reckon I can tell you that. Some of them at any rate."

"How d'you come to know that, Sid Carrot?"

"'Cos I was on my way to the Duster, wasn't I? Going towards Freemen's Square where all the cars were parked. And there wasn't many of that lot who didn't come in a car an' have to park it, was there? Anyhow, I passed some of 'em I reckoned was coming here and they'd be among the first."

"Did you recognize them?"

"Two lots, I did."

"Who?"

"Old Fred Croft and his missus. Mean old sod, he is, too. Keeps a big ironmongery place. Does central heating, double glazing and sells every damn thing he can think of short of cornflakes. Carpets, crocks, paint, soap, glass, anything anybody else might set up in he starts to sell to finish them off. Supposed to be a Christian, too. Leastwise he's allus going to chapel, though I only reckon he goes 'cos it's good for business. A fortnight ago he started selling bicycles because a young bloke had set himself up in the summer doing it with his redundancy money."

"Okay," said Green. "Where do I find him?"

"I know, sir," said Sibley.

"Right, Sid. Who else did you see?"

"Young Bob Frame and his little missus. I know him because he used to be agent for my pools. He's in charge of a builders' merchant's yard. Calls hisself a quantity surveyor, though all he does is measure out yards of sand. He's with Blade and Youngs."

"I know them, too," said Sibley.

"Is that the lot?"

"Isn't it enough? Oh, Bob Frame's missus is a typist somewhere in the middle of town. I don't know where."

"Thank you. Now . . . "

Green was interrupted by a knock at the door, and Constable York looked in.

"What is it, lad?"

"Message for you, sir, from Mr Masters."

Green held his hand out for the envelope.

Cleveland found the address of Jack and Norah Jagger, who were hosting Miss Whitehead, by the simple expedient of ringing the music shop which was mentioned on the handbills and placards as booking agent for the *Messiah* performances. The proprietor, it turned out, was a member of the choir committee and so knew the arrangements that had been made.

"Member of the committee!" said Cleveland to Reed. "I'll bet he is. All hundred and fifty people in that choir buying their music and other bits and pieces from him. It strikes me sitting on that committee will be very good for business. Very good indeed."

"If you will direct me, sir, please."

"To the Jaggers? Beverly Way? That's straight on and second right. Out to the east of the main centre, actually. Almost at the end of the old tramway lines when we used to have them. Pity we haven't got them now. No matter where you wanted to go in Nortown and round about, a tram would come along inside three minutes. Nowhere was more than five minutes' walk from a tram stop."

"I can just remember seeing some in Glasgow when I was up there as a child, sir."

"Ah, yes! Do you know what I used to do when I was a kid? I used to put pins — you know, ordinary dressmaking pins — on the wide part of the line, so that the tram wheels used to flatten them. Did you ever see one?"

"No, sir."

"Wide and flat and thin, they were, with a sort of flat beret at the top. Just like miniature daggers. We used to put them in the lapels of our jackets, crossed like those swords they put on maps at the sites of old battles." Cleveland sat back in the luxury of the Yard car. "Kids would never think of innocent pleasures like that these days. Now they go around in twos and threes threatening to disfigure babies in prams if the mothers don't hand over their wedding rings."

"Copycat stuff, that, sir. Nobody had ever heard of it happening till the telly mentioned the first case, and then within a month there'd been over a hundred incidents clocked, with some of the babies actually bruised and lacerated."

"Seeing you're a believer in the influence of TV in causing copycat crimes, Sergeant, what about these cases we're on now? Are they copycat? Emulating the Ripper and a few others like him?"

"Difficult to say what might have influenced your man, sir. You heard the Chief last night half blaming himself for not averting Miss Festival's death because his instincts were working overtime and he was uneasy. If Mr Masters could have guessed what was influencing the killer, he might really have come up with the answer yesterday."

"He's that good?"

"If you don't mind me saying so, sir, none of your investigating officers have got themselves anywhere near the position where they could even claim to be to blame, like the Chief did."

"They wouldn't have hinted that any of the blame could possibly lie with them even if they had got as far as Mr Masters, simply because they haven't got a brain box as well filled as his."

"But to get back to influences, sir."

"Yes?"

"The Chief probably didn't mention this to you, because it came up in conversation in the car on the way home last night. What he hinted at was that these days people think they're entitled to anything they may think they want, and that gives them the right to use any means to get it. That's the influence of the times, sir."

"Mr Masters said our man was after some form of objective? Something he thinks he wants?"

"That is a view he takes, certainly, sir."

"Not just haphazard?"

"Definite objective in view, sir."

"In that case . . . what you're saying, Sergeant, is that Mr Masters knows more than he's told us."

"I'm not saying that, sir. I'm just warning you of how the Chief works. He works out every possible solution in that brain box you were talking about. Then he sets them up like mental Aunt Sallies.

"As he gathers facts he knocks them down. Some go straight down, others may appear to be bolstered up for a bit. But in the end he only has one standing. And that, sir, has no fact to knock it down, and lots of facts to prop it up. That's the successful one. Like his picking the dates for these murders, sir. You all tried. . . . "

"And failed to find a pattern."

"Mr Masters probably did exactly the same as you, sir. I'm no mathematician, but I do know about arithmetic and geometric progressions. He was using them. He was tying in the alphabet and letter frequencies and all manner of things. That was why, eventually, he was so sure he was right, despite what a lot of people up here thought. He could shoot down scores of likely theories about the date, except one. He gave you that one and he proved he was right by forecasting the next death. He'll be doing the same, mentally, with the whole business. So he may have possible ideas, sir, but he'll never hold back any positive information. Just the opposite, in fact. He'll make sure everybody working in the team knows everything everybody else knows. That's why we'll be meeting at lunchtime, to talk. And I'll let you into another secret, sir. That's why he's made sure there's one of your chaps with him, and one with Mr Green and Sergeant Berger — he wouldn't want anybody to think we'd be holding anything back from you. After all, sir, he could have found his way round Nortown with a street map, like everybody else."

"He's going to those lengths to make sure there's no misunderstanding?"

"The Chief can't cater for that, sir. We've been to places where we have co-operated with local forces, and they've had as much information as he's had, but because they haven't made as much use of it as he has, they've not come to the same eventual conclusions and so they've accused him of holding back. But his thought processes are not facts and because he can't give those, there could be misunderstanding."

"Thanks for the warning, Sergeant. Turn left at the small crossroads ahead. Beverly Way is in the dip about two hundred yards along the side road. Turn left to get to the houses."

Reed followed the instructions and two or three minutes later was drawing up outside the 'fifties-built Georgian house owned by Jack Jagger.

"Mrs Jagger? Police. I am Detective Chief Superintendent Cleveland and this is Detective Sergeant Reed."

Norah Jagger invited them in and escorted them to what the house agents these days are pleased to call a utility room to the left of the front door.

"We have come to see Miss Whitehead. Is she up and about yet, please?"

Norah didn't reply. Instead she went to the door and called: "Jack."

"I know who you are," said Jagger, waving aside the introductions. "In fact I was expecting some of you, that's why I didn't go into the office this morning."

"May I ask why you didn't go in, sir?"

"If the police are calling at my house, for any reason, I prefer to be here." He laughed. "Not because I look on you as ogres or anything of that sort, but I think you'll agree that women prefer a man around at such times. I know my missus would prefer me to be here."

"What about Miss Whitehead, sir?"

"Can't speak for her, of course. She's a very level-headed, sensible woman, and she held up last night until we got her home. Then she went to pieces a bit. Dosed her up with brandy. It helped, didn't it Norah?"

"Margaret was a lot better when she went to bed," agreed Norah. "And she's had a bit of breakfast. Shall I fetch her?"

"She's fit enough to answer a few questions?"

"She was clearing the table when I left her," said Jack. "A bit white around the gills, but otherwise pretty normal. But I think you ought to know that she and Nancy Festival were friends. Not bosom pals, exactly, but they had worked together quite a lot these last few years and Margaret thought a lot of her as a woman, not just as a singer."

"Thank you. That is useful background information."

They got to their feet as Norah brought in Margaret Whitehead.

"Oh, I was expecting to see Mr Green. He was the one who talked to me last night."

"He's busy elsewhere, ma'am," said Reed, bringing up a chair for the newcomer. "He asked me to tell you how much he enjoyed your singing last night and then meeting you, despite the circumstances."

Jack Jagger said: "Well I'm damned. Coppers going on like that. Paying compliments and going to oratorios. I'd never have believed it."

"Well," said Cleveland, "there's not much point in not behaving like reasonable human beings, even though this is a murder investigation."

Norah gave a squeak of dismay.

"Definitely murder?" asked Jack.

"Definitely, sir." Cleveland turned to Margaret. "Now, ma'am, as I suspect you've guessed, Miss Festival died of ingesting some form of poison. The forensic specialists are not quite sure what it was yet, but they do know it was toxic."

Margaret nodded gravely. "And I was alone with her in the dressing-room. Is that the point you wish to make, Mr Cleveland?"

Cleveland regarded her for a moment or two and then smiled. "Naturally we take everything into consideration, ma'am, and as you have brought the matter up, I must confess that we realize you had the opportunity to poison Miss Festival. But so had a number of other people, probably scores of other people. So opportunity alone is not worrying us very much at the moment — the obvious opportunities, I mean. But for form's sake, and to give you the opportunity of denying that you gave Miss Festival anything of a toxic nature, I'll ask you the usual question. Did you give her anything poisonous?"

"No."

"Did you give her anything at all?"

"I handed her a cup of tea. It was brought to our door by a girlie at the interval. I took two cups and handed one to Nancy."

"Did either of you take sugar or any form of sweetener?"

"No. We're too figure-conscious to take sugar."

"That's that, then," said Cleveland. "Now, if you have been worrying about our reactions to the fact that you shared a dressing-room with Miss Festival, please forget it."

"You'll take her word for it, just like that?" said Jack. "I mean, I'm not saying Margaret was implicated. In fact I'd stake my life she wasn't. But just to accept anyone's word seems a little . . . "

"A little what, sir?"

"Trusting."

Cleveland grinned. "Simple-minded perhaps?"

"I wouldn't go so far as to say that. I'm surprised, that's all."

"No need to be, sir," said Reed. "We do a bit of work behind the scenes, too. So what you've just heard has only been said because of Miss Whitehead's earlier remark. Had she not said what she did, the matter would not have been mentioned at all."

"Because you already know Miss Whitehead is not involved?"

"That's it, sir."

"Then why this interview?"

"Because what Miss Whitehead said and did and who she saw and the timings and so on are very important, sir. Maybe without her knowing it. So Mr Cleveland is going to question her at length."

"Oh, I see. Sorry to have been so obtuse."

"Not at all, sir. It's better to have things clear."

"Right," said Cleveland. "First of all, Miss Whitehead, when did you arrive at the hall? A detailed description of your arrival, please."

"Mr Jagger drove Mrs Jagger and myself there. He dropped us outside the hall at about five past seven. He then drove off to park the car. Mrs Jagger went into the main doors. I slipped down the side entrance to the stage door. I have sung here before, so I know the way."

"Did you see anybody in the passage?"

"There is a light on the wall but it is not very bright down there, but I did see two or three people ahead of me. Two women and a man, I think."

"Were they together?"

"Oh, yes. They were all talking. I took them to be part of the chorus. I think there were others coming behind me, chattering."

"Then what?"

"I went in, straight to the dressing-room. I knew where it was from previous visits, and in any case I'd been in there yesterday afternoon."

"Why yesterday afternoon?"

"For a cup of tea. There was some hang-up over the piano, and that fool, Butcher, wanted to run through the Pastoral with his orchestra before we rehearsed. Actually we only wanted entries and a few bars here and there. Desmond Darren and James Capper were involved before Nancy and me, so we had a quick cuppa made by a committee woman who was there. Wrigley, I think her name was. She was fussing around with a tin of biscuits and telling the caretakers their business."

"Thank you. When you arrived in the evening, did anybody

meet you?"

"No, I went straight to the dressing-room."

"Where you had twenty minutes to spare."

"If you like to put it that way. Actually I wanted to do a few breathing exercises and so on."

"So on?"

"Settle myself. I'll let you into a secret, Mr Cleveland. I get stage fright rather badly. I have to . . . well, pull myself together by various means."

"I understand, ma'am. You were alone until when?"

"Nobody came until Nancy appeared. That was about twenty-five past seven, I think. I remember mentioning to her that she was cutting it a bit fine, but she just laughed and said they couldn't start without us. Then she did my hair and . . . "

"Did your hair?"

"Tucked the ends in for me. I'd been exercising a bit and a few strands had come out. While she was doing that, Butcher stuck his face round the door to say he was sorry he hadn't been along sooner but he'd been busy teaching James Capper his job. Nancy asked him to go because we needed a bit of privacy to touch up our make-up. Butcher said he'd see us at the interval."

"I understand Miss Festival brought two bags with her?"

"That's right. Her music case. She had her score in there and one or two other bits of music she was learning. And a book. I expect she intended either to study the music or just read her novel while she wasn't on stage in part two. Oh, and her evening bag. Just a little white one with a compact, lipstick, handkerchief and a few tissues in it for taking on stage. Nothing bulky."

"In her music case, was it?"

"Yes. Her other case — a vanity case I suppose you'd call it . . ."

"One moment, ma'am. Did you have a music case with you?"

"Oh, yes. With my score, a clip-top make-up bag and a little evening bag."

"Miss Festival's other case?"

"It had been specially made for her. With padded indentations to take three or four throat sprays."

"You had no throat sprays, but Miss Festival had three or four.

Why was that?"

"I think the easiest way of explaining it is to say that we all have our different problems. I've told you mine. Stage fright. I'm as nervous as a kitten until I actually start to sing. Nancy was not like that. I don't mean she didn't have the delicacy of feeling to put on a beautiful show. You know she could do that. But she was always assured, almost bubbling over at the prospect of singing. That's how it seemed to take her. But her problem was a certain weakness of the throat or sinuses. Nobody seemed to know exactly what it was. Some said she could have been slightly asthmatic. If so, I think it was probably an allergic form — like hay fever. She never sang with her throat, of course. Head tones always, but the voice was heavy and full, and I think it probably took a greater toll of the nose and throat area than would, say, my piping treble. Anyhow, whatever it was, she found the need to use sprays."

"She used them before she went on last night?"

"No, no. I don't think she ever used them before singing because that would affect the organs adversely. No, after singing, to repair the damage, as it were. They weren't so much preventative as curative, I'd say."

"So why take them to the hall? Why not use them when she got back home?"

"Because she'd finished singing by the interval, and she'd use the sprays as soon as we were back on stage and she was left alone."

"By jove," said Jack Jagger. "Somebody had doctored the sprays."

"It seems a very likely answer, sir. But who? Doctoring aerosols is no easy matter. And when? That's what we've got to discover." He turned back to Margaret Whitehead. "Who visited you at the interval?"

"The little girl with the tea and Rodney Butcher. He came in with his cup and waffled for about five minutes. Mostly about himself and what a struggle he was having with the orchestra."

"Then you were called back to the stage?"

"Yes. I left Nancy alone."

"Do you think she would stay in the dressing-room?"

"I can't imagine she would leave it."

"Not even to visit a lavatory?"

"We had our own — just off the dressing-room."

"Could anybody have been hiding in there?"

"There wasn't when I paid a call during the interval."

"Excellent," said Cleveland.

"I don't understand."

"Well now, I can hardly see Miss Festival letting somebody into the dressing-room, while she was there, to tamper with her sprays, can you? Besides, from what you said, she would have used them straight away after you'd left her. And nobody touched them in the dressing-room before the show or you'd have seen them doing it. So that means that they were got at during the first half, between half-past seven and nine, when they were lying there on the table and nobody was in the room."

"That seems very reasonable."

"If the sprays were the things that killed her."

"Yes."

"Right. Now you got there in good time, but you saw nobody sneaking into the Central Hall. But we have heard there was a chap seen going down that passage earlier on, and he was carrying a parcel or bag. Any ideas about him, Miss Whitehead?"

"Ideas? Couldn't it have been literally anybody?"

"It could spark off an idea, if you would just talk. Who could it have been or who couldn't it have been?"

"Before seven o'clock?"

"Yes."

"The obvious answer would be a member of the chorus, though why any of them should arrive so early I can't think. Nor can I guess what there would be in a parcel. On a night like that a girl might wear heavy shoes and carry light ones in a bag to change into."

"It was a man."

"Well now, I don't think it would have been a member of the orchestra. They're too used to playing at shows like that to get there that early, and I don't think it would be one of them carrying his instrument because all the players were there in the afternoon and they left their instruments at the hall. There's a lock-up instrument-room there. No musician carries his instrument if he doesn't have to."

"None of them? Even the ones with little flutes and things like that?"

"Not usually, and they wouldn't arrive so early. They're a blasé lot, the musicians. They're always there in time, but not before time. None of them except . . . " She stopped in mid-sentence and clapped a hand over her mouth.

Cleveland waited a moment and then asked: "What were you going to say, Miss Whitehead? Except something or another."

"The trumpeter," she whispered. "Maxwell Mawby. He took his trumpet away with him in its little case after rehearsal."

"And?"

"He'd be back earlier than you might think, seeing he doesn't appear till part two."

"Early at the hall? Why?"

"To warm his trumpet up."

"To what?" demanded Cleveland.

"He's a very good player, but he thought his trumpet was crackly during rehearsal — on the tricky runs, you know. He's talked to me about it before. He likes to warm it in a gentle heat for quite a long time so that it can get thoroughly warm so that it will play properly, or at least play how he likes it to play."

"So he could have got to the hall early to put his trumpet on a radiator or something like that?"

"I think so, but he wouldn't . . . I mean, he's a nice little man."

"Nobody's said he's not, Miss Whitehead, but when we see unknown characters sneaking around the scene of a murder, we like to identify them, if only to eliminate them from our enquiries. Had Mr Mawby played here in Nortown before?"

"Often. I have the impression he knows the Central Hall like the back of his hand."

"Thank you, ma'am. That's all from me, unless you have any other suggestions to make about the man who arrived early."

"None."

Cleveland turned to Reed. "What about you, Sergeant? Any questions you'd like to ask Miss Whitehead?"

"Yes, please, sir. Miss Whitehead, can we talk about Miss Festival for a minute?"

"What about her?"

"You must have been wondering why such a woman should have died like she did last night. Why anybody should kill her."

"A madman," growled Jagger.

"A madman, certainly. But what do you mean by madman, sir? One who just kills haphazardly without reason?"

"Yes."

"But Miss Festival's death was not a haphazard affair, sir. It was planned. Well-planned, if those sprays were tampered with."

Jack Jagger grunted.

"Or, perhaps," said Reed, "you think the killer didn't know who his victim was going to be. That he might have thought either of the two ladies would do, or even that he was after Miss Whitehead and made a mistake in thinking the sprays were hers."

"Oh, no," breathed Miss Whitehead.

"It has to be considered, ma'am, though I think you can rest assured that the killer got the victim he intended."

"How can you know that?"

"Because he knew of the sprays, ma'am. He was prepared. Well-prepared. So, in spite of what Mr Jagger says, he knew what he was about, which leads us to think he had some reason for killing Miss Festival."

"Oh, no."

"Oh, yes, ma'am. So what was it about her that caused somebody to want to kill her? Had she some startling defect of character?"

"That made enemies, you mean?"

"Yes."

"She was a charming woman. She was nearly twenty years younger than me, but she treated me as an equal not only by ignoring the age gap, but as a professional, too. That was kindness, because I never was her equal professionally. And I don't believe in mock modesty. I've been successful, highly successful. But only among my own kind. She was paramount. She had taken the whole world by storm in a very few years. Yet she'd come into a dressing-

143

room and laugh and joke and put my hair up for me."

"So could her success have roused jealousy?"

"Lots of it. But not among men. Only among women contraltos, and even then not to the point of murdering her."

Reed nodded. "She was the same with everybody?"

"Not quite. She didn't like fools and she wouldn't allow anybody to interfere with her profession. For instance, she had no time for Rodney Butcher, and she wasn't too friendly with him last night when he suggested James Capper didn't know his stuff."

"But otherwise she was a happy woman?"

"Yes."

"Always happy?"

"Which of us can be that?"

"I think you know what I mean, ma'am."

"Yes, of course I do. I'm sorry to be so stupid, Mr Reed. We singers are human, you know. We may be blessed with voices, but we're still cursed with all the usual emotions. We fall in love, have children, and so on, just as other women do."

"Are you saying Miss Festival has had an unhappy love affair?"

"Mrs Saltwell had a quite unhappy time for a year or more."

"Mrs . . . you mean Miss Festival was married?"

"To a Graham Saltwell. Until the early summer of this year. May or June, anyhow. There was a divorce. The year or so leading up to it took the edge off most of Nancy's happiness. Or so it seemed to me. We performed together on a number of occasions during that time. We even made a long-playing record of duets. So I saw a good deal of her and talked quite a bit. I think the process of divorce to any but the most uncaring of women must be a very upsetting time. Nancy was far from uncaring. But once it was over she seemed freer. More like her old self before whatever the trouble with Graham was blew up to the decision to divorce. And she seemed to me to get happier and happier."

"Was there another woman involved, do you know?"

"Haven't a clue."

"Was there another man in Miss Festival's life?"

"Before the divorce, I'd have said not. But there were a lot of men buzzing round her, always. Sycophants as well as genuine admirers. Whether any one of them was special, I wouldn't know, but I can tell you she was often out to lunch. It's the best time for people like us, you know, who often can't go out to dine at a reasonable hour."

"Thank you, ma'am."

Margaret Whitehead smiled. "I can't think that a man who has been pursuing her these last few months has committed a crime of passion."

"Maybe not, ma'am."

As they drove away from the Jagger household, Reed said: "I think we should let DCI Green know about the trumpeter, sir."

"We can do that on our way to seeing this Mundy woman we've heard about."

"Route directions, sir?"

"Back the way we came. And, Sergeant Reed . . . "

"Yes, sir?"

"In your estimation, was that interview helpful?"

"Very helpful, I'd say. You conducted it very much as the Chief would have done."

"Is that meant to be a compliment?"

"I couldn't pay a greater one, sir."

Chapter Six

ON HIS SECOND visit to the Butcher household Masters was shown
into the room at the front of the house. Normally, this would, he supposed, have been furnished as the family sitting-room, but now it was obviously Rodney Butcher's music studio.

A large grand piano occupied much of the space. Whoever played it sat in the bay window so that the light could fall on keyboard and music. The boarded floor was bare, with no hint of carpet or rug, or even of staining and polishing. Indeed at one spot — Masters guessed it was where singers might stand if Rodney was accompanying them — the wood was scuffed bare. Music was everywhere. Sheets in piles a yard high on the floor, on the piano top and on all manner of cupboards and shelves. The only places to sit other than the piano stool were two old upright dining chairs with brown rexine seats. Rodney Butcher was now wearing old grey slacks and a roll-neck, bottle-green sweater.

"I shan't keep you long, Mr Butcher, as I have learned something of what I was going to ask you elsewhere. But perhaps you would care to sit down."

Rodney took the piano stool and sat sideways to face Masters who drew up one of the upright chairs.

"Let me say at the outset, Mr Butcher, that I was present at the performance last night and I was most impressed by it. The soloists were marvellous, that goes without saying, but I thought the chorus was excellent, too."

"Yes, it was, wasn't it? Of course, I train the choir myself. Unfortunately, I don't have the same control over the orchestra. Some are local musicians and we have to import others, so it is a struggle for me to get them playing as a coherent whole."

"They didn't let you down. But now, let us talk of other things."

Softened up by the genuine compliments Masters had made

him, Rodney leaned forward as if anxious to hear more in the same vein.

"Your performance of *Messiah* is, I believe, an annual event?"

"We put it on every year in the first full week of December."

"Always for the three nights of Tuesday, Wednesday and Thursday?"

"Always. We use the Monday evening for rehearsing the choir in the Central Hall. Not singing, actually, though we may polish up on one or two small weaknesses, using the ordinary hall piano. No, it is mainly getting them into the right order for filing on to the stage, and marking their scores at the points where they must stand up. Getting them to do it quietly is so important. For instance they have to get up between the two soprano recits that come before 'Glory to God'. Noisy shuffling and creaking can put a soloist off. And turning pages does, too. They all use the same scores and follow the performance closely, of course. That is vital. But when a hundred and fifty people turn pages together it can be disturbing."

Masters nodded his thanks for this less than useful information. "So you know the dates of your performances, should you wish to consult the necessary calendars or almanacks, for years ahead. Is that right?"

"Quite correct."

"You book the Central Hall well in advance?"

"Oh, yes. At least a year ahead. We would not want some minor affair to interfere."

"Quite. How far ahead do you book your soloists?"

"Anything up to two years ahead. You see, these top-line singers always like to get their main engagements into their diaries as soon as possible, so that they know when they will be free for other things. Those who have *Messiah* in their repertoire are always in great demand around the Christmas and Easter periods, so we have to make the bookings very, very early. Not so early in the case of people like James Capper, of course. He's not really top-line and is very much a second choice. We hung on, hoping to get a better bass. In fact, I think he was only booked three months ago."

"And Miss Festival? When was she booked?"

"I can't give you the exact date, but on the Friday after the performance, the President of the choir and the committee have a dinner."

I'll bet they do, thought Masters. The non-playing members whoop it up.

"And I remember that it was announced at the dinner last year that Nancy had agreed to sing for us this year. So it was probably some time last November that the agreement was reached."

"Thank you."

"The others would be about the same time, including Maxwell Mawby, the trumpeter, whom we have every year. The exception was James Capper, of course."

"Understood," Masters drew his coat around him preparatory to getting to his feet. "Mr Butcher, among other people I have spoken with in connection with this case was Mr Logan, the blind piano tuner. I was concerned to see that his forehead and one of his cheeks were both heavily plastered and he told me that one of his spectacle lenses had been broken. Out of courtesy, I asked him how the damage had happened. He was not willing to tell me at first, but as I am very concerned at the moment with death and injury at the Central Hall, I insisted on an answer. Now, what went on between you and him is no concern of mine, but I suspect that you, immersed in your music and away from the ordinary workaday world, know very little about industrial injuries and compensation for them."

"I did nothing to . . ."

"Please hear me out, Mr Butcher. You hired your concert grand, and the music shop which supplied it employed Mr Logan to tune it after it arrived on stage. If Mr Logan were to consult his solicitor, the music shop, as employer, could well find themselves facing a claim for injuries. But once they had heard Logan's evidence, they would almost certainly, in their turn, try to shift the blame on to you."

Rodney Butcher stared aghast at Masters who got to his feet before continuing.

"I would suggest that any committee dinner on Friday night would, this year, be highly inappropriate. In view of Miss

Festival's death, merrymaking would be in bad taste. I, therefore, suggest that a very sensible gesture would be for the money that would have been spent on the dinner should be handed to Mr Logan to pay for his replacement spectacles and as some recompense for the injuries he sustained."

Butcher gawped in dismay.

"Perhaps you would be kind enough to sound out your committee at tonight's performance — before it, actually — and phone their decision to me at the Station Hotel before I dine at seven-thirty. The reason I ask for such prompt action, Mr Butcher, is because after dinner tonight I am meeting a local solicitor who already knows of Mr Logan's injuries. If I can report a magnanimous gesture from your committee, he may decide not to pursue the matter. Now, I'll go. Please don't get up, Mr Butcher. I can see myself out."

A few minutes later, Masters was being served with coffee. He had started his second cup before DC York joined him.

"Nothing among her belongings, sir. Miss Jane Fenny was with me and she has packed them up."

"Thank you. Help yourself to coffee. There's still some in the pot and I took care to get you a cup and saucer and a Chelsea bun."

Green read the note from Masters and then handed it to Berger and Sibley.

"Right, Sid and Elsie, I've just got some new information. Two sinister characters were seen sneaking down your side alley just before seven last night."

"I know nowt about it," said Sid.

"I'm sure you don't, otherwise you'd have said, wouldn't you, chum? Two characters. One in leather-soled shoes carrying a squeaky case, and one in rubber-soled shoes."

"I still know nowt. And how could you know what soles they were wearing?"

"One of our secrets, Sid."

"I knew somebody had been wearing rubber soles round here last night," said Elsie. "When I mopped this corridor this morning I seen the marks close to the wall out there."

"And you mopped over them and wiped them out?"

" 'Course I did. That floor! Whoever heard of a concrete floor painted green as 'as to be mopped an' polished? It's the bane of my life."

Green sucked his partial denture. It wasn't clear whether he was showing disgust at the composition of the floor just described or the loss of possibly valuable evidence.

"So you reckon our man could have come in by this entrance, Elsie?"

"Only me and Carrot's supposed to use it, an' we don't have rubber soles. Sid wears boots from the army surplus store an' I don't have size nines."

"You and Sid walk down the middle of the passage, do you?"

"You've only to look to see that. These rubber marks were on the shiny bit at the side near the door leading to the dressing-room block."

"We're getting on. It sounds as if this chap knew where to come and where to go once he got here, to say nothing of keeping himself hidden for some time. So, it sounds as if he'd been here before." Green looked from Sid to Elsie. "Who visits you here?"

"Coming in this way? Nobody."

"I'll put it another way then. Who has visited you here?"

"Nobody."

"Come off it, both of you. What about the blokes who read the meters and mend the boiler and all that malarkey. Who delivers your tea and milk?"

"Most of 'em won't come this far. They come to the stage door."

"And you're telling me nobody has ever come to this door of yours."

"I'm not saying that," said Sid. "Not over the years."

"What are you saying then?"

"That chap selling cleaning stuff." He turned to his wife. "He found his way in here before you nabbed him."

"Oh, yeah! Wanted to sell us big tins of polish an' jerricans of washing-up liquid. Him. I found him wandering about here one day, oh, about three months ago, I reckon. I know it was good weather, 'cos I'd got the door wedged open an' he said finding it like that he just walked in. 'Course I told him we got all our stuff from Alderman Wrigley. He's chairman of the Hall committee."

"Is he?" asked Green. "And so he gets the trade, does he? How much does he charge you?"

"Dunno," said Sid, "he keeps the books, but he's never stingy. We get what we ask for."

"I'll bet. Now this stranger. How old was he?"

"How would I know?"

"A youngish lad? An old man?"

"In a suit, he was. About . . . what shall I say . . . thirty-five? No more than forty."

"Right. How long had he been in here when you found him?"

"Lord knows. I'd been working in the main hall and had come out here for a cuppa. I caught him looking in the kitchen."

There was a noise in the corridor. "See who's out there," said Green to Berger.

"Mr Cleveland and Sergeant Reed, looking for you."

Green got to his feet. "Hallo, Matt, what brings you here?"

"Could I have a private word? Outside?"

Green joined him in the corridor.

"Have you got anywhere with the business of the chap who was seen sneaking down the side alley?"

"Chaps, in the plural," said Green. "George sent me a note a few minutes ago. Here you are. Read it for yourself."

Cleveland read the note and handed it back. "I'm here about that, as well. I didn't know there were two, but the one with the squeaky case was most likely the trumpeter, Mawby. Miss Whitehead reckons he'd get here early to warm his trumpet up on a radiator."

"Thanks, I'll look into it. These two characters here found a bloke snooping about inside a few months ago. Said he'd come to sell them cleaning materials."

"Got anything else?"

"Not much. You?"

"Reed says we've got a goodish bit, and I agree there are a few points."

"Okay, I'll hear them at lunchtime. Now I've got a solid fact to work on I'd better get on with it."

Cleveland and Reed went on their way. Green returned to the staff rest-room.

"Now, you two," he said to Sid and Elsie. "I've heard that the bloke with the all-leather shoes and carrying the case with the squeaky handle was very likely the trumpeter chap, Maxwell Mawby. Evidently he got here early to warm his trumpet."

"There, now," said Elsie, "I'd forgotten him."

"You mean you'd forgotten between last night and this morning that you'd seen him?" asked Berger disbelievingly.

"Didn't see him," retorted Elsie.

"Then how could you have forgotten him?"

"He always comes, dun't he? Plays every year. Uses the little storeroom with the gas fire. Knows his own way."

Green got to his feet. "Show us."

The storeroom was opposite the room they had been occupying and between the kitchen and the outer door.

"Just look at that, you Sid. Been smoking in here something chronic, you have." She pointed at the butt ends on the floor.

"Don't be so daft, woman. I don't smoke posh fags like that."

Green looked around the small gloomy room. "We never use it," said Sid. "Except to put these old bits in."

Green was crouching in front of the old-fashioned gas fire. "There are rings in the dust down here. That's where he must have stood his trumpet on its wide end." He straightened up. "You say this is the only room with a gas fire?"

"That's it. Shouldn't be here by rights. It was the gas tiffies when they came to run the central heating in. Winter time it was, and it took them weeks on end. They said they weren't going to work without somewhere with a bit of heat, and they couldn't turn the system on, so they brought along this old second-hand fire, ran a bit o' pipe from the main and shoved a flue through the window. So's they could have their breaks in the warm, like. They forgot it when they went an' I wasn't going to remind 'em."

Green turned to Sibley. "Find out where this Mawby chap is staying."

"I can tell you that," said Elsie. "Leastways allus before he's stayed with that chap Wadland who conducts the brass band. They were bandsmen in the army together, I think."

"Wadland?" asked Sibley. "Where does he live?"

"I don't know that, but all you've got to do is ring the foundry. It's their band."

"Get the address, lad, while we have a look round."

Sibley left them. "Any other cubby holes like this?" asked Green.

"Instrument room," said Sid, "but that's always locked. Orchestra put their instruments in there for safe keeping."

"And where do you store your buckets and mops?" asked Berger.

"Broom cupboard."

"Where?" demanded Green.

It was next to the back-stage lavatory for men and about as big as the average house loo.

"You've been in here, this morning?" asked Green.

"Not to say in," replied Sid. "I've reached in to get one or two things."

Green was crouching again.

"This could be it. Yes. Look here, Sergeant. He must have been sitting on an upturned bucket. Those are footprints. Rubber soles, would you say?"

Berger got down beside him. "Fairly common pattern of tread, too, I'd say. Hello, what's this? Do you eat Polo mints, Sid?"

"Course not."

"Elsie?"

"Never. If I has anything it's wine gums."

"He must have chewed a packetful to while away the time." Berger picked up the familiar paper roll, torn in a helix, using tweezers from his breast pocket to do so. He dropped it into a specimen envelope from his inside breast pocket. "We'll want shots of the footmarks but the bags are in the Rover with Reed."

Sibley joined them.

"Got a photographer at your HQ, son?"

"Yes, sir."

"Get him down here pronto. Sergeant Berger will wait for him. Tell him it's just shoe-sole marks he'll be snapping. He won't get

153

casts."

Sibley left them again.

"Stay here until the shots have been taken," Green told Berger. "Then get back to HQ and wait for us there. I'm going to see this son-of-suction, Mawby."

Berger said quietly, "Something's struck me."

"Such as?"

Berger drew Green further away from the Carrots. "Nancy Festival was off-stage all the second half, last night, so it's likely somebody planted some poison for her in the first half. This Mawby bloke was the only one not on stage during the first half. And he took good care not to be seen. I know Sid was off to the pub like a long dog as soon as he'd opened the place up, but his missus was around all the time, brewing up for the interval, and she never saw him."

"Right, lad. Actually I had thought of that, but his nibs has given us the news that there were two sneakers. One has been accustomed to coming down here and hiding himself away in that storeroom to warm his trumpet. So he's been acting normally. But another cove comes along wearing brothel-creepers and hides himself away in this closet. Why? Mawby had a reason. Rubber soles didn't. We know Mawby. We don't know the other bloke. I could go on and on, but the fact would still remain that rubber soles is the suspicious character where Mawby isn't. Of course I won't lose sight of Mawby, but I'm more interested in the other chap just now."

"Fair enough."

"Try to get a better description out of those two of the chap who came in to sell them cleaning materials."

"Right, I'll cadge a lift back to HQ with the photographer. Here's Sibley now."

"On his way, Mr Green. He's bringing laser equipment, too. He says it'll pick up prints in dust probably better than the ordinary camera."

"Nice work, lad. What about this Wadland character?"

"I asked HQ to get the information. I'll call up on the blower when we get back to the car. They should have it by then."

"Good thinking."

After Green and Sibley had left, Berger returned to the Carrots who, by now, had gone back to their own room.

"The others gone, have they?" asked Sid.

"That's right. There'll be a photographer here soon, though. Now, you two, I take it you'd rather not go along to the nick for a session with the artists and photo-fit experts?"

"Too true," said Sid. "Who wants to go to a cop shop?"

"Right. Then let's try and get a description of this thirty-five-year-old salesman who was wandering around the premises a few months ago."

"I've told you . . . " began Elsie.

"No you haven't, love. Now, you're an intelligent woman. If you saw that man again, you'd recognize him, wouldn't you? You met him, talked to him about cleaning materials and so on, didn't you?"

"Yeah. I said."

"What did he talk like? Posh? Yorkshire accent? Like me? Like Sid?"

She thought a moment. "Lancashire, I think. Not right Lancashire, you know."

"Scouse?"

She shook her head. "No. Lancashire, but with a bit of . . . you know . . . as if he'd learned to talk proper on top of it."

"Fine. Did he wear glasses?"

"No."

"A moustache?"

"No."

"Good. Did he have a face as fat as mine or was it thin, like Sid's?"

"Skinny," she said. "That's it. Sort of boney. Nose sort of thin, but not hooky."

"You're doing fine. Colour of hair?"

"Dunno. Mousey, I think."

"Curly? Flat? Short? Long?"

"Brown," she said. "Definitely brown."

Berger waited. He didn't want to interrupt the mental struggle for recollection that appeared to be going on.

"He wanted a haircut, I know that," said Sid.

"Yeah," said Elsie, prompted out of her effort to remember. "I felt a bit sorry for him. His hair was a bit straggly round his collar, like. Not a lot of it. Thin wisps. An' his face was thin an' boney an' white. I remember thinking I wish I could have given him an order, an' thinking he could do with a good meal, an' yet he was well-dressed. Nice suit an' tie. Funny that. Must have put all his money on his back an' none in his belly."

That was all Berger could get. He offered Sid and Elsie cigarettes which were half-smoked by the time the photographer arrived.

Cleveland and Reed ran Alice Mundy to earth in the little wool shop she owned, just twenty or thirty yards down a side street off a small shopping centre. As they entered she was serving an elderly woman with hanks of blue wool.

"You'll just take the four, Mrs Curtis?"

"An' you put the others away for me. I'll be back for them next week sometime."

"Right, Mrs Curtis."

They stood aside as the woman left the well-stocked shop.

"Mrs Mundy?"

"Yes. I know you. You're two of the policemen who were at the hall last night."

"Quite right."

"What can I do for you?" She moved round the counter and turned the OPEN sign to CLOSED. "I shut early for dinner. My hubby comes home for his, you see, so I have to have it ready."

"You live on the premises?"

"Yes."

"Is your husband here now?"

"Yes. I'd just got the food out when that customer came in. He'll have served himself by now."

"So much the better. Could we come through? I'd rather he was present while we talk to you. You can have your dinner while we chat for a minute or two."

"If you must . . . " she began.

"It would be better. Women prefer their men with them when the police call."

"Come through, then."

It was a neat little all-purpose room with a kitchen-scullery behind. The square table was pushed under the side window and an old-fashioned Yorkist range glowed on the other side of the room.

"Policemen, Danny," Alice said as they went through the door with coloured glass panels. "To talk to me."

Danny looked up. Reed guessed he had some minor clerking job where the employees were sent off for lunch on a rota system, Danny being first away. The biros and pencils in the breast pocket of his well-worn jacket argued clerical work of some sort.

"Please go on with your dinner, Mr Mundy, we don't want to make you late."

"I'll wait," decided Alice. "Sit down."

There were two Windsor chairs, one on each side of the fire.

"We've been speaking to a lot of the people who were at the hall last night," began Cleveland. "We got to hear you're something of a soloist yourself, Mrs Mundy."

"I do quite a bit. Sacred and otherwise."

"May I ask if you, as a soloist, ever use throat sprays?"

"The only things I use are Pulmo-Bailey and Kosylana."

"And what are they exactly?"

"Pulmo-Bailey is for strengthening the throat and chest and Kosylana is a soothing linctus."

"You use them in sprays?"

"I use a medicine spoon. Pulmo-Bailey is a bit horrid but Kosylana is sweet like a liqueur."

"I see. Thank you for that information. Now, I'd like to ask if you saw anybody wandering round the dressing-rooms who wasn't a member of the choir or known to you as a musician."

"I don't know all the musicians."

"Anybody not dressed ready to go on stage, then?"

"Nobody."

"Now, Mrs Mundy, I don't know what you think was behind

Miss Festival's death last night."

"I heard she was poisoned. Your questions about throat sprays mean she probably died that way."

"Maybe. We don't know until the pathologist has finished his examination. Also, what we don't know is why she was killed. It could be, you know, that whoever did it thought he would be killing the other woman using that dressing-room."

"Margaret Whitehead?"

"Yes. We have to keep all possibilities in mind."

"I can see that," said Mundy. "P'raps he didn't mind which one he got."

"That is another possibility, too. But we've been asking questions of a lot of people about who could bear a grudge against Miss Whitehead as well as Miss Festival." Cleveland looked sternly at Alice. "Several people have told us, Mrs Mundy, that last night you had some not very nice things to say about Miss Whitehead. When we're on a case of murder, we have to take note of such things."

Mrs Mundy made no reply. She leaned heavily on the back of the chair behind which she was standing.

"Alice," said her husband sharply.

"I didn't mean to . . . "

"You've been at it again, haven't you? Spreading gossip. Now look where it's got you. I've told you before that tongue of yours would get you into trouble."

Cleveland got to his feet. "Mrs Mundy, if it had been Miss Whitehead who had died, we'd have been obliged to go round and get statements from witnesses of exactly what you had said, and then we'd have had to ask you for an explanation. That wouldn't have been very pleasant for you, and it would have been a waste of our time. So please pay heed to what your husband has told you."

"She will," said Danny grimly. "I'll see to it."

"Thank you, Mr Mundy, I'm sure we can leave the matter safely in your hands."

"It's this amateur crowd," said Mundy. "They're always backbiting. Singing's supposed to be their pleasure, but it's more like a cat and dog fight, they're all so jealous of each other."

Cleveland and Reed let themselves out.

"Ready to go?" asked Masters.

York wiped the grains of sugar from round his mouth. "Yes, sir, thank you, sir."

As they left the café, Masters said: "I'd like you to take me to a big pharmacy. Choose one where you can leave the car and come in with me."

York obeyed his instructions to the letter. Only a matter of minutes later the car was being parked in a quiet minor road. "If we go down to the main street, sir, and turn left, only fifty or sixty yards up is Wilson's. It's the main shop of a small chain of three or four in Nortown and roundabout."

"It sounds ideal. Lead on."

Masters showed his card to the girl behind the pharmaceuticals counter. "I would like to speak to the pharmacist, please."

"Which one, sir? Mr Wilson himself, or Miss Jeffrey?"

"Why not both if they're available? But please tell them not to be alarmed. I only want a bit of information."

A moment or two later they were led into the dispensary.

"My name is Masters. I'm a Detective Chief Superintendent from Scotland Yard. This is Detective Constable York from your local force who is acting as my guide to Nortown. Could I pick your brains for a few minutes? I am investigating the murder of a singer at the Central Hall, last night, and I'd like a bit of expert advice."

"Be our guest," said Wilson. "We've only bench stools to sit on, but you're welcome to make yourselves as comfortable as you can."

"Thank you." Masters opened his coat and perched on one of the high stools. "I'd like to talk to you about sprays, aerosols and that sort of thing."

"We sell scores of one sort or another. Medical ones, cosmetic ones, gardening ones."

"Can we discuss the medical variety, please?"

"Ad nauseam, if it helps or, rather, if we can help. Miss Jeffrey is much more recently trained than I am, so she's probably better informed about these comparatively modern gadgets."

"That sounds as if, between you, you will be able to help. The pathologist and forensic people have not yet sent me their reports, so I am jumping the gun just a bit, but I am convinced Miss Festival was killed by some toxic substance that had been introduced into one of her throat or nasal sprays."

"One of them?" asked Miss Jeffrey.

"She had four, all nicely tucked into a custom-made vanity case for carrying about with her."

"Four? Golly! She either overdid it — if they were all the same. Or it may be she liked a bit of variety."

"They were all different."

"In that case," said Wilson, "in spite of what Sandra has just said, Miss Festival was probably choosey and maybe even very sparing in their use."

"Meaning?"

"She would self-diagnose her need, and use the best one to meet it."

"Thank you. What would they be — at a guess?"

"No guess needed," said Sandra, "unless she was an asthmatic which is unlikely, being a great singer, or she was a crank, which I take it she wasn't?"

"For crank read hypochondriac," said Wilson.

"As far as I know she was neither. A very normal, rather happy-go-lucky sort of woman and not over-endowed with artistic temperament, though with more than her fair share of artistry."

"They seem to have called you in very quickly," said Wilson.

"I was already up here on a visit. In fact, I was present at the performance last night and saw Miss Festival collapse. I was asked to investigate her death."

"One of the girls in the shop was there," said Sandra. "She's talked of nothing else all morning."

"In that case there is no need for me to describe it for you. But to get back to throat sprays. You said you would know what they contained, Miss Jeffrey."

"One would be a local anaesthetic for pain and soreness. Something like methyl chloride. It comes out very, very cold.

160

You've probably seen them on telly spraying something like it on sports players who pull muscles."

"In the football games?" asked York.

"Yes. Then there would definitely be a mouth deodorant. They used to suck cachous in the old days."

"Sen Sen and Sweet Lips," murmured Wilson, then added, "Sorry. I'm maundering."

"There would likely be a mouth freshener, too."

"Not the same as a deodorant?"

"No. It would likely be antiseptic, with a few other essential oils in it to make it faintly analgesic, perhaps."

"I see. And the last one, Miss Jeffrey?"

She turned to Wilson. "My guess would be an antibiotic for infection. Something like benzocaine, which is also a mild local anaesthetic."

Wilson nodded. "You've got all four there, Sandra. Anaesthetic, analgesic, antibiotic and deodorant. They will be basically right." He turned to Masters. "I say basically, because many of these sprays are combinations or have several active ingredients."

"I understand."

"Is that all you wanted to know?"

"Not quite. You say there are a great number of sprays on the market?"

"Oh, yes. All sorts of atomizers. The biggest medical sale, of course, is for asthma, but the others are readily available. For instance, if you go into the shop you will find all manner of hair sprays, fly killers, wasp killers, garden sprays and so on. Go round the corner to the paint shop and you will find them there. The ironmonger will sell you easing oil in an aerosol, the stationer will sell you gums and resins. The list is endless."

"How easy are they to tamper with?"

"Meaning to add something nasty to their contents?"

"Yes."

"The ordinary aerosols are pretty well foolproof. By that I mean you'd find it hard to add to your wife's can of furniture polish. But what you haven't to forget, Mr Masters, is that a modern cigarette lighter is an aerosol which can be replenished from another aerosol, just so long as you have the right nozzle attachment."

"Cans of lighter fuel are often supplied with a variety of such nozzles, I believe."

"Just so. Cheap little bits of plastic all moulded on the same tree. All one has to do is break off and then attach the appropriate one, and the transfer of the contents is an easy matter as thousands of smokers prove every day. You see the mechanism is basically extremely simple. A spring-loaded washer inside the cap blocks the hole through which protrudes a short stem. The stem is usually a pretty good fit, leaving only a little space between its own circumference and that of the hole, just enough, in fact, to allow a controlled escape of the contents when pressure is applied to the stem. As you know, in most cases, the pressure itself is applied through the little finger stud which protrudes from the top of the can, and which is, itself, a primitive valve."

"The stud which has a side hole in it and usually an arrow indicating which way to point the spray?"

"That's the fellow. It is made so that no matter how hard you press, it can only force the other valve stem down a minute distance, otherwise you might get an unwanted whoosh of the contents."

Masters nodded. "Those are ordinary aerosols, I think you said?"

Wilson turned to Sandra. "You've been in laboratories and research departments much more recently than me. Perhaps you'd better tell Mr Masters what you know about the modern uses and types."

Miss Jeffrey smiled. "It all seems so simple one never thinks that it could be very important. What I mean is, if I'd ever thought Scotland Yard would be questioning me about them I'd have paid more attention to the wretched things and not just taken them for granted."

"Does that mean you are unable to help me further, Miss Jeffrey?"

"Oh, I didn't mean that. I know a bit about them. But first off I think I should tell you that I have seen an advertisement for refillable aerosols. I didn't read the ad. It was one of those small ones you see in daily papers on a Saturday morning and I just skipped over it."

"That information could be useful, Miss Jeffrey."

"I thought I'd mention it. Now, we sell, for medical purposes, inhalation aerosols and they are, in effect, refillable, in that the inhaler itself with its mouthpiece and so on can be used any number of times, while the container for the medication is replaceable."

"But the container is not refillable?"

"No. And I think I can be absolutely sure in saying that if anybody tried to introduce a toxic liquid into them, all the propellant gas would have escaped before they managed to do it. And without the propellant gas, you've got no aerosol."

"I understand that, Miss Jeffrey. So what you are telling me is that the aerosols in Miss Festival's sprays would not — could not — have been tampered with."

"Right. But they could have been replaced."

"But the replacements would have had to be tampered with to make them toxic, and you have told me that is impossible."

"What I'm saying is that they could have been specifically made for that purpose."

"Ah! Now we're getting somewhere — if you can tell me how."

"Nothing easier, I'd have thought."

"Please explain."

Miss Jeffrey reached up to a shelf and took down a small carton. From this she took a small cylindrical metal container painted white. It narrowed towards the top where a small gold-coloured cap, pierced by a plunger, was crimped round the rim of the neck.

"These are usually of standard size; two inches tall and one inch diameter. Some — like this one — are of metal, some are glass and I believe there are some made of plastic. The big thing to remember is that the people who make these don't make the contents."

"Firms buy them in to fill for themselves?"

"To fill and seal, Chief Superintedent."

"I can see that. But that would be on a production line, and to interfere with that would be tricky, because one could never be

163

sure of picking out the right one at the end."

"True. But every factory in this country, and when I say every factory, I mean the vast majority, has a crimping machine for these little chaps. They have to have, because before you can go into bulk production, you have to have tests for things like stability and corrosion. Will the contents react with the metal? Will light coming through the glass spoil the colour? Will the propellant gas make the goods inactive? And so on and so on.

"What I mean is, that even a food producer might want to produce a salad dressing that the housewife could spray on to her lettuce leaves instead of tossing them in home-made dressing. He would want to know if the vinegar would react with the metal, if the oil would clog the nozzle, if the gas would affect the mixture and so on. So, somewhere in his factory, he would have a pull-down filling and crimping machine, no bigger than some of the power tools the ordinary householder uses.

"He would fill his container first — half or two-thirds full — put it into the machine which incorporates a bottle of freon, which is a very volatile liquid and turns to gas in the expansion chamber left by only partially filling the cartridge, and then pull down the handle. The measure of liquid freon would go in and the cap be crimped on before the liquid freon could become gaseous. One specially prepared aerosol refill coming up.

"I think you'll find that Miss Festival's refills are all of this standard size. Any or all of them could be standard preparations or, as she is obviously a wealthy, famous singer, she may have an ear, nose and throat consultant who makes up special prescriptions for her which he could well put into the cartridges on his own premises or which could be put up specially for him — at a price."

"Thank you very much indeed, Miss Jeffrey. Would I find such machines in Nortown?"

"Probably about forty, I'd say. There's a lot of experimentation goes on in R & D departments and control labs in the most unlikely factories, both large and small. As Mr Wilson told you, everything from spray-on glue to graffiti paint."

Masters grinned. "You've helped me a lot. I'm very grateful."

164

"Don't be. I'm not much into that sort of singing myself, but I know how I'd feel if somebody did it to Elton John."

They were all gathered in Cleveland's office at the Nortown HQ.

"I saw Mawby," said Green after reporting his visit to the hall. "He'd gone down the side alley at about seven o'clock to warm his trumpet in the storeroom with the gas fire. He said he saw nobody in the alleyway or the hall. He's played there so often he knows his way about well enough and doesn't have to ask the Carrots. One thing worried me and I questioned him closely about it."

"What was that, Bill?"

"Why he should go there so early to warm up, seeing he wasn't going on stage till the second half. He said Wadland, his host, was going out to a brass band practice and offered to take him to Freemen's Square by car if he'd go that early. So he went with Wadland rather that get a cab."

"And he just sat in his storeroom alone?"

"That's right. Evidently he'd got the blues and didn't want company, so he stayed put. According to him he's getting a bit fed up because really he's a pianist and composer but the only recognition he gets is for playing the trumpet. He wanted a good old brood on the unfairness of the world in general and to himself in particular. I'd say he was of no interest to us, George, but I pointed out to him that he was the only performer off-stage in the first half and Nancy Festival was the only one off in the second."

"Did he grasp the significance of that?"

"Not until I'd explained to him that he was the bloke with the best opportunity to do the lass in. Then he woke up a bit. But the trouble is, George, nobody knows how she died yet. Even we don't. If he'd agreed with me, I'd have begun to think he knew something I didn't."

"I get that point, Bill. The genuine innocent couldn't know we think Miss Festival's sprays were interfered with before the interval. Is that the lot?"

"I saw the Frames and the Crofts. None of them saw anybody or anything near the hall. I reckon we can discount them."

"Thank you. Matt, can we hear from you?"

Cleveland complied and then Masters described his interviews. By the time he had finished it was nearly half-past one, but the forensic reports had not arrived.

"Sandwiches," announced Masters. "Everybody go off now and get yourselves fed and watered. Back here at two-fifteen."

"Any ideas, George?" asked Cleveland as the two of them, with Green, made for the senior mess.

"I'm very sanguine. What about you?"

"I'll have to mull over all that lot we've just heard before I can honestly say I can see our way forward. Shouldn't we set up an incident room to collate it all?"

"I'd rather not. I find them inhibiting. But if you want to. . . . "

"You're the boss."

"Bill?" enquired Masters.

"No incident room for me," said Green. "I reckon this is beginning to gel. I can feel it in my water. But I'll tell you what, Matt. As soon as we've nobbled this joker, you're going to need an operations room with filing and cross-checking to nail him for the previous jobs. He'll have to be tied in to them."

"I can see that. We've got to be quite sure about the others in order to close the files, even if we get him dead to rights and send him down for this one only."

"You've got to know," agreed Masters, "and so have the public. You can't leave any hint of suspicion that the chap who did the other eleven jobs is still at large."

They entered the mess and read the chalked-up menu. "Sandwiches various?" grunted Green. "And what would they be?"

"Try a couple of fried bacon butties," advised Cleveland. "Or they'll make you one up with something like fried liver or sliced stuffed heart."

"I'm spoiled for choice, am I? Would they put me a fried egg on top of the bacon?"

"Ask 'em," said Cleveland.

While they were eating, Cleveland was called to the internal phone. When he rejoined them, he said: "Forensic and path reports are here, George. I've asked for them to be put on my desk for you."

"Excellent. I'll go up and read them now. Please don't hurry if you'd rather finish your . . . "

"We're coming," grunted Green, getting to his feet. "I've been thinking about those sprays while we've been feeding our faces. Only one of them would have to be changed."

"Quite right, Bill. And it would make a hell of a difference which one it was."

"How do you mean?" asked Cleveland as he hurried along with them.

"I think that will be explained when we get the report."

Masters slid open the envelope.

"Nothing wrong with the two cups," he said. "Ordinary tea dregs."

They waited while he read out:

"Death due to respiratory failure and cardiac arrest consequent upon . . . " Masters turned the page " . . . the ingestion of a thion insecticide, a virulent pesticide of the organo-phosphorus group. Thions are cholinesterase inhibitors . . . nothing found at autopsy which is diagnostic, though miosis and pulmonary oedema were present . . . amount of thion ingested was some 55 mg (oral doses of 15 to 30 mg have previously caused death so that fatal dose is reckoned as 0.015 – 0.030 grams). Normally with parasympathetic excitants such as physotigmine and choline derivatives death occurs within two hours, but with insecticides of the thion group death may be delayed by several hours. However, as the amount ingested was almost four times the minimum fatal dose and almost twice the maximum fatal dose, it is suggested that death was not delayed beyond two hours after ingestion and could have occurred well within that time. This view is supported by the fact that though the urine was found to contain paranitrophenol and the brain cholinesterase activity was only twenty per cent of normal, there was no increase in bronchial mucus, nor was the bowel haemhorrhagic as would be expected if death did not supervene before all bodily functions had reacted in the normal way to thion poisoning."

"Meaning, I suppose," said Green, "that she got enough of it to do in her heart before it had time to complete all its other nasties."

"I imagine that to be the case, Bill, because as far as we know she didn't vomit or have diarrhoea and both are mentioned here as typical reactions." He paused to read a little further. "Oh, yes. They go on to say that the thions are metabolized first to paraoxon which is the active cholinesterase inhibitor, then to paranitro-phenol which would normally be excreted by the kidneys but which seems not to have happened in this case."

"Meaning she didn't go to the loo for a leak?"

"I imagine so."

"So she didn't feel ill at all," said Cleveland.

"They deal with that. They suggest that she probably passed out, in a light coma, and then recovered, thinking she had dropped off to sleep."

"And if she did that," said Green, "she was probably feeling krank but put it down to the fact that one often feels like death warmed up after a cat nap. I know I do."

Masters nodded. "I think you've got it, Bill. If she did pass out, she was probably brought back to consciousness by the applause at the end. She realized what it was and though feeling definitely off-colour, knew she had to get on stage immediately, without having time to visit the lavatory either to be sick or to empty her bladder. Being the professional she was, she managed it and then col-lapsed."

Cleveland said he could not fault that reading of events, so Masters turned to the rest of the report.

"Analysis of contents of inhalation aerosols taken from the dressing-room of the deceased." He looked up. "What's the betting, Bill?"

"Millions to one on."

The phone rang. Cleveland answered it and then handed it to Masters. "Professor Barzey, the pathologist."

"Good afternoon, Professor. Masters here."

"Ah, Mr Masters. Have you read the reports yet?"

"I am doing that at this moment."

"Good. There are just two points I thought I ought to make which are probably not facts in this particular case but are, nevertheless, fairly widely held medical opinions. I say that because I've just been consulting the literature about them. The first is that the thions produce coma before death. Now that seems incompatible in this case, where the woman was, I believe, standing up and acknowledging applause from her audience before collapsing and dying immediately."

"We were speculating on that point, Professor."

"Don't worry any further. There are a number of recorded instances where the victims have become unconscious to a degree where they are not fully aware of their surroundings, but have then reacted to a stimulus, particularly one which they recognize. In this case, Miss Festival would react to clapping and applause because, being an artist, she would be very accustomed to it. The point is, could she have heard the applause from where she was at the time?"

"Very easily, I would have said. She was in the soloists' dressing-room immediately behind the stage."

"Excellent. That settles that. I should just add that something of the sort goes on sometimes with children who are in a long-term coma. Doctors can often evoke a reaction by playing them tapes of their favourite pop groups or their school friends singing."

"I've read of instances of that, Professor."

"Fine. So you know where you are on that point. Good safe ground there, Masters."

"Thank you."

"Now for the second clarification. Miss Festival seems to have missed out on some of the expected consequences of ingesting poison. Don't let that fool you. She took a large dose, consequently her blood levels rose very quickly to the point of toxicity and beyond. As you must know, the higher the blood levels, the more severe the reactions they cause, particularly in — to put it in lay terms — in the working parts of the body, such as heart, brain, lungs and so on. So these stop working long before the poison has had time to eat through tissue such as bowels and membranes. So, though I have estimated the time of poisoning as about one and a half hours before death, that could be a little on the long side. If an hour suits your timings better, that will be fair enough, but not less than an hour."

"Thank you, Professor. I don't think the exact moment of ingestion will be too important, as long as it was after the interval at the performance."

"Good. Anything else I can help you with, just get in touch. I'll be glad to help."

"Thank you, again."

Masters put the phone down and proceeded to tell his two colleagues that their own original assessments had been confirmed. He was just turning to the report on the analysis of the spray cartridges when the remaining four members of the team joined them.

"Only one had been tampered with. It contained a thion derivative, a virulent pesticide of the organo-phosphorus group. The contents are from the concentrate used by farmers for watering down for crop spraying."

"Just like that," said Green. "He wasn't taking any chances on failure, was he?"

"The others . . . methyl chloride . . . local anaesthetic . . . very cold. Mouth freshener . . . harmless essential oils. Mouth deodorant, harmless." He looked up. "It seems our friend replaced the one Miss Jeffrey said would contain an antibiotic for soreness and infection, and that, gentlemen, is likely to have been the one with the throat nozzle. . . . " He consulted the report. "Yes. It says here it was the one with the long tube for the back of the throat. The one with the expansion chamber apparently was for the methyl chloride. The other two had normal apertures."

"So we can work it out," said Green.

"Work what out?" asked Sibley.

"Why she didn't know she'd sprayed her innards with some foul-smelling, corrosive pesticide, lad. Haven't you wondered why she didn't stop after the first little shot? Why she didn't realize it wasn't her normal stuff and immediately do something about it?"

Sibley shook his head.

Green shook his, too, sadly, and then turned to Masters. "She used the cold spray first, George. Froze her gullet, so that she couldn't tell from the taste what she popped in next."

Masters nodded. "There's no other explanation for her failure to

170

realize she'd got the wrong liquid."

Cleveland said: "The mechanics fit, George. The very cold spray had an expansion chamber which means, I suppose, that it spread its contents far and wide inside the mouth and throat, anaesthetizing the whole area. Then she must have used the poison spray with its long throat nozzle, so that she squirted it right down her gullet, without feeling any burning sensation or other effect, after which she would use her mouth deodorant and then the freshener, so that there would be a pleasant smell and she again wouldn't notice anything amiss."

"I agree with that completely," said Masters, much to Cleveland's gratification. "So, gentlemen, we are now all aware of how Miss Festival died, we have a report of a stranger being seen in the area of the alleyway at seven o'clock, and the DCI's report of a man having hidden in the broom cupboard for some time last night. Does anybody disagree with the obvious presumption that the stranger was the killer, that he hid until all the singers got on stage and Mrs Carrot was otherwise engaged with laying out her teacups. . . ? "

"Making a hell of a rattle with them," said Sibley, "so that an army could have moved about those corridors without being heard, let alone a single man in rubber soles."

"Very good point," said Masters approvingly. "Our man got into the female soloists' dressing-room in the sure knowledge that nobody would return to it to disturb him for the hour and a half or so before the interval. So he had plenty of time in which to effect the change of aerosol which is, I presume, a job which takes seconds only."

"Straight in and out, Chief," said Berger. "As easy as replacing a light bulb."

"Good. He had plenty of time at his disposal, so though he hadn't to hurry, I imagine he did the job carefully without wasting time. How long? Two minutes? Then out again immediately, providing the coast was clear."

"Which it would be, Chief," said Reed. "We reckon Mawby was safe in front of his gas fire and the only other person about was Elsie Carrot. I can't see her hanging about in draughty corridors for long when she'd got that little snug to sit in when she wasn't in the kitchen."

"So if we say twenty to eight," added Cleveland, "we'd be about right for his leaving the alleyway. Are you wanting us to try and find a witness to him leaving, George?"

"No. There'd be no point. A report of a figure muffled up against the cold? I think another blind man's observation would be more useful — rubber soles and so forth. Logan was very useful to us."

"He was that. I'll make sure he gets that money out of Butcher, George, even if only for that bit of information."

"I'm hoping you will, Matt."

There was a moment or two of silence. At last Sibley, who was fidgeting, as if anxious to be about his business, said: "What now, sir? Who have we got to go and see this afternoon?"

Masters looked at his watch. "It's almost three o'clock, so we won't have a long stint this afternoon. Matt, will you and Reed get hold of Mr Festival and see if there's anything relevant to be got out of him? I don't have to tell you what to do, except to ask you to treat him fairly gently. He'll have just identified his daughter's body, remember, and could be in a bit of a state."

"Anything in particular you want to know, George?"

"I think, really, that it's a job of elimination, Matt. A formal one. Where was he last night? Did he know about her sprays? Who else knew about them? Had she a boy-friend? I'm not expecting you to get much, Matt, if anything. But it has to be done, diplomatically, for form's sake."

"Right."

"Bill, I think your team ought to talk to the two male soloists, Darren and Capper. Again I'm not expecting anything, but one never knows."

"What about you?"

"I'll try and learn a few facts about her former husband."

"He was rid of her already," said Sibley. "Will he be interested, sir?"

"Interested or not, Sergeant, he may know something we'd like to know."

"I see, sir. Sorry."

"Don't be. If you have doubts or queries, voice them. The same if you don't understand anything. Any point, however trivial or even silly it may seem, could spark a fresh line of thought. And that is what we're after." He glanced round. "Shall we say five-thirty here, gentlemen? I don't expect there will be much to discuss, so we ought to be away by six."

The Yard team returned to the hotel shortly before seven.

"I forgot to tell you, gentlemen, that I cancelled whatever entertainment had been laid on for tonight, with the excuse that we would be working on the case."

"Going out again, are we?" grumbled Green.

"After dinner. I accepted a completely different invitation for us all, from Mrs Fenny. I think you'll enjoy it more than the brass band concert."

"You didn't forget to tell us," snorted Green. "You held back till we were alone. You wanted to get away from the locals and have a bit of a knees-up without Matt Cleveland and some of his mob."

"I confess I kept the information back, Bill, but I assure you we are going there to work or, at any rate, to ask the odd question, which amounts to the same thing."

Green grunted equivocally. "Early dinner then?"

"I want us to be standing at the dining-room door when it is opened. In fact, we could ask for a prior glimpse at the menu so that we can order before we sit down."

"In that case, I'll see you in the bar in ten minutes."

"It's a date."

Soon after half-past eight, the Yard Rover was nosing into the driveway of the Fenny house.

"Are you sure we won't swamp you, Mrs Fenny?"

"Perfectly sure, Mr Masters. And is this Mr Green whom you said I should enjoy meeting so much?"

The introductions went on. At last Mrs Fenny brought forward the girl who had sold them programmes the night before.

"And this is Cissy Spring, a friend of David's. This is Cissy's first visit, too. She was on duty at the Central Hall last night, and is on again tomorrow night."

When Reed was introduced to her, he said: "I've met you before, Miss Spring."

"I sold you programmes. . . . "

"No, that's not it. I recognize your face from somewhere else."

"A face known at Scotland Yard," laughed David. "That doesn't sound too good."

"Your name is Spring? I've got it. Is Mr Jagger your uncle, by any chance? You're very like him."

"No. I know him of course, but . . . "

Mrs Fenny broke into the conversation. "I feel sure everybody would enjoy a drink, Peter. I shall take Mr Masters and Mr Green into the sitting-room. Bring ours to us there, please. You young people can find somewhere else to sit and talk. We'll see you all later on."

As Masters closed the door of the sitting-room, Mrs Fenny said quietly: "I'm sorry to have interrupted the conversation Sergeant Reed was having with Cissy, but he was on dangerous ground."

"Putting his foot in it, was he?" asked Green with a grin.

"Very much so," said Mrs Fenny as she sat down. "He was quite right, of course. Cissy does look very much like Jack Jagger who is, I need hardly say, a very handsome man, whereas Spring resembles a Pekinese, facially."

"Ah!" said Green. "A question of paternity, perhaps?"

"Exactly. It is a mystery to me why nobody in Nortown has ever tumbled to the fact that Jagger is Cissy's father."

"You know," reminded Green.

"Yes, I know. But then, I ought to. My husband and I were in London, many years ago, and discovered that Jack Jagger and Mrs Spring were using the same hotel as us, for a . . . well, they call them weekend or high-life breaks now, I believe. We took good care they didn't see us. That would have been so embarrassing for them, but when on the appropriate date Mrs Spring had a baby which resembled Jack so much, we had no doubt as to its parentage. Other people seem to have missed the connection — all except Cissy's mother and Jack Jagger, of course. He knows. I've been present when they've met, and though the child suspects nothing, I've noted a father's pride in Jack's demeanour. I suppose

Sergeant Reed has interviewed Jack Jagger today?"

Masters nodded. "He is also a trained observer and quite a bright young man."

"I guessed as much." She laughed. "And has the bright young man been primed as to what to ask the other bright young things he is with at the moment?"

"Both of them have," said Green.

"I wouldn't like you two on my trail if I were a criminal."

"There's no answer to that," said Green. "Except to say that I've never met a criminal who resembled you, ma'am. But I'll keep you in mind in case we hear of a gang of five operating up here."

Mrs Fenny laughed again. "And what have you come prepared to ask me, Mr Masters?"

Masters stretched his legs. "May I smoke my pipe?"

"By all means. But please don't try to parry all my questions by asking others."

"I had to, because there is no question I want to ask you immediately."

"You surprise me."

Masters was rubbing Warlock Flake in the palm of his left hand. "But I want to talk and I was hoping to meet Mr Festival."

"He went up for a short rest after dinner. He promised to come down to meet you."

Masters smiled. "That is when the questions could start, Mrs Fenny."

"You see, ma'am," said Green, offering his hostess a cigarette which she declined, "we've so far regarded the murder of Miss Festival as just the latest in a series of twelve killings which you've no doubt heard about."

Mrs Fenny nodded her head. "Spread all over this area, I believe. Are you telling me you don't now think it is the latest in that dreadful catalogue?"

"No, ma'am. We still hold strongly to the view that it is. But until we get sure evidence we are right on that score, we can't afford to ignore the possibility of it being just a one-off murder."

"I am sure you must take every possibility into account, Mr Green, but murder is murder, whether it is the latest of twelve or, as you put it, a one-off event."

"To you, ma'am, perhaps. A victim has been killed. It's the same difference as being knocked down by a Rolls Royce or a Mini. They'll both kill you. But to the chaps investigating the crimes, they are very different and the solving of them involves different techniques and methods."

"You interest me, Mr Green." She looked up as her son entered, carrying a tray. "Your usual," he said handing his mother a long gin and tonic. "I brought the whisky decanter for you, gentlemen. There's water, soda and ginger if you wish to ruin it."

"Thank you, Peter. Is there any sign of Mr Festival yet?"

"None. Would you like me to tap on his door to say our visitors are here?"

"I think so. He promised to be down, but he seemed very tired. Perhaps he's fallen asleep after all."

Peter nodded understandingly and left them.

"I think I had better tell you what I was about to when the drinks arrived," said Green. "Before Mr Festival comes down, that is. You see, ma'am, where a multi-murderer can be just any old psychopath, the single victim killer is, statistically, more often than not a member of the family."

Mrs Fenny considered this for a moment. "I'm sure I don't see all the implications of what you have just told me, and I cannot doubt its truth. But surely you are not suggesting that Mr Festival could have killed his daughter?"

Green looked across at Masters. "I'm allowed to say that nothing is further from our minds, am I, George?"

Masters straightened up in his chair. "Of course you are." He addressed Mrs Fenny. "That is the truth. But you should realize, that without even meeting Mr Festival, Bill Green and I — or any detective — could make out quite a good case on paper against him."

"But he was in London last evening, Mr Masters."

"Quite so, Mrs Fenny. But somebody substituted a cartridge of poisonous liquid in one of Miss Festival's throat sprays. The substitution could have taken place in London yesterday morning. Miss Festival, I imagine, did not use the spray until last evening here in Nortown. The opportunity was there for Mr Festival — or so I could argue."

"I see."

"However, ma'am, I am not here in your house to harass Mr Festival. That would be insensitive and unforgivable. But you will appreciate that I must talk to him, and I think he would prefer to talk about his daughter — might even like to talk about her — in these very pleasant, relaxed surroundings, with you present to reassure him if he needs reassurance."

"You think he may need that?"

"We are not unaware that whatever the circumstances in which we meet them, some people find police officers forbidding. After losing his daughter so tragically, I should hate Mr Festival to feel we were hounding him."

Mrs Fenny turned to Green. "Is Mr Masters always so considerate?"

"Don't let him fool you, ma'am. He may use fair means as opposed to foul, but he always gets his way."

"And you?"

"We're a team, love. We play to orders from the boss."

She smiled. "You are forgetting your drinks, gentlemen."

Masters drowned a small measure of whisky in water.

"Has Graham Saltwell been informed of Nancy's death?" asked Mrs Fenny.

"I tried to get hold of him myself, this afternoon," replied Masters. "I didn't succeed. But he should have the news. All the papers and broadcasts have featured it."

"He'll be out calling on his customers, I suppose."

Green was about to ask a question when the door opened and Peter brought in Mr Festival. The newcomer was a man of above retiring age, but despite the shock he must have suffered, appeared spritely enough, even quietly cheerful, though the lack of colour in his face argued that such cheerfulness could be bogus.

Mrs Fenny was on her feet immediately and advancing to meet him before he was fairly through the door. "Mr Festival, I hope you have had a good rest."

"Not actually. Well . . . I suppose I have, Mrs Fenny. I've been thinking, you see. About our Nancy and her mother. Good girls both of them. And that's done me a bit of good. But Peter came to say these gentlemen would like a word."

"I'm sorry you were disturbed, Mr Festival," began Masters.

"Call me Harvey," said Festival. "That's what they always called me at the bakery. Everybody did. Nancy did, and her mother. Harvey Festival — short for Harvest, you see." He gave a little laugh at his own joke. "Real name's Josiah," he said. "Never did like that."

Mrs Fenny sat him down and Peter poured him whisky before leaving.

"You do know we're policemen, don't you Harvey?"

"Mrs Fenny said you'd be here. I've heard about you in London, Mr Masters. Never thought I'd meet you though." He sipped his whisky and put the glass down. "Met one of your lot this afternoon, or rather he met me. Nice chap. Mr Cleveland. Very nice and kind. Asked me a few questions, but I couldn't help him. I don't know who'd want to harm our Nancy. She was a great lass. Everybody thought so."

"Tell us about her," said Green.

"Nowt much to tell, really. She were a very ordinary girl. Pretty and nice. Mother and me, we thought the world of her. Did everything we could for her, too. She had piano lessons right from being a little lass."

"She played well, did she?"

"She was never all that good at it. Too high-spirited to practise properly, her teacher said. Even when she left school to become a typist in an office she was always up to her larks. But she knew her notes all right, and that turned out useful when she started to sing."

"When was that, Harvey?"

"Let's see. It would be when she was about nineteen or twenty."

"She went off to learn singing?"

"No, nothing like that. She were a natural, our Nancy. Nobody knew how. She didn't do any singing at school except in their little choirs and things. But she was always fooling about, like I told you, and mimicking people to make us laugh. I was in hospital for a few days, and she came in to see me. In the morning it were. It wasn't visiting hours, but Nancy had sweethearted the sister to let her in. Told her some story about having travelled up overnight from Brighton to see me and she had to get straight back. She was a right card in them days."

Festival took another sip of whisky and accepted one of Green's cigarettes. As Masters had foreseen, talking about his daughter was helping him. He seemed keen to continue.

"Anyhow, Nancy came in and decided we all needed cheering up. Men's medical ward, it was, and there were cleaners going round and nurses rushing about. The hospital barber was there too, doing haircuts. Little fella, he was, about forty. Very neat and trim. Spoke a bit prissy-like. The lads were a bit rude about him, actually. But our Nancy didn't care what was going on. She started to act and sing an old bit of music hall stuff I'd taught her on my knee when she was little. 'Can anyone kindly tell me have you seen my Mickey Flynn?'."

"I've never heard it," confessed Mrs Fenny.

"Nor have I," added Masters.

"I know it," said Green.

Almost by consent, the two older men started to sing:

"Can anyone kindly tell me have you seen my Mickey Flynn,
It is no joke, his nose is broke, an' he's got one eye in a sling.
He hopped away on his wooden leg
And the thought of it makes me cry.
He makes a round hole in the mud with his pole,
And that's what you can tell him by."

Mrs Fenny and Masters applauded the effort, and when Festival had got his breath back, he said: "I can tell you, our Nancy, with a lump of bandage round her eye and one of the cleaner's brooms for a crutch, was a sight for sore eyes. But it was the barber, Smith his name was, who came up to talk to her. He'd stopped barbering the bloke in the bed just two down from me to listen. Then he came up to her and said: 'You're a singer, young lady.' Anyhow, it turned out he conducted a Ladies' Guild Choir. They used to go off an' give little concerts in old people's homes and go in for little music festivals in the villages round about.

"Somehow he persuaded Nancy to go along to this choir, which she did for a year or two, and he put her in for some of the solo classes after a bit. She began to win, and then one day they happened to have a doctor of music called Bessborough to adjudicate. Evidently he'd been born in this village and came up for a day or two every year to judge the classes. When he heard Nancy sing, he said he'd never heard a voice like it and she ought to do something with it.

"The upshot was, he sent her to a pal of his who was a voice teacher nearby, and when this one heard her he set about putting right all the things she was doing wrong. We had a bit of a time of it, I can tell you, round about then."

"There were some snags, were there?" asked Mrs Fenny.

"You've no idea. Well, first off this new chap told our Nancy she had to work and work hard for about three hours a night, every night. But she was still only a young lass and doing her office job in the day, and she'd started courting Graham Saltwell a bit before then. Three hours' work each night was no joke to her. Fortunately, Graham was a commercial traveller, so he wasn't usually about Monday to Thursday, but weekends! She was having lessons all Saturday morning and then having to practise nearly all the rest of the day besides keeping house for us. Clara, my missus, that is, was ill, you see, and couldn't do much. Our Nancy was marvellous, but she couldn't see her singing leading anywhere."

"Why was that, Mr Festival?"

"Because her teacher wouldn't let her sing anywhere. He said she wasn't going to be heard until she was good and ready. He was going to launch her ready-made, he said. He said it would have been different if she'd started early and gone to a music school and so on. But she hadn't, and this was the way he wanted it. As I said, our Nancy began to get a bit fed up. Then Clara died, and that did it. Nancy said she wasn't going on singing because it wasn't worth it, and about three months after Clara had gone, she upped and married Graham."

"Had she stopped singing?"

"Yes. She didn't go near it for the best part of six months. Of course her teacher was running wild, but I reckon he saw he'd made a mistake. He'd piled too much on Nancy without giving her owt in return. So he asked her to go back an' said the break would probably have done her good. Our Nancy had one for him, though. She hadn't stopped, not completely. She'd learned a lot of stuff she wanted to sing, an' when she went back she sang it to him."

"What happened?"

"He'd overlooked something, hadn't he? Besides not seeing he'd been driving her too hard, I mean. He'd been so hard set on getting her voice just so, he'd not bothered to find out about how Nancy could interpret a song. I told you she was an actress. She acted that stuff she'd taught herself and he found it hard to fault, even though he'd expected to tear it to bits. You know how these blokes are. They'll find something to chew you up about if it kills them. But this one couldn't. He was so surprised he couldn't, he carted Nancy off to London to let some other bigwig hear her sing her bits, in case there was something he'd missed. Our Nancy came through with flying colours. She still had to work, of course, and she had to learn a proper repertoire, but by the time she was twenty-five she was ready to take engagements. She had a few little ones for a quid or two a time, and then she was asked to come and sing *Messiah* here in Nortown. It was her first big professional appearance and it was a success. After that she never looked back. But she was still taking lessons, you know. Right up to last week."

"Miss Festival stayed here with Mrs Fenny on that first occasion, I believe?"

"That's right. And has done ever since."

"Did you come to hear her début here?"

"I was a baker, Mr Masters. We're in the bakehouse at night."

"Of course. Her husband? Did he come?"

"Graham? Yes, on the second night, I think. He drove over from wherever he was on his round and then went back again to where he was staying, to start again next morning."

"Didn't his wife know he was there?"

"Not until the end. He wanted to surprise her. He just went behind when it was over and gave her some flowers. She was that pleased. She hadn't expected him, you see. When she got home she told me all about it. How Graham had suddenly appeared with . . . I think she said they were freesias."

"They were," said Mrs Fenny quietly. "I remember it very well. She was so excited by the success of the occasion and Graham's appearance. She was just lovely to watch and have about the house."

"So Graham liked her singing did he?" asked Masters, nonchalantly.

"Oh, yes. He liked to hear her."

"I meant her going away on engagements and tours and so on."

"Ah, there you have it, Mr Masters. I'm her father, so I'm probably not quite fair about it. Graham wasn't too happy about our Nancy giving up her office job. They'd counted on the money, you see, and he wasn't sure she'd make as much each week by singing. I was a bit surprised at that, because she liked doing it, and he was away so much, it seemed to me to be ideal. And she turned down all engagements on Fridays, Saturdays and Sundays unless they were local, because of him being home then. I reckoned he shouldn't have tried to stop her, but I needn't have worried because in no time at all she was earning a lot more money than she had done in her office, and more than Graham himself. And by then she could pick and choose where to go, so he didn't miss out on anything. In fact, he was on the pig's back, you might say, because he had only himself to provide for, and not even that, really."

"How d'you mean, Harvey?" asked Green.

"Because they'd had a little maisonette place when they first got married. Not far from me it were. Then Nancy found she needed a bit bigger place. Graham said they were quite happy where they were and he wasn't going to pay more mortgage, which was a bit of a sauce seeing it was our Nancy's pay from the office that had always gone straight into the building society. But that's by the way. Nancy was beginning to get all sorts of people calling on her. Conductors and the like. Nobs she used to call them, and she wanted somewhere for them to sit down when they came or stay the night if they had to. So she bought a little house. Well, I say little, but it was big compared with the maisonette, and she took it because one of its rooms was very big. And she paid for it herself. She told Graham he could sell the maisonette and he could have the money he got for it. So you see, Mr Green, he didn't have to pay a mortgage or any rent from then on. That's cheap living, especially if you're a commercial traveller and get all your meals paid for in hotels and your car given to you."

"Quite right, Harve, lad. He'd got the life of Riley. It was a bit ungrateful of him to feel narked."

"Don't get me wrong," said Festival. "I liked him. And our Nancy had married him, which to my mind says a lot for any man. And I could understand his attitude a bit. I've often seen it cause trouble when a wife finds herself financially independent and then starts to call the tune."

"But from what you've said," prompted Masters, "all your daughter was doing was running a business. Her expenditure seems to have been solely for the purpose of making a success of her career. She didn't fritter the money away, I take it?"

"Not our Nancy. I've told you she wanted this house with a room a bit bigger than usual. The reason for that was she wanted a baby grand piano. Until then she'd made do with a secondhand upright for learning her notes. But as she got on, she began to have to employ professional accompanists. You can't learn all these operas without somebody like that to help. Well, these upstage players don't like pianos that sound as if they'd had twenty years' hard labour in a pub bar. But when Graham heard she was going to spend several thousands on a baby grand, he couldn't or wouldn't see the need. He thought she was just getting too big for her boots."

"You should have told him, Harve," said Green. "Pointed out the facts of life."

"I did," said Festival. "Told him and asked him what he had to worry about. He was getting on himself, you see. He'd got himself a better job. Still in the field, of course, in water-treatment sales."

"What is that, exactly?" asked Masters.

"His firm design and construct treatment plant for water and waste products. There's a big call for them, you know. His markets, he told me, were industrial and towns and things — what do you call them?"

"Municipal clients."

"That's right. Sales executive he started to call himself. But when I spoke to him about the things our Nancy was buying because she needed them, I got to the bottom of the trouble."

"And what was that?"

"He wanted to be her manager. He thought the money she was spending should have been saved to pay his wages for arranging things for her."

"You mean he would have liked to leave his job as a representative?"

"That's it. But it wouldn't have been any good. He didn't know anything about it. And as for music, well, when I was a nipper they used to say somebody couldn't tell a bee from a bull's foot when they knew nowt about music. And that about described our Graham. Besides, Nancy had an agent in London. He did all her work for her. All she had to do was keep her diary of engagements and see she got there on time, knowing her stuff. She had an accountant to deal with her tax and all that lark."

"Saltwell took to heart what you said to him?"

"In a way. As I said, he wasn't a bad sort of bloke, and he settled down for a bit after that, because after the piano there wasn't much she spent a lot of money on except her dresses and hair. She didn't want a car, you see. Said long drives would tire her out before engagements and she didn't like the atmosphere inside — too hot and stuffy or blowing cold if you opened a window. Very careful about her voice and throat, she was. I often used to think she'd got a what's-his-name about them. A thing, you know."

"A phobia, perhaps?"

"Yeah. She said it was so that she could always be sure of being in perfect voice, but I reckon it was nerves."

"Probably. We all have our funny little ways."

"Yeah. Nothing to it really."

"So she and Graham settled down after you'd had a few words with him?"

"For a bit. But he was a funny character, too."

"How do you mean?"

"If it wasn't one thing it was another. First he started saying he wanted kids. Nancy would have wanted a couple, too, but she was still young and only just beginning to get well-known, really. She reckoned that if she'd dropped out for a year or two just then, she'd have had to start all over again later. Anyhow, it didn't please Graham, but I reckoned it was only his way of trying to stop her."

"He wanted to do that?"

"Not really. I reckon he wanted to show her who was boss by lashing her up with a couple of kids to stop her getting big ideas."

"There were no children, were there?"

"Never a sign. I don't know whether our Nancy tried to have them and couldn't, or what. But she never started one to my knowledge."

"And after that phase what happened?"

"Nothing you could really put your finger on except that Graham found he couldn't get on with the people she met. She always took him with her if he was available when she was invited out, which she was, more and more, of course. But from what he said, to put Graham in among all those music buffs was like asking me to carry on an intelligent conversation with Jonathan Miller, Enoch Powell and Bernard Levin all at once."

"You didn't attend any of these parties, did you?"

"When they went out? No, I never went. No reason why I should be included in the invitations, was there? But when our Nancy was having a few people round herself, she used to say to me, 'What about one of your nice fruit cakes, Harvey, and a couple o'dozen sausage rolls?' Always the same. 'Course I made her all sorts of things, but it was always fruit cake and sausage rolls she said she wanted. I'd take them round for her, all the little savouries and fancies, and once or twice she made me stay. Fooled me into it the first time by saying she wanted me there to heat up the things like sausage rolls in the kitchen oven. I fell for it, and then she dragged me in to the party. Great it was. I never understood why Graham couldn't get on at them, I could. An' she never had to fool me into it again. If she asked me to stay, I stayed. I got to know one or two of them quite well. Cracked a joke or two with them, you know, and saw they'd always got a drink. Gave away a few recipes, too. It was good fun."

"I'm sure it was, and they liked seeing you there. But Graham was different, was he?"

Festival shook his head. Green rose at Mrs Fenny's nod to refill his glass.

"Ta," he said to Green.

"Pleasure, mate."

Masters, a little put out at this interruption, refused more whisky and waited patiently for the older man to continue his story. At last Festival began again.

"I couldn't understand young Graham. He liked parties. I know it was always those reps' dos with his pals that he liked most, but these others were all right. I met some interesting people at them. But Graham . . . well, he wasn't happy about them. First he suggested Nancy should stop going to them or having them. Then he started refusing to go out to dinner invites with her, at the last moment, when it was awkward and then he started criticizing her pals. That did it, because you see Nancy reckoned she owed a lot to some of them. Nancy said if he couldn't live with her chosen way of life she certainly wasn't going to try to live with his any more. She'd leave the house and go and live in London. She didn't, of course. She tried to make things work, but Graham seemed hell bent on not letting them. Then last year, just before Christmas, a German bloke called on her.

"I've forgotten his name, but he was some big bug in music over there who'd been appointed director of some big festival that lasts a fortnight. He'd come over in a hurry because he'd seen the programme the chap who had the job before him had left and he'd realized there were some gaps in it or it was out of balance or something. Anyway, he'd come to ask Nancy to sing in some extra concerts he was trying to arrange at the last minute. For this August it was, but they call it the last minute. I know Nancy was wanted to sing on two mornings as well as some nights.

"Our Nancy really wanted to do it, because this festival was quite something in her world. So she got out her diary and said yes, she could do it as August was her slack month anyway. She was just agreeing to all this when Graham came in and, according to our Nancy, said she couldn't go because he'd arranged his holiday for that fortnight and his firm wouldn't change the dates.

"Our Nancy was flabbergasted, but apparently this German stepped in and said nothing could be better. Herr Saltwell could go to Germany with Miss Festival as the guest of his committee and he could have a feast of sausages and beer as well as music. But Graham wouldn't wear it. And that got Nancy's dander up because she knew Graham didn't have to arrange his holiday that far in advance anyway and his firm had always been easy-going about booking holidays at quite short notice. So she took the agreement this German had brought with him and signed it there an' then, where she'd usually have sent it to her agent first, like. She got the German out of the house quick."

"I reckon he'd be pleased to go," said Green. "Having got what he'd come for."

"Right. Then there was a flaming row, of course. Graham took her diary and started turning over the pages saying she hadn't left a free time in the whole year long enough for them to go to wherever it was he said he'd decided they should go.

"Anyway, the upshot was Nancy told him she'd had enough and was going to see her solicitor about a divorce, and she asked Graham to get out of the house. He wouldn't go. Said she'd like that of course, so's she could accuse him of desertion or some such. An' that's how they stayed. His solicitor told him not to leave the house whatever he did, but he also told him not to start trying to lock Nancy out or there'd be ructions and he'd do himself a lot of no good. Mark you, Nancy started making sure she was away at weekends when he came home. Her solicitor said Graham's man was trying to get evidence of hanky panky with other men."

"Which there wasn't, I take it?"

"Never. But to make sure, Nancy rented this flat in London, an' got me to go down an' keep house for her, which I have done, ever since. She mucked in, of course, when she was at home — dusting an' stuff like that that I wasn't very good at — but I did all the cooking and shopping. We had a good time. 'Make me posh stuff for the nobs,' she used to say when anyone was coming, 'but let's have real food for ourselves.' She was fond of a bit of steak an' kidney pud an' a stew with dumplings an' the like." For the first time, Festival showed signs of emotion. "We had a grand time, me and our Nancy."

"I'm sure you did," said Masters quietly. "Just you and your daughter."

"Aye. I used to listen to her practising in the mornings as I did our cooking or read the paper, and wondered where it had all come from. Her voice, I mean. If she was singing at night she'd rest in the afternoon, so I'd go out a bit, shopping and looking round, and get home in time to see she was fed before she went off. Sometimes she was recording or rehearsing in some hall, or away like this time. But I had the telly and a decent little pub. . . . "

They waited for him to regain his composure.

"The divorce was heard in the spring or early summer, was it?"

"Aye, and a right mucky do it was. As I said, I'd never thought Graham was all that bad, but he said that as our Nancy made a lot more money than he did, she should pay him maintenance every month. I ask you! And him in a decent job. But he was a fool there. You see, Nancy had a lot of friends who'd heard an' seen things. They didn't do Graham a lot of good, and that German was there, too. He came over an' said his piece an' he could speak our lingo better than most of us, I tell you. An' the judge settled Graham's hash. Told him straight that as Nancy had bought the house an' was letting him keep it for nothing, he should count himself lucky. An' he went on to say if Graham had ideas about leaving his job an' then claiming he was destitute just to get money out of Nancy, he could forget it. Divorce courts weren't there to give cash to the greedy, an' so on an' so on. An' that was that. Our Nancy was free of him and we've not heard a word from him since. She was happier without him, Mr Masters. Me and her. . . . well, I knew she'd probably get married again and our little set-up wouldn't last for ever. . . but we got on well together. And in some ways, knowing she wouldn't always want me, I'm prepared for it, like. I'll be able to go back again, I reckon, easy enough, but it won't be the same, knowing Nancy's gone."

Green poured Festival another whisky.

188

Masters said quietly, "Miss Festival was a lovely woman. Full of personality. She had a great presence."

"She had that."

"She would take a lot of living up to, for a husband, I mean. What sort of a man was Graham Saltwell? Could he match her intellectually, physically, creatively?"

"He was an ordinary sort of chap. Actually, if you like, I could show you a photo of him. I've got a lot of Nancy with him on snaps, and I brought the album with me. I don't know why, but I've spent a few evenings putting them all together in one of these long flip-over books and I just thought it would be company to have it with me, so I put it in my case."

"I'd be delighted to see them," said Masters. "Can I come up to your room with you to get the album?"

"I'll go, George," said Green. "I want to have a private word with Harvey about whether he puts onions in beef pie or not." He got to his feet as Festival did the same. "Come along, Harve. Now I like mine without onions, but I don't mind a mushroom. . . ."

The door closed behind them.

"Are the questions about to follow, Mr Masters?" asked Mrs Fenny.

"I think I'd better not pose any, ma'am."

"Humbug," she retorted.

Masters didn't reply.

"Humbug, because you've already asked them."

"I've merely listened to another of your guests talking, Mrs Fenny. He obviously needed to talk about his daughter. He'll feel better for having a number of sympathetic listeners."

"I'm sure he will."

Chapter Seven

THE THURSDAY PASSED in furious activity. Masters asked Cleveland for more officers to help and got them. He then asked Cleveland to supervise their activities and left him to do the job. Green was kept busy with his team, while Masters and DC York spent the day on the telephone. The last chore of the day fell to the Northern Counties DCI, Sandy Finch.

Masters and his team were due to dine with the Chief Constable and his wife. Matthew and Philippa Cleveland were also in the party. The two cars arrived at the Pedder house together, Cleveland having acted as guide for the Yard men.

"I hope we haven't interrupted any serious investigation," said Mary Pedder to Masters. "I expect you must be busy. I've asked Alf how you are getting on with this dreadful business, but he says he doesn't know."

"He doesn't," smiled Masters. "Your husband has behaved impeccably for a senior officer by not badgering us once for information. He has left us to get on with it in our own way, after ensuring that Matt and the whole of the force would be ready to give us maximum help and co-operation."

Mary Pedder laughed. "That must have been a job for Alf. He likes to poke his nose in."

"Can I poke it in now?" demanded the CC, "and ask what you'd like to drink, Judder?"

Before Masters could reply, Cleveland asked: "Have you got any champagne on ice, Alf?"

"Champagne? What the hell do we want . . . ?" He stopped in mid-sentence and regarded the slight grin on Cleveland's face for a second or two. Then he turned to stare at Masters who stood quiet, and at Green who gave nothing away. But the silence spoke for itself.

"There's something going on, here. Champagne? That's for toasting victory. D'you mean you've cracked it?"

"George has," said Cleveland. "Our man is in the nick, right now."

Pedder put down the gin bottle he was holding.

"The bloke who did for Nancy Festival?"

"The bloke who did for them all, sir."

"I don't believe it. Who is he?"

"Chap called Graham Saltwell," said Green.

"Who's he?"

"Divorced from Nancy Festival six months ago."

"Divorced from her? Then why would he want to kill her?" asked Mary Pedder.

"It's a long story, love," said Green. "You and Philippa wouldn't want to hear it."

"Perhaps not," said Pedder, "but I would."

"It is written up, sir," said Masters. "For the most part at any rate. I'll put the finishing touches to the report and let you have it by ten in the morning before we set off for home."

"I want to hear it now," said Pedder emphatically.

"And so do I," said his wife. "But first, Alf, you haven't given these gentlemen their drinks. You've only served Philippa to sherry, and . . ."

"Help yourselves, gents," said Pedder. "It's all there. I'll be back in a couple of minutes, and we'll hear what you've got to say over dinner." The CC left the room at a half-run.

"Oh dear," said Mary. "Now what's got into him?" She turned to Masters. "You'll have to tell him, otherwise he'll get no sleep tonight, and neither shall I."

"It would be unforgivable of me to rob you of sleep," said Masters, smiling. "And as your husband is my superior officer, I shall have to obey orders."

"Rubbish," said Philippa. "You'd never obey any order you didn't want to, George Masters, and you know it. Bill Green told me last night that you give every appearance of toeing the line, but you still manage to do what you want, always, no matter who says what. He says you can jaw the hind leg off a donkey to get your own way and from what little I've seen of you, I agree with him." She smiled suddenly. "That's a bit of plain Nortown speaking for you."

"And totally deserved," said Green.

"Are you being got at, Chief?" asked Reed.

"It would seem so."

"I'll have to tell Doris about this," said Green.

"Doris?"

"My missus. She thinks George can walk on water."

"And can he?"

"My missus is a very wise woman."

Philippa Cleveland laughed. "You're all as bad as one another. Now you've pulled George out of the situation I'd just got him into and I do so like having men like him at a disadvantage."

Berger said: "Have another sherry, Philippa. You might as well get the Chief Constable at a disadvantage by drinking his booze in his absence."

"Thank you." She held out her glass and then turned to Masters, Green and the two sergeants. She raised the glass and said: "Actually, I want to say a big thank you to all four of you. If you've done what you say — and I don't doubt that you have — you'll have laid a spectre that has been haunting Matt for a year. And that is worth everything. I'm speaking as a wife, but there'll be other women, too, who'll sleep easier, knowing of your success."

"That's handsome of you," said Berger, and the rest of the team felt his reply was sufficient response.

Ten minutes later, they were sitting down to dinner.

"Start talking, Judder," said Pedder, sharpening the carving knife on a steel, preparatory to tackling a roll of roast topside well over a foot long. "I can listen while I'm doing this. And don't leave anything out, because the ladies will want to hear and I'm a lot better at absorbing the spoken word than I am learning from some high falutin' report you've written."

"In that case," said Masters, "I'll begin by just mentioning that there had been eleven deaths, one every month since last January, and though there was ostensibly no pattern to the killings, they did seem to coincide with the dates of the full moon and all the victims were murdered after achieving a minor triumph of some sort. By

192

using the dates of the full moon it was, therefore, easy to suggest that, if we were right, the next murder would take place this week — December the third or soon after — and that the victim would be some woman who had achieved her triumph, major or minor, actually on the third."

"You actually knew some girl would be murdered on the third and you did nothing about it?" asked Mary Pedder, scandalized.

"Quiet, please," said her husband.

"We couldn't do anything about it," said Masters, answering his hostess, "because though we could guess the date, we had no possible means of knowing who the intended victim was to be."

"How sad," said Mary. "I mean, if you could have guessed . . ."

"Mary," growled her husband, "you're not thinking straight. If no murder had happened between Tuesday and now, it would have meant the theory was wrong and we'd be no further forward. That murder proved these lads were right and so we knew that if we caught whoever killed this latest victim, we'd got the bloke who did the other eleven."

"You mean Miss Festival was the sacrificial lamb?"

"Miss Festival or whoever it was who was killed," said Masters. "I assure you, Mary, I'd have given anything to have been able to prevent her death, but the previous killings had taken place over a huge area, many thousands of square miles, including many towns and cities. It was impossible even to hazard a guess as to the next victim."

"And yet you happened to be on the spot when it happened."

"Entirely fortuitously," said Cleveland. "George had nothing to do with it. I booked the seats, purely for his entertainment. If I hadn't done that, there would have been no policeman present when she died on Tuesday night."

"I see. I'm sorry, George."

"Please don't be. I've been castigating myself for not having foreseen the tragedy. I had been uneasy throughout the day, but I assumed it was because Tuesday was the day I had forecast. I did not connect my feelings with one particular person."

"Understandable," grunted Green, accepting a plate of beef and Yorkshire pudding. "Nobody could have foreseen what happened because there were no clues to the killer's identity and consequently to his likely victim."

"Thanks, Bill. I'll push on a bit faster, if I may. When Miss Festival collapsed and died, we had no doubts whatsoever that this was the multi-murderer's twelfth victim, because the day was right but, even more important, she had scored a great, great triumph with her audience. They were standing and applauding as she died.

"But there was something different this time. Always before, a woman had achieved her triumph and then died because of it. The murderer of Nancy Festival knew before it happened that she would score a triumph that evening." Masters looked along the table towards Pedder who had now sat down. "And that told us a lot, sir."

"Us?" asked Cleveland. "You."

"What?" demanded Pedder.

"It suggested that Nancy Festival was to be the last victim. That everything that had gone before had been carefully planned to lead up to her death in the certain knowledge that the performance in Nortown would be a triumph!

"It brought us no nearer to the killer, because hundreds of people would know that fact. The choir, orchestra, fellow soloists, her hosts . . . many, many people who knew that she was liked, loved, adored even worshipped in Nortown. Her triumph was a certainty in the town where she began her glorious career and so tragically ended it. I do not suggest that her murderer knew just how dramatically she would die — at the very height of a standing ovation — but he knew that she would at least have won, by the time she died, the hearts of her audience.

"And that told me that the killer knew the mechanics of a performance of *Messiah*. Knew that the triumph would be scored in part one and that Nancy Festival would be alone, in her dressing-room in part two. Again the numbers who would know that were large. Choir, orchestra, fellow soloists, her hostess and, indeed, anybody who had ever attended a similar performance.

"From the moment Bill Green went to her dressing-room and discovered her case of throat sprays, we considered we knew the means used for killing her. There were four sprays, and it became clear to us that if all four had been tampered with, our killer would not be familiar with the routine Miss Festival always followed in tending her throat."

"How do you make that out?"

"If he did not know the routine, sir, he would have to poison all four sprays in case, haphazardly, she should only use one. But if he did know her routine, he would realize that there would have to be only one toxic spray capsule."

"I realize just one would kill her. . . . "

"She used them in a special order, sir. First a methylchloride spray which was a local anaesthetic and so very cold that, for a time, it virtually numbed the throat and membranes of the mouth and tongue. That meant she would be unable to taste the next spray, which, normally, contained an antibiotic to combat soreness and infection. After that she used a mouth freshener and, lastly, a deodorant. Our man had to be somebody who knew which spray she always used first, in order to avoid it, otherwise Miss Festival might have tasted the poison and realized something was wrong before she had given herself a toxic dose."

"Got you," said Pedder. "So he poisoned the second."

"Quite right, sir. In fact, he didn't poison the capsule already in the spray, he put in a totally new refill containing a thion insecticide, one of the organo-phosphorus group of virulent pesticides. Highly lethal in the amounts sprayed down her throat by Miss Festival.

"This, I felt, narrowed our field a great deal. Her fellow soloists, her immediate family, and probably her hostess might, I believed, have known that fact. Her companion in the dressing-room that night was Miss Margaret Whitehead who had access to the pack of syringes and who admitted to knowing, at least roughly, how Miss Festival used them. So the means and opportunity were there for Miss Whitehead, but for a number of reasons we discounted her. First, we could think of no probable motive; second, the character of the woman herself argued against it; third, she had been on stage throughout part one, during which time we believed the substitution to have been made; and fourth, it was impossible to imagine

Miss Whitehead in the role of killer in the eleven previous deaths."

"Good point that," said Green. "It helped to clear the decks."

"The other two soloists, the men, Desmond Darren and James Capper, did not visit the ladies' dressing-room as far as we could discover, and the four points which applied to Miss Whitehead applied equally to them.

"So the probable field was narrowing. Miss Festival's hostess, Mrs Sarah Fenny, her daughters, Jane and Juanita, and her sons, David and Peter, were all with Miss Festival in their home during the early part of the evening, and they even accompanied her to the Central Hall. I must confess that they seemed so unlikely to have killed their guest that I never seriously considered them as likely suspects."

"I should hope not," said Mary. "The Fennys? They don't rate quite as high as the occupants of Buckingham Palace round here, but after the present incumbents of the throne room the Fennys would come in as a good second family in a local referendum."

Masters nodded. "My impression was much the same. However, we persisted. We even interviewed Mr Rodney Butcher, but discounted him for slightly different reasons."

"Old Jelly Bags?" said Philippa. "His mummy wouldn't have let him out long enough without her for him to get near any woman. I've heard she listens at the keyhole when he's teaching a female pupil lest some twelve-year-old totty should make a pass at him."

Masters smiled at this bit of gossip and then returned to his report. "We had — or rather Matt had — started his men making enquiries near the hall. We learned that one figure, heavily muffled against the night and carrying a case, had been seen to slip down the alleyway at the side of the hall at about seven o'clock. Then, by a little stroke of luck, we discovered that the blind piano tuner was sheltering from the wind in a doorway near the entrance to the alleyway. He was able to tell us that two men, not one, had gone down the alleyway. First a man in leather-soled shoes, carrying a case the handle of which squeaked in its metal rings, and shortly after him a man in rubber-soled shoes had gone the same way.

"The man carrying the case was the trumpeter, Maxwell Mawby. His instrument was in the case, and he had arrived early to warm his trumpet at a gas fire in a little storeroom at the back of the hall. He knew the place of old and had used it on a number of occasions. Please don't ask me why he should wish to warm his trumpet, but I am given to understand it plays better when warm than when cold.

"But the second man was a different kettle of fish. We could not identify him, but we did discover that he had been hiding in a brush store and we were able to photograph his footprints in the dust on the floor.

"So we now thought we had narrowed the field even further. Miss Festival had been divorced some six months ago and since then had lived in a flat in London with her father, a retired baker. He came up to Nortown at our request and the four of us spent the evening as guests of Mrs Fenny, who had also invited Mr Festival to stay with her overnight. So we had a long, long chat to Mr Festival. This achieved two things. It convinced us we could rule Mr Festival out of our list of suspects."

"Why was he ever on your list?" asked Mary.

"Because he fulfilled many of the criteria of a prime suspect," said her husband. "He'd know about her reputation here, he'd know all about her sprays, and it's ten to one she didn't use her sprays after leaving home until after she'd finished singing. So they could have been changed before she ever set out."

"Oh, yes. I was overlooking that."

"And," went on her husband, "when it comes to murder, a member of the victim's family is involved more often than not, and Nancy Festival didn't have much family, apparently." He turned to Masters. "Sorry for the interruption, Judder. You had just told us one of the things your conversation with the old boy had achieved."

"The second was that the husband Miss Festival divorced six months ago was a very likely candidate for our attention. I won't go into details except to say that the marriage broke up because he was insanely jealous of his wife's success. And that meant we had to start getting positive proof. You see, Saltwell obviously knew of his wife's popularity here, because he had been present at her very first performance, and on that occasion had even gone backstage to present her with flowers. So he was familiar with the layout concerning the ladies' dressing-room. He would also know of the existence of the sprays and, I suggest, her routine use of them.

"Mr Festival had brought a photograph album with him — for company for himself and to show Mrs Fenny. Some of the photographs were of Graham Saltwell. I managed to borrow those, because I wanted a good supply of copies for Matt and his officers, and also for another reason. Bill Green had discovered from Mr and Mrs Carrot, the caretakers at the hall, that some time ago they had surprised a man reconnoitring the layout backstage at the hall. They said he looked like a rep to them, and they said he even tried to sell them cleaning materials for their work. That is by the way. Bill had done a good job on getting the Carrots to remember this character on Wednesday morning. This morning we showed them half a dozen shots, among which was one of Saltwell. They picked him out as their visitor."

"Have a bit more meat before you go on, Judder. There's plenty of roast spuds and veg, too. You as well, Bill. Come on, pass your plates up. There's more than enough for seconds."

Masters sat back and enjoyed the rest for a few minutes. Then when everybody was again settled down, he continued his report.

"Then we had a stroke of luck. Mawby called us this morning to say he remembered that a man had just looked into the storeroom he was occupying. He even knew the time. Ten past seven. So we showed him a handful of photographs, too. He wasn't very sure because he'd not had much of a sight of the man and he wasn't paying attention anyway. But he picked out three characters who, he said, he thought looked like the intruder. Saltwell was one of them.

"So there was a number of things to do all at once, today. We knew from old Harvey Festival that Saltwell was a rep for a firm which designs and constructs water- and waste-treatment plants for industrial and municipal clients. Matt visited the company and asked to see the hotel bills supporting Saltwell's expense claims over the past year. It was a long business but at last Matt got to know that Saltwell had stayed in hotels within twenty miles of the scene of all eleven previous murders on the evening of the day the individual murders were committed or were presumed to have been committed."

"I like it," said Pedder, a forkful of food poised before his mouth. "Well done, Matt."

"Not only that," continued Masters, "but Matt discovered that some of the hotels he had used were not those he was accustomed to using, but the company thought nothing of it at the time as they give their reps a fairly free hand so long as they bring home the bacon.

"So we had begun to tie Saltwell in with the previous murders, but I wanted to know where he had stayed on Tuesday night and the firm wouldn't have been able to tell us that because Saltwell's expenses sheet and bills for this week wouldn't have reached them. So DC York and I spent a lot of the ratepayers' money on countless phone calls to hotels within striking distance. At last we ran him to earth, less than fifteen miles away and, by great good fortune, the girl at the desk there told us where he usually went on to after leaving her hotel. She was right. So we knew where he had booked in for tonight. Matt's boys picked him up there when he arrived just before five o'clock. They were waiting for him outside the hotel, and brought him straight back to Nortown, luggage and all. In his case was a pair of rubber-soled shoes the pattern of which, we were told by forensic after an hour's comparison, exactly matched those in the dust on the brush store floor. Also his fingerprints match those on the paper wrapping from the tube of mints he ate while waiting."

"So you've got him dead to rights, George."

"We have, sir. There are just one or two things I should add which will, I think, relieve your mind."

"Such as?"

"The final row between Nancy Festival and her husband, which led to her suing for divorce, concerned the timing of an engagement in Germany she had accepted. He said it would clash with his projected holiday. The details don't matter at the moment, but during the disagreement, Saltwell took his wife's engagement diary and went through it very closely, in order to point out to her that nowhere in the forthcoming year had she left a gap big enough for the two of them to have a decent holiday together. The point to note is that this conversation took place in mid-December, just before Christmas. Quite when Nancy Festival agreed to visit Nortown for this week's performances is not yet established, but we know her acceptance had already been announced on Friday the fifth of December at the annual dinner of the choir committee. So the Nortown engagement would be in the engagement book for the third, fourth and fifth of December this year."

"Meaning Saltwell would know of it, or could have noted it?"

"I think the latter, sir, because don't forget he had come to Nortown to hear her sing on the occasion of her first big engagement. Such things stick in the mind, and we all take note of things and places we know or have visited. We seem automatically to pick them out of a host of other facts that have never concerned us. So, I think Saltwell noted that date and location. Also, we found this year's pocket diary on Saltwell when he was taken in. It's a very ordinary diary — one of those with a double-page spread for each week. On the top line for each day is a printed note. . . ."

"Christmas Day? Good Friday? That sort of thing?"

"Just that, sir. And the phases of the moon on appropriate days. For December the third there was a minute circle and the two words, Full Moon. I think that is what gave Saltwell the idea. He knows the Nortown Hall, he knew when his wife would be going there, and as likely as not he had that diary in his hands by mid-December or soon after. While he was still toying with the idea of making his wife pay for starting divorce proceedings, he consulted his diary. He'd do something to her at Nortown on the third of December. Full-moon day! And I think that triggered the whole thing. He'd kill her at the height of her fame on full-moon day. The idea must have grown like a maggot in his brain. By now he must have become psychotic about successful women. He hated them. Wanted to kill them. He would kill them. One a month for the whole year on full-moon days, culminating in the last and most important of all — Nancy Festival in full triumph in Nortown."

"Another good point," said Pedder. "Counsel should be able to work that up in court."

Masters laughed. "I know I didn't express myself very well, sir, but please don't make it so obvious."

"Didn't mean that at all. You were talking off the cuff. Prosecuting counsel will have all the time in the world to tart it up to appeal to the jury. Now, what other points were there?"

"Having given you cause to accept the original opinion we sent from the Yard . . . "

"Now who's rubbing it in?"

" . . . there is the matter of where Saltwell could have obtained his cartridge of virulent pesticide. We have not discovered that yet. But remember his job. He was visiting industrial sites to advise on the disposal of all manner of toxic materials. I am sure a thion derivative would not be too hard for him to find. Finally, I have been informed that most industrial plants these days have a filling and crimping machine for aerosol cartridges. Their preparation is swift and easy. It will be up to Matt to discover what he can about those two points. By following Saltwell's selling calls — from information supplied by the company — he should run them to earth."

"And the other eleven jobs?"

"The early ones may not be so easy, sir, because memories fade. But the killings in the last three months should give him a chance to complete those files. I don't think the full eleven cases will matter, just so long as Saltwell is tied in with the series which, by and large, I believe he already is."

"I reckon so, too, and my people will welcome the chance to polish them off." He addressed his wife along the length of the table. "What's for duff, Mary?"

"Cheesecake."

"Proper cheesecake? Not the stuff made with yoghurt?"

"Proper cheesecake with proper cream cheese and sultanas. But why the interest?"

"Let's have it then."

"All you men can think about is your stomachs."

"It's not that, love, it's the champagne."

"Champagne?"

"Yes. I whipped out to that off-licence round the corner and got a few bottles. Didn't take me more than a couple of minutes. But I put them in the fridge. I don't want them in there too long. They'll get too cold."

"I tell you what, Alf," said Green. "Wheel 'em out now and we'll drink 'em with the cheesecake. It's a long time since I had real cheesecake, so we might as well make it a celebration."

"Celebration? I'd call it a triumph. I've had that word on my mind ever since Judder used it in that opinion of his."

"Don't let it haunt you," counselled Green.

"I don't intend to. I'm going to drown it in bubbly."